In The Mists of Time

RICHARD D. BALDWIN
ROBERTA BALDWIN

The Reading Glass Books
1-888-420-3050
www.readingglassbooks.com
fulfillment@readingglassbooks.com

Contents

Dedicated

To my dearest friend and helpmate

My Wife

Roberta May Baldwin

ACKNOWLEDGMENT

FIRST AND FOREMOST, I must thank my wife Roberta for her kind generosity in giving me countless hours of encouragement, and revising clumsy, ungrammatical and mistakenly spelled text. Every hour she graciously gave to me was an hour taken away from her busy creative schedule of designing original cloth dolls and Christmas tree ornaments.

Professor Karen Elias, an experienced author and teacher of college English, first reviewed the mantuscript and kindly suggested cogent modifications which reflected no t only experience but the insight of a sentient soul.

The critique of this work's commercial value, editing, and unstinting advice and personal encouragement by Dione M. Coumbe, author and sagacious literary connoisseur, were, and are, of a humanity and power which can never be forgotten. Such wisdom is priceless!

Map by Roberta M. Baldwin

PREFACE

I HOPE THE reader will enjoy the mystery which forms the plot of this novel. As the mystery unfolds an additional matter occupies the major characters: a common enough action, a "political giveaway."

One aspect of this romance touches on a disturbing aspect of our time: the unbridled corruption of our society by masters of greed and delusion and how it adversely affects the quality of life for us all. Americans have historically been encouraged to regard our national entity as a republic " . . . of the people, by the people and for the people . . . ." Howard Zinn's, monumental epic, *"A People's History of the United States,"* leaves little doubt about the mythic quality of that aphorism; a doubt which is strengthened daily by the motives and actions of our "public servants." Consider, for example, the unconstitutional and brutal action of the domestic military (the police). Their behavior in suppressing peaceful public remonstrances, beating, gassing and imprisoning citizens, is a clear warning of grave national peril.

In dealing with "the news" I have tried to keep a basic principal of Logic in mind, namely that . . .

An object is validly described by its properties.

For example, consider the term, "terrorist." What are the properties which define a terrorist? The term likely strikes you with terror, fear arising out of ignorance. Scholarly research into and discussion of well studied properties of terrorists would lead to understanding why a person commits terror and how such motivation might be mitigated. But that, of course, would defe at the purpose of those whose object in broadcasting the term is to purposely instill irrational fear and equally irrational reactions.

As someone recently said on the Internet, "The function of News is to inform. The function of Public Relations is to delude." What do the properties of the for-profit-media define its function to be?

iii

. . . to provide reliable information? . . . Truth? . . . the facts, all the facts and nothing but the facts? . . . or propaganda? Your study of the properties of the for-profit-media will answer that question for you. As an aid you might look into *www.medialens.org* and *www.fair.org.*

With the exception of the name "Boofy Quimby" which I took from the name of a fire department in western Maine, all characters and events in this book are fictitious, and any resemblance to persons living or dead is purely coincidental.

Some years ago I saw the following carved in a lobby wall of The Second National Bank of Boston:

> "My country right or wrong
> When she's right keep her right
> When she's wrong put her right."

To labor at that endless task, it helps to know what is wrong and needs to be put right.

PROLOGUE

FRANCOIS LOUIS ST.HILLAIRE, old, white bearded, starving and weak, his once beady black eyes now clouded with terror, lay shivering, confined in a tough canvas hammock swaying and bucking as the doomed ship violently tossed and rocked, a doomed wooden fragment, already smashed and beaten, now in the death grip of a malevolent sea.

Rope coiled about the hammock protected his skull from being split on the erratically pitching floor. Starved, bruised, his clouded brain clung to the desperate hope that he might not be killed on this cockleshell of a ship, an insignificant speck in a raging sea.

In the year 1761 this wet, painfully chilled, terrified old man was held helpless prisoner in a ship assailed by roaring wind and thundering plumes of violent surf precariously anchored off a terrifying granite cliff. Held in the unyielding grasp of a dreadful nightmare this terrified old man reflexly relied on his ineffable skill to frustrate Fate.

Clinging to the hammock, a tall black man, a chain of small links riveted around his left ankle, branding him a slave, danced to retain his footing . . . a slave oddly solicitous of the old man . . . a slave whose proud bearing bespoke paradoxical pride . . . a slave who realized the ship, creaking and straining at her anchor, would disintegrate ere reaching a safe harbor. The ship's voyage from Hispaniola had been beset by awesome waves of opaque ocean, ferocious winds and torrential rain in the realm of overcast days and impenetrable nights. This nightmare, the slave knew, was the end of their terrible ordeal.

The old man turned his head, and meeting the gaze of the black man's sad eyes, his broken mind brightened and he was mercifully thrown back almost half a century to the year he purchased this slave, the year of our Lord 1720.

In the fall of that year, the ship "Olympus" anchored off the northwest coast of Africa beneath the blazing tropical sun, in a sea so limpid, fish appeared to fly over the white sand. Now an old, barely seaworthy, three masted, thirty six sailed ship, the sleek design of her hull still proclaiming a once vigorous youth, when, her hold filled with plundered new-world gold, she outran pirate corsairs waiting beyond the offing, ready and eager to spring upon Spanish treasure ships.

One moonless night she struck a rock unmarked by bell or marker buoy which ended her proud career of treasure transport; thenceforth her task was hauling cargoes of molasses, trade goods and slaves.

Her timbers creaked as she rocked in the gentle waves, for she was now aged and would soon spread her sails for the last time, embark upon to her final voyage to her final port and there be rendered into scrap.

A line of barefoot, bearded, unshorn men, their heads swathed in strips of sailcloth canvas to keep burning sweat from their eyes, extended from the hold of the ship to a cable hoist dangling at the deck edge.

"Jolly Roger 'aport, lads . . . Heave the powder, heave the shot . . . Sweat or die, lads, sweat or die . . . Old Neptune waits below . . ." rhythmically beat an incessant chant as they passed crate after crate to the edge of the deck and lowered them into a waiting long boat whose gunwales sank ever lower.

St.Hillaire heard again the echo of the helmsman's cry—"Push away, boys! Pull on the oars for all you're worth!"—as the laden boat, oarsmen straining and groaning, rowed slowly ashore.

Boatload by boatload, the ship's hold was emptied of all save rats, stale air and a regular pattern of staples nailed to the dark, damp floor of the hold to chain, needed to restrain the cargo of slaves in the dark. That cargo waiting to fill the empty hold was a cohort of slaves, kidnaped by raiders whose skins were as black as theirs and hearts much blacker.

In the first boat ashore sat a thin, secretive, shifty eyed man in his twenties who appeared nearer forty, adept in the crafty wiles of commerce, rich, greedy, suspicious. A man to whom sharp bargaining was a challenge, a compulsion, and if the capacity resided in such a heart of granite, even a joy. For two years he had owned a prosperous sugar plantation on the West Indian island of Hispaniola, inherited on the death of his father, but this was his maiden trip around the established "Molasses, Rum, Slave Triangle."

His eyes and ears missed nothing. Daily he recorded important details of the commercial activities in which he was engaged: molasses from plantations in the West Indies to the colonies of New England, a miscellany including flintlock rifles, salted fish, cooking utensils and woven fabrics from the New England colonies to Africa, finally, full circle, slaves from Africa to the West Indian plantations. This man, like a prudent spider, was spinning a clever web of profitable revisions to his customary processing, transporting and selling of molasses. He was now shore bound at this African port to assess what profit might be made as a broker in the sale of human beings.

The long boat docked at a crude but substantial wharf onto which the sailors unloaded the heavy crates which were then transferred to donkey carts. Over the wharf blew gusts of dust and sand, raised by donkeys and carts trundling along the dry cart way. Along this windblown cart way a cluster of hut-like sheds offered items to seamen casting about for spices, trinkets of ivory and leather, rum, opium or the services of a woman.

"Halloa, senor," hailed a Portuguese, holding back a canvas flap to reveal a light skinned, scantily clad young woman. St.Hillaire passed, heedless of the man; whores stirred no passion in his breast.

He made his way toward the far end of the cart way to where a chained mass of helpless black humanity awaited transport to the Olympus and other slave ships. There he mingled inconspicuously with the group of slave brokers assembled before a wooden platform on which an African warlord auctioned the choicest women and strongest men culled from the latest lot captured by his black marauders.

A hush fell as the attention of the white men was arrested by a chained black giant. A boy, perhaps sixteen or seventeen, with muscles of a Hercules, was pushed onto the block. Standing above six feet in height, he dwarfed the white men, who considered five feet an admirable height. A disdainful smile twisted the slaver's thin lips as his cruel, cold eyes surveyed the white men. Were they afraid of this giant? With a half snarl, half yell, he cracked the leather thongs of the whip in the air and snapped them into the giant's back. The nearest bidders reared back to avoid splatters of the boy's blood.

It was the policy of St.Hillaire to select slaves needed to work the plantation from those who survived the hellish voyage to Hispaniola. However, he had no doubt about this boy surviving. The slaver was about to gavel the sale of the boy closed when, having made his decision, St. Hillaire entered a successful bid, and the giant was his.

Arrangements for his slave's transport on the Olympus completed, St. Hillaire turned to leave when he felt a tug on his sleeve. He turned to face a white man: small in stature, skin tanned and wrinkled by the scorching sun, and black eyes shining beneath massive white eyebrows.

"You are a man of purpose," he said with a slight bow. "May I lead you to another treasure which may interest you?"

Francois, always armed with sword and a pair of ready pistols, nodded and followed the strange old man to a hut of reeds and mud, roofed with dry, brown palm fronds, and dimly illuminated by a feeble light which diffused through the smoke vent in the low roof. The old man motioned Francois to a seat on one of two stools at a table of polished ebony then clapped his hands. Through a curtained doorway a figure robed in black entered. The man spoke in unintelligible guttural tones at which the figure quickly slipped back behind the curtain.

A woman as old and wizened as the man re-entered the room accompanied by a black girl in the bloom of youthful beauty, her naked body draped in a pale transparent saffron colored gown, her lovely face flushed with maidenly modesty.

"A virgin, sir, kindly raised and trained to charm her master. She is healthy, virtuous and obedient, and I offer her at a fine price." He looked into Francois' eyes and smiled. "Does the gentleman fancy this maiden?"

Francois' cold, calculating heart was not touched. He shook his head and asked himself if this old man, this likely dealer in contraband, pirate loot, and flesh, had anything else of possible interest? Was flesh his only ware, or was this girl bait to stimulate his interest? The old man smiled and motioned for the girl to be taken away.

"You are a man with all his needs satisfied?" he asked. Francois nodded, not deigning to speak and began to withdraw toward the entrance. "Pray, dear sir, allow an old man to bring a treasure of a different kind to your notice." Francois again seated himself at the table. "You have access to gold?" the man watched his eyes intently. Francois dipped his chin in affirmation, at which the man then reached beneath his robe and withdrew a small casket of lead which he placed upon the table and covered with both hands.

Two men, daggers thrust in sashes about their waists, stepped from behind the curtain.

"Be not alarmed, my friend; they guard me and intend no harm to you."

The old man spoke with a calm assurance which did not totally allay St.Hillaire's apprehension. "Will you exchange gold for wealth more easily concealed from the covetousness of greedy men?" Francois looked directly into the eyes of the old man who, recognizing his interest, raised the casket's lid revealing an oval gemstone the color and clarity of pale blue crystal. Even in the feeble light coming through the roof vent, it threw off glistening rays of red and sparkling blue. As the old man moved the casket, stars of every rainbow hue flashed across the sky-blue surface of the large diamond.

"The `Aqua Adaman', dear sir, a stone of India, renowned for its beauty for three hundred years." With these words he drew a knife from his robe and struck the blade with the stone, leaving a mark on the glistening steel.

"Old man," said Francois, "will you have a pliable leather belt made for me by one of the craftsmen hereby?"

"Assuredly," answered the old man.

"This stone must be securely concealed in a pouch attached to the belt? I put my life in your hands; for if one person aboard the ship knows what I have about me, my body will be thrown to the sharks!"

Slowly the old man nodded his head. "Under your own eyes I will, myself, secure the stone within the pouch."

He gestured to the two silent men, "If anyone threatens harm to you before your ship departs, he will be a dead man by the hand of one of my sons! Let the concealment be done the day you sail. At the same time I will weigh and inspect the gold which you will pay me and return it to you. Once you possess the stone, these two will guard you until you leave our shore.

Just before you board the long boat, avoiding notice which might excite attention, you will hand the bag of gold to my sons."

On the crowded wharf the exasperated crew pushed and shouted unintelligible orders to the confused slaves awaiting transport to the ship. St.Hillaire and the two bodyguards stepped to the rear of the pliant blacks and the impatient crew; the bag of gold changed hands, and the two men disappeared among the hangers-on surrounding the dock. St.Hillaire unprimed the two pistols concealed in his cloak and stepped into the long boat.

The cargo of slaves climbed aboard the "Olympus" on their own shackled legs. Despairing of mercy this side of the grave, their fates sealed, forever shriven from homes and families, they were herded, cursed and prodded into the hold. Nights they lay chained to the rusted staples on the rotten boards of the stinking floor, fending off rats as best they could. Days were spent sleeping wherever they could on deck.

The heaviest burdens on that leg of the voyage were black bodies weighing little enough, dead of dysentery, pneumonia or heartbreak, casually tossed over the side. A low moan then rose from the living chattels, a hymn to Charon on their stygian voyage, and they all turned to face the ship's bow to avoid witnessing what was to follow. The crew, as they always did, watched from the stern the corpse toss on the waves then slowly roll and sink. Silently they counted the seconds until in a watery explosion, the corpse was suddenly dragged below, torn apart and devoured in a feeding frenzy by the ship's constant companions, the eager sharks.

A fair wind carried St.Hillaire, the giant, and the `Aqua Adaman' to Hispaniola. The diamond was his assurance against misfortune; a pirate raid, a slave mutiny, the ferocity of a tropical hurricane were always possible catastrophes. Such easily concealed and portable wealth was a wise precaution; St.Hillaire was a cautious man.

The risks to shipping from accidents, pirates, and privateers were too great for an undivided transport of the plantation's annual molasses production. Therefore, St.Hillaire entrusted this to four smaller shipments in two convoys composed of his two well armed ships. Year after year, decade after decade, he accompanied the first convoy of the season to the town of Providence in the colony of Rhode Island, where he was noted for the excellence of his molasses, the rum which it yielded, and the bargains he drove.

Though unknown to all, St.Hillaire was never without the diamond secured about his waist. Humorous and quizzical reactions were prompted by his giant black bodyguard. It did not go without notice this astonishing, formidable and well armed companion was always within ear shot. To some that made St.Hillaire's fear of robbery or murder a certainty, and they pondered the reason why.

The molasses transported in the remaining convoy was pledged to that rum distiller who had earlier contracted to pay the highest price. Woe to the purser to whom he entrusted this shipment if he failed to return to Hispaniola with the exact payment due. Only one had the temerity to steal that due to St.Hillaire. The persistence of his search, his success in tracking the thief's overland flight, and the criminal's grisly fate made certain no one would again risk such an attempt.

St.Hillaire was not a humane man. His slaves were branded, poorly nourished, worked without mercy from dawn to sunset, beaten if wearied from overwork, and died early deaths, but not so the giant. He was treated preferentially, marked only by a chain and medallion encircling his ankle, and given a pretty wife with whom he dwelled in a cabin adjacent to the main house. St.Hillaire's purposeful indulgence evoked the loyal attachment of the giant, whom he called "El Negro Grande." El Negro Grande guarded his master assiduously.

St.Hillaire unkennelled two fierce hounds, manageable only by himself and the giant, chained one by each entrance to the house at night, secured the shutters on the windows, and bolted the entrance doors. He slept alone, his door securely barred and a loaded pistol under his pillow.

Four decades passed without any untoward incidents other than the theft noted and several attempted raids: one by a British man-of-war which his speedy crafts outran and several by pirates which were sunk or disabled by his well armed ships.

A favorable south wind brought summer heat to Hispaniola early in the spring of 1761. St.Hillaire, now a man in his mid-sixties, wished to embark on his annual voyage nearly a month earlier than was usually prudent. Because of the premature onset of winter, weather had closed the North Atlantic, and the last molasses shipment of the previous year still remained in his warehouse.

He was anxious it be delivered as soon as possible, before its color and flavor deteriorated.

"It is not wise," said Captain Slocum, "to risk your ships. Winter storms on the North Atlantic are fierce and unpredictable. Many's the ship and many's the crew they've claimed."

"I have made the voyage often, Captain," retorted St.Hillaire. "We will stay within the Gulf Stream and follow the coast. If, God forbid, the weather threatens, we will then seek safe harbor and anchor until it passes."

Captain Slocum was a bold, courageous man, but while a boy in the family home on Nantucket, he had seen furious winter storms drive in off the Atlantic. No ship could survive such fury! Who would provide for his wife and family if he perished? He could not take the risk! "Sir," he said, "you must find another captain, for I cannot do what experience and common sense rebel against. I tell you it is folly and warn you not to go!"

St.Hillaire's small fleet of two ships had a captain responsible for each. What one would not do, perhaps the other would. Captain Alfonso Alvarez was a Spaniard, younger than Slocum, of a gayer more daring temperament, whose father and whose grandfather had sailed the Spanish Main, brave men undaunted by the pirates who infested the route of the gold bearing galleons on route to Spain.

It is a risk, thought Alvarez, *. . . but a bonus of gold! Fair weather! A challenge! I cannot resist!*

And so they departed, the ship lying low in the water, with double the usual cargo of molasses, St.Hillaire, El Negro Grande, and the diamond. The first week at sea was a sailor's delight, balmy days, a rolling sea and a brisk following breeze filling the sails. West of their course, the coast, a thin line above the water, was always in sight. Alvarez was pleased; the voyage was going well.

In the darkest hours of a moonless night, a fierce gale from the southwest suddenly was upon them with such force the ship, with all canvas secured and dragging a sea anchor, was driven to the northeast. By morning the shoreline was no longer visible. The depth of the sea rendered fruitless any thought of anchoring. Day after day the wind beat the sea into wild, dangerous, mountainous waves. The ship, a mere triviality, was, at a moment of threatened inundation, raised onto the terrifying height of a wave crest then plunged into the swirling abyss of its trough. Rain assailed the ship in torrents; seas crashed aboard; a sodden, lurching, rolling, gale-blown hell, she was driven farther and farther into the dreaded northern sea, under dark skies by day and an even blacker shroud by night.

The free edges of the furled sails caught the shifting wind with loud thundering claps as it screamed through the rigging. Never glimpsing the sun through the low black clouds, they were swept helplessly into the northern ocean where no ship was safe at that time of year. One storm passed; then another was upon them, mercilessly battering the ship with harrowing gales and towering waves. After thirteen days the wind moderated, but the sails were no sooner unfurled, than it swung to the southeast, driving the ship farther north and westward. The sky remained overcast, and in the absence of stars and sun, Captain Alvarez lost all reckoning of the ship's position. At last all hope nearly gone, they sighted land and dropped anchor in a storm-tossed sea off an unknown coast on the evening of April 13, 1761. Fortunately, the anchor wedged and caught on the rocky sea floor, holding securely.

Day was departing and stormy night was gathering. Dark threatening clouds rolled in from the east when St.Hillaire, awakening from his reverie, was assisted from the hammock by El Negro Grande who wrapped him into the fur cloak which contained, sewn under the lining, his store of gold. St.Hillaire, urged by nature's necessity and supported by his faithful servant, stepped onto the cold, wet, heaving deck. The crew, drenched by the cold sea, frozen by icy blasts and weak from lack of food, now exhausted lay below. In his quarters Captain Alvarez, near his physical and mental end, knew not where they were nor what land they had touched and thought only of the preservation of his ship. Overcome by sleep, his head fell forward onto the desk.

St.Hillaire grasped for balance the gunwales of a boat which rested on the mid-deck, ready for a party to go ashore, as soon as a suitable place for a landing was found. He gazed at the dark forbidding cliff of great rock slabs against which storm-driven waves crashed in plumes of spray and booming roars. Black silhouettes of conifers standing atop the cliff were etched against a wan, gray, fast fading twilight. The air was frigid; his breath congealed into frost on the fur collar covering his lower face.

As he turned to return below, his unbelieving gaze fixed with horror on the eastern horizon where a watery precipice bore relentlessly shoreward. Higher and higher loomed the rogue wave as it sped toward the anchored ship. In frenzied terror he sprang into the proposed landing boat, crouched in the bottom and clung desperately to the gunwale.

The mountainous wave raised the ship onto its awesome breast and heeled it over until the small boat slid from the deck and sped away on its boiling crest. The wave overturned the ship and bore the small boat above a ledge of jagged rocks which jutted out high on the cliff face and there splintered it. The gigantic wave sank back into the sea. A sea soaked mass of flesh, fur and sundered planks remained in the recess behind the rocks.

Trapped below deck, the helpless crew of the Olympus perished. The power of this monster wave created a raging mass of water more powerful than that rushing over the edge of the mighty falls at Niagara. The loaded ship, totally insignificant to the God of Destruction, was ground in its fearsome jaws and spat out in splinters of timbers and lifeless bodies. In the wake of the awesome wave, timbers tossed in the froth of lesser waves while the bodies tumbled, sank and were seen no more.

The cliff on which the body of St.Hillaire was stranded formed the buttress of a promontory where stout, gnarled conifers, their tenacious roots entwined in rocky cracks and crevices, clung to the very verge in stubborn defiance of winter gales. In the still, cold pre-dawn hours, fog blew in off the sea, condensed and dripped from festoons of gray moss hanging from their branches.

The crescent of a waning moon appeared then quickly disappeared; the clouds, so long persistent, were breaking up. The cadence of breaking waves and a dirge-like wind sighing through the trees, nature's requiem, seemed to mourn the death of the ship and all the souls she carried.

Steadily brightening pre-dawn light laid a gentle glow upon the wide expanse of storm lashed sea, heralding the emergence of a bright point of sun on the distant horizon, which sent hundreds of raucous sea birds into the air. Dawn painted the ocean radiant silver and the sky glowing azure as the full disk of golden sun emerged from the sea and mounted a sky washed clear of clouds for the first time in many weeks. A glorious day proclaimed the long spell of storm and gloom had ended.

A meadow dotted here and there by ice age, glacier borne rocks and granite outcrops stretched an estimated 400 yards from the edge of a dark forest of oaks to the cliff edge of the sea. Against the forest stood a house, from which the sweet smell of burning wood wafted on the morning air, while from an adjacent barn there issued the lusty crowing of a cock and the lowing of cows ready to be milked.

A farmer, not aged but near the end of his prime, left the house and trod toward the cliff wondering what a horde of screeching sea gulls had found to forage. There he came upon timbers, barrels, tangled lines and canvas surging in the storm riled waves and saw, wedged in a crevice behind a craggy outcrop not far below the edge of the cliff, pieces of shattered wood and a matted brown bundle from which protruded an arm and a leg.

"There has been a shipwreck, Seth, and I need your help. Bring a rope and that bit of sail from the loft and come along!"

"There's no point in risking a young life," Abner Gibbs said to his son as they stood looking down on the body of St.Hillaire. "Tie the rope around me, and I'll see if he's dead or alive."

Warily, Abner descended the slippery rock, lifted the sodden beaver cloak and looked on the contorted body of a man frozen in death.

"Is he dead, Father?" yelled Seth.

"Cold as ice," replied Abner. "Drowned and with a broken neck from the look of it."

He untied the rope from his waist, secured it under the arms of the corpse and said, "If I push and you pull we can get him up. So haul away!"

It took all Seth's strength to haul up the sodden body. When it reached the top, he pulled it over the edge then flung down the rope for his father.

They placed the remains of St.Hillaire on the remnant of canvas sail and, each grasping a corner, dragged it to the barn.

After freeing the heavy sodden coat from the stiff arms of the drowned man, they considered the pressing problem of burial. To dig a pit in the still frozen earth with pick and shovel was clearly impossible. However, the layer of soil immediately beneath the manure pile, warmed by the decaying matter, might be deep enough for a shallow grave. They attacked the ground beneath the deepest part of the steaming manure until the spade struck partially frozen dirt.

With much effort Seth was able to hack out enough soil before he was stopped by rock hard frost.

While Seth dug, Abner searched the body for any clue to the man's identity. In so doing he found the belt containing the diamond. This he fastened about himself and covered with his coat. He would say nothing about it until he knew what made such a hard bulge in the pouch. A purse containing an abundant treasure of Spanish gold coins found in the cloak astonished and delighted his wife and sons. It was indeed a treasure!

Standing by the make-shift grave with his wife Sarah and his three sons by his side and with the large family Bible in his arms, Abner offered a homely prayer:

"Heavenly Father, we have no notion who this man was, where he came from or was bound. The poor soul perished by drowning in the stormy sea. Ye know best if he was kind and good. I ask Ye, if he was, his soul be admitted to Heaven and his virtues bring him peace and life eternal. Amen."

Thus the remains of St.Hillaire were interred. Before replacing the manure, Abner laid several slates over the grave. Using a leather piercing awl, he gouged on one: "Drowned man unknown to us. Laid to rest April 14, 1761."

Abner found the diamond. He guessed what it was and knew it was valuable for why else would a man hide it on his person? The discovery startled and alarmed him. The gold might be carefully spent, but this stone must be kept for whomever might come seeking it with proof of rightful ownership.

This was not without hazard; for if word reached the authorities, the stone would be confiscated and become property of the hated English Crown. If no one knew of it, there could be no dangerous rumors, no attempted theft or murder. He would say nothing about it and conceal it until it was claimed. The coins salvaged and spent over the years, were acknowledged in the family as "the shipwreck treasure." The strange clothes in which the body was garbed were a curiosity to be shown to friends and passed down from generation to generation diminishing in interest and eventually stored in a box, stowed out of the way and virtually forgotten.

In the large family Bible, that repository of births, marriages and deaths of his ancestors, Abner briefly recorded the date of finding and burying the body.

An itinerant stone carver, who annually canvassed the need which Death occasioned for his craft, paid his call during the summer; Abner's attention was drawn to the large boulder which he had placed as a monument over his parents' graves twenty years before. It still lacked a suitable inscription, and he engaged the man to carve his parents' epitaph.

Following their names and dates of birth and death, the following verse was inscribed:

LET NONE FORGET
In truth let all ye
Befriend each lost
Outcast wanderer

In September of that same year, a stroke robbed Abner of speech. Three days later, after uttering the single word "treasure," his days on earth ended. He was laid to rest by the side of his parents, his name and dates of his birth and death were eventually carved below the verse he had composed.

While he lived, no inquiry had been made about either the wreck or the stone. With his passing all knowledge of the diamond vanished.

Chapter 1

IF A WORD sufficed to characterize Isabella and William McLeod, that word would be "simple," for simplicity distinguished their life together, a hardworking, clear-thinking couple of uncomplicated morality, instinctively guided by the Golden Rule. Having fallen in love, they lived together happily, closely contented and caring.

For forty-five years they bore the hardships and sorrows of life with stout fortitude, grateful for life's blessings, kind to the poor and helpless, wary of those with the power to inflict suffering and deprivation on others, and were, in a sense, courageous, not in a sword-rattling, flag-waving way of bullying, boastful cant, but in unwavering faithfulness to the imperatives of humane conscience.

Coming upon them as one might, sitting side by side on the modest porch of their modest house on the modest street in Halifax, Nova Scotia, one could not fail to note the merry twinkle in their eyes and the loving tones in which they conversed nor lack conviction that love, honesty, loyalty, common sense, and humor were sound roots of their happiness.

However, one cold, gray, unforgettable morning long ago, Bella and Will had stood on the Clyde quay in misting rain, dreading that moment of parting, when Will must board the waiting ship to America, so far, so very far from their home in beloved Scotland. Raindrops dotted Bella's soft brown hair, and tears in her clear blue eyes belied the fleeting, brave but wan smile on her trembling lips. Will held his darling in a gentle, firm embrace.

The desperation of poverty, its awful hopelessness, had brought them to this awful moment. Will had no choice. He had no other choice but to leave the beloved "auld country" in search of work while Bella stayed behind supporting the children in the slums of Glasgow. She and the children must survive as best they could on a housemaid's wages until Will saved enough to bring them across the sea to what they hoped would be a materially better life. It was a desperate gamble.

She sobbed tears of fear and loneliness as the ship pulled away from the dock, leaving her more isolated and afraid than she had ever been. They would be together again; they must be together again! To doubt that certainty for a moment let in the awful icy grip of soul-crushing loneliness. "Dear God," she prayed, "keep my Will safe and sound. Oh God! Please dinna take your eyes off him before we're back together again."

Will waved to her with a brave smile and a heart as heavy as her own until the tugboats turned the ship, and Bella was suddenly lost to view. In wild desperation he ran breathless to the other side of the ship that he might not lose sight of her, but his effort was vain. Among the people on the quay, now too small to distinguish in any detail, was his wife while he, wretched in heart, was now too far out upon the Clyde to see her. An emptiness fell upon him so powerfully, he grasped the handrail for support. "Dear God, Father of us all," his inner voice implored, "hold Bella and the wee 'uns in the palm of your hand till I hold them in my arms again!"

As he descended to steerage, he noted the faces of others, mostly men but a few families, bound in the same direction, faces of desperate people doing what they must, lacking feasible choice, hoping for the best, human beings as desperate, as lonely, as disconsolate as he.

Time dragged slowly by as he sat alone in the tiny cabin, feeling unbearably lonesome, unconsciously contemplating its cheerless narrow upper and lower sleeping berths. Minute after minute marched dully by to the regular muffled *thump, thump, thump* of the great engines until he heard the welcome fumbling of someone at the latch.

The door opened, and a man of about his own age, dressed as was he in the cheap, black Sunday suit of the British workingman, stepped in, small valise in hand.

The stranger looked at Will, noting his light brown hairbrush mustache, dark blue eyes, and frank, honest countenance, then smiled and extended his hand. Will looked at the stranger and saw at once intelligence and jolly good humor written on his face. The sadness of both remitted, and a welcome relief from loneliness caused each to grasp the other's hand.

"Andrew Duncan," said the stranger, "fra' Hawick!" "Will McLeod, fra' Glasgow!"

"Ha'ee a trade?" Will asked, after the question of who would sleep in the bottom bunk had been settled by the toss of a coin.

"Oh, aye," Andy replied, "train dispatcher. An' ye mon, what o' ye?"

"Afore the war, I was a hoose painter . . . but there's na' work there the now," Will replied. "And whether there ever will be again, nay 'en kens."

The two Scotsmen, avoiding by common consent their combat careers in World War II, quickly found they shared much in common. Both had learned the dear old ballads from their mothers and agreed that never were there such incomparable tales of ghostly haunting as those told by Scottish grandmothers whose belief in their veracity was unshakable. Many were the winter nights when menacing shadows were cast by the fire's glowing embers and the candle's flickering light, shadows in which unspeakable horrors lurked just out of sight. Be it in Hawick or Glasgow, the dear old ladies filled the imaginations and raised the hair on the necks of two wee frightened lads. Overwhelmed with fear, it was then to dark, cold bedrooms for the wee 'uns, who disappeared at once beneath homemade patchwork quilts until merciful sleep overtook them.

"It was me granmither's half sister," related Andy, "who froze afeared for her life while awaiting a friend on a dark Edinburgh street and felt a hand placed on her shoulder from behind, sure she was aboot to be strangl'd by Burke and Hare when a bobby happened rounded the corner in the nick o' time. Though 'twere a hundred years lang syne, the terrible, everlasting moment lives on in the telling."

Never to be forgotten were the colorful legends of Wallace and Bruce, the border raids of Rob Roy, the glorious battles won and the sorrowful battles bewailed by a coronach, and of course, the immortal romances of Mary Queen of Scots and Bonnie Prince Charlie.

Tears of laughter and melancholy rolled down their cheeks. "I dinna doot they felt they were there their-ain-sel's, and hadna doot o' it, at the time, but saw it a' and felt it a' . . . ye were there yersel', mon!"

For blessed moments they were back in the local pub, and the ballads and poems of Robbie Burns, taken warmly to heart in youth, reechoed somewhere in the engine's droning bass. The music, the feelings, the words, the images were there; and voices forever silent in the grave sang lustily in their memories.

Days and evenings of lonely longing for home and family were relieved by sharing beloved memories of happier times. They talked of their favorite novels by Scott, sang old songs, and in so doing, welded links in a chain of friendship which time could not tarnish nor distance rust.

"Will," said Andrew when they were about to part at Ellis Island, "Mind we dinna fail t' keep in touch, lad!"

"Oh, aye, Andy," replied William, "I ha' the place where ye'll get letters and will write to ye when I find a job and a place to bide. But gie us a hand, my trusty friend, and here's a hand o'mine."

They embraced, shook hands, and parted with little hope of ever seeing each other again, but both were as good as their word. Not a year passed without a letter, on the average of one a quarter.

So many weeks went by after his first letter to Andy that Will feared they had permanently lost touch. However, a letter arrived at last—from Canada! Andy had found work there, a job which paid a wage, not a grand wage but adequate for a life of few material wants, and was eagerly longing for his wife and family.

William found employment with the Erie Railroad and after a year of frugality was reunited with Bella and the children. The unfortunate former owners of a small house at number 7 Park Terrace being unable to keep up the mortgage payments during this time of stressful unemployment, the bank foreclosed and immediately put it up for sale. The monthly payments were a formidable expense, two weeks of Will's scanty wages, but they bought it and, with Bella's careful management and eventually the earnings of their daughter and two sons, were successful in keeping it. By the time Hawkins came to live there more than a decade later, the last mortgage payment had been celebrated.

The neat white house with the green roof and the large cherry tree in the front yard at number 7 Park Terrace was built in the bungalow style popular in the years after the first of the Great Wars, and it was there Hawkins Shortreed spent his early childhood. He lived there with his maternal grandparents, Will and Bella, who adopted him following the death of his parents in an auto accident when he was two years old. Bella and Will were devastated by the death of their beloved daughter, but the strength of their faith and their love for each other sustained them. Their grandson Hawkins, very like his mother with his sensitive, loving, happy nature, in a way known only to Providence, brought her back to life in their hearts.

For a quarter of a century, Will and Andrew never failed in their correspondence. Andrew had settled in Halifax, Nova Scotia, and worked in its large rail and ship terminal. Each knew the other was a grandfather, how many grandchildren each had, how old they were, and such promising youngsters they were. Andrew's granddaughter Mary had been born but a year after Hawkins. What farfetched possibilities might that portend to two doting grandfathers? For even wise grandfathers indulge in wishful thinking at times.

What a dreadful day it was in 1970 when Will found himself out of work at fifty! Bitter news to tell, but there it was. The truck revolution was in full swing, the Interstate Highway System nearing completion, and the railroad forced to close.

Putting it as mildly as he could in a letter to Andy, imagine his astonishment at the following prompt reply:

> Lose no time, my friend, and get here as soon as you can. There's a job here. I've spoken for you, and it's yours if you want it. There aren't any physical tasks. It will take a bit of time to get used to. You'll have an easy boss to get along with, and it pays enough to get by.

So Hawkins left number 7 Park Terrace with its wonderful cherry tree when he was about to enter grammar school's second grade. Will and Bella, heartbroken to leave their grown sons, old friends, and familiar places, once again picked up the pieces of their lives and moved to Canada.

In the seaport city and rail complex of Halifax, Nova Scotia, the two old friends were joyfully reunited. The two families became closely linked in fondness, and many were the new friends waiting to be made known to them.

In Halifax, trains from throughout Canada and freighters from all over the world met to exchange cargoes. Will's new job was in Andy's department where they matched the transits without tangling them up.

Andrew and his wife Flora lost no time in introducing the newcomers to their family and friends. A Scot away from Scotland was quick to befriend another Scot away from Scotland; the "new Scotland" of Nova Scotia did indeed remind them of home. Bella and Will soon looked back on the loss of Will's job in a less tragic light. His new job, their new home, and new friends were a blessing for which, true to their upbringing, they gave thanks to their Maker.

In August of their first year in Nova Scotia, they set out to the Highland Games, that festival of nostalgic national pride so dear to the hearts of Scots, who flocked from near and far. There were marching bands of kilted pipers and drummers resplendent in ceremonial highland tartans and tall bear skin hats. Burly lads tossed the caber and pitched the woolsack; border collies herded sheep, and lassies frocked as highland maids danced the highland fling, sword dance, jigs, and reels. Hawkins was delighted when he spied that one wee lass in diminutive tartan hose and dancing slippers was Andrew Duncan's granddaughter, Mary Ayrshire; he waved and she smiled.

The screel of the beloved bagpipes brought tears to Bella's eyes and a lump to Will's throat; they were back in Scotland among their own that day. In later years, when Hawkins marched with the Pipers of the Loch, they smiled at each other, recalling earlier days when the boy was learning to play "the pipes."

The powerful longing of adult immigrants for all the customs of their past lives and for the land left forever behind, the romantic historical fables, their hometown, its festivals, and lifelong friends, never failed to spread its powerful effect to their children and to their children's children. Even the heart-wrenching grief attached to graves of babes who succumbed in childhood, parents, grandparents, in fact, their entire ancestry, left an unfilled blank in their identity. A word here, the bit of a memory there, provided most of the links in the chain. When the McLeods and Duncans sat late around the dining room table, as they often did, enveloped in the delicious spell of rampant nostalgia, the children were forgotten; but not a peep was to be heard from them. Wide of eye and sharp of ear, not a nuance, emotion, or tale passed them by. When this familiar party of friends broke up and the tired bairns were borne home in loving arms, they were not the bairns they had been a few hours before. They were infected with the deeds of tartan-clad heroes and heroines, which replayed in their waking dreams much larger than life. Perhaps it is true the Scots are natural dreamers, romantic souls, and perhaps not, but Mary and Hawkins certainly were. Their love of a culture of which they only experienced exported excerpts bound them in an ever- faithful friendship. Young as they were, they knew the power of love: for their families, for their puppies, and for each other.

Hawkins chose the bagpipe, and Mary, an old bass drum with which she followed behind Hawkins. A rope wrapped behind his neck and under his arms, attached to the front of Mary's decrepit drum, just kept it clear of the ground. Oh, the forbearance of the neighbors, the crying of babies awakened from naps, the howling of dogs—it couldn't last!

"Hawkins, while aroond the hoose," Will was forced to occasionally plead, "use only the chanter! Think of the neighbors! Why not use the bag and drones doon at the train yard while you're learning the pipes."

"I love the pipes, Bella," he would confide, "and I dinna like to complain to the lad, but the racket he makes is awfu' at times. When he and Mary are both at it, a saint couldna' stand it. Oh, aye, they must practice, I ken that well, but . . . but dammit! We must have some peace in the hoose!"

The determined children did find a spot in the maze of railway tracks at the terminal where their squawks and booms blended with the noise of the trains. The trainmen, faces streaked with grease, grinned and waved as they shuffled engines and freight cars about the yard.

The day came when Mary grew tall enough to support her drum unaided, and she and Hawkins began marching to her *boom, boom, booms*. Imaginary clans brandishing gleaming claymores rushed to battle behind them, incited by their rendition of inspiring martial airs. If a moment of silence could have descended upon the imaginary battlefield, the martial airs might have sounded suspiciously like squawks to others, but not to them. The grins of the greasy trainmen became even broader, and the waving arms, more enthusiastic.

"Look, Mary!" Hawkins shouted, convinced that their enthusiastic effusions soared above the grinding and chugging of the trains. "They like our music!"

Mary was a lithesome sylph who loved to dance! While little more than a baby, pigtails flying and merry eyes sparkling, she laughed and pranced to her mother's clapped beat of a hornpipe, reel or jig. There never was a more beloved, happy, and winning child.

With and without her grandparents, she spent many pleasant evenings at the McLeods over the succeeding years. After an evening pint of beer, Will would take up his fiddle, and Mary would dance. Nothing would do for Bella but to have Hawkins dance too; she was certain he could if he would but put his mind to it. To please her, Hawkins reluctantly complied, but dancing was not his strongest skill. The efforts of the good-natured lad soon had them all laughing so uncontrollably Will had to lay down the fiddle and wipe away his copious tears.

"Now, lass," he would say, again taking up the fiddle, "show us how it's done! If Hawkins doesna' practice he'll be the death of me! Ach, how I ache from laughing!"

How they missed Mary when she and her parents moved far away. But fathers must go where their jobs take them, and the job of Mary's father took the family across the continent to British Columbia when she and Hawkins had been close friends but for a few precious years. Mary and Hawkins knew not the strength of the puppy love they bore each other until parting intruded upon them when Hawkins was age fourteen and Mary tender thirteen. Unbearable sadness pervaded the first weeks of separation. Of course, they promised each other they would write, but the promise faded, and the letters dwindled until after a couple of years, they were reduced to Christmas cards and finally to none at all: puppy love and friendship tucked away and hidden; childhood memories and promises, once so poignant and destined to endure until the end of time, were now temporarily eclipsed by the irresistible enthusiasms of adolescent life.

One summer evening, as Will sat smoking his pipe on the porch, a sad and puzzled young Hawkins, intensely missing his recently departed friend, came and sat beside him.

"Grandpa, I wasn't chosen to play on the baseball team."

"Oh?"

"I don't have enough 'fight' in me. I don't try hard enough to win."

"Do you like to play baseball?" Will asked. "Yes, but not the way they want me to."

Will was unsure what he meant. "How's that?" he asked.

"To practice a lot and keep my mind on winning," Hawkins replied, "for losing is bad, and nobody likes a loser."

Will became thoughtful. Muscular Christianity and the Civic Gospel of the 1880s were still a strong influence in Scotland when he was a boy. He thought about the soccer games he had enjoyed in the old country and about what he had been taught was the spirit and purpose of sport. He could only pass on to Hawkins what he had learned and felt to be right.

"Winning is not all, lad. A wee bit o' competition a'tween friends is fine as long as it doesna' become o'er important. It's no', as they say, whether you win or lose that counts, it's how you play the game. Sport is supposed to teach lads and lassies how to play honestly and courteously by the rules of the game. It's how they learn what fairness and justice are and how to win and loose wi' grace; it builds good character!

"It's no disgrace to lose if you do it wi' good humor. Losing shouldna' make you think less of yersel. It's as much a part of games as winning. Like a seesaw, when one end goes up the other goes doon. One end's as important as the other, for it takes both to make it go.

"Winning is fine as long as you remember your opponent is a friend who loves the game as much as you do. Treat him kindly and with respect, and if he's a worthy opponent, he'll do the same for you."

Hawkins put his arms around his grandfather's neck.

Damn those people whoever they are! thought Will indignantly. *What right have they to judge this gentle boy and tell him he's not good enough for them?*

"Best stay away fra' anyone too keen on winning," he said. "Vanity and selfishness are apt to be stronger than friendship and fairness."

Hawkins saw Will was angry. "They're greedy! They cause strife and misery. That's not how life should be lived!"

"Should I stop playing ball, Grandpa?"

"Not if you enjoy it, lad. Just be more particular who you play with. If they're hell-bent on winning at all costs, you'd best play with somebody else!"

That brief lesson stayed with Hawkins. It made good sense to him, and he never forgot it!

Hawkins matured into a gentle, handsome young man with a talent for drawing and painting people and scenes which captivated him. It was something natural—it was his way. To say he enjoyed it would be to miss the point; not doing it was impossible and something which never crossed his mind. Bella and Will recognized his skill, and because he would always be modestly provided with income from the insurance trust left by his parents, they fondly envisioned his future as an artist.

The years passed peacefully and uneventfully until the inevitable day when Hawkins said good-bye to Bella and Will. He was to study at the Art Students League in far away New York City, where Bella and Will had entered the United States so long ago. For a weary time, they listened for a voice they didn't hear, for footsteps which did not fall, and their lives seemed empty indeed.

Will's two sons, Ken and Alex, had not emigrated to Canada and still lived unmarried at number 7 Park Terrace. They were soft-spoken gentlemen of retiring nature, delighted to welcome Hawkins back to a home he had been fast forgetting but where he now would spend such pleasant holidays during his years in the city.

Hawkins was not able to go home as often as he wished during his student days. He saved what he could from the insurance annuity to establish himself in a modest home and studio when this phase of his training ended. Now it was finished; he had amassed a small sum, and it was time to try his wings. It was a happy, zestful time of life when the future beckoned, and exuberant youth eagerly responded with hope and boundless expectations.

During her years in secondary school and university, Mary never completely forgot Hawkins and what to her were the wonderful girlhood years in Halifax. Though she longed to see her grandparents and the McLeods, her education was foremost in her mind and its expense, in those of her parents.

Shorthand had been an essential skill when Mary's mother, Heather Ayrshire, was employed; but not having worked outside the home since emigrating, she was unaware of its obsolescence. With modest pride in her skill and believing it still useful, she taught it to Mary. It was like a game to Mary, a game she was eager to learn. Though no more vain than most, she was flattered by the admiration and envy of her friends.

When she went on to university, Mary found it very useful for taking lecture notes and for copying reference sources. It enabled her to write and rewrite drafts of the compositions required in her study of English literature, getting everything just as it should be before making a final copy.

As Mary entered the house one afternoon shortly after her graduation from university, her mother excitedly grasped her arm.

"Mary! A letter has come from your aunt Martha today with a newspaper clipping from the *Dirigo Vigilance*. It's an ad for someone interested in newspaper work who knows shorthand! Why don't you write and ask about it?"

The question of why anyone still needed shorthand in this day of electronic recording had crossed Mary's mind, but working on a newspaper interested her and might do very well until she published her first novel. She replied to the ad. After all, for her too, it was a happy, zestful time of life when the future beckoned, and exuberant youth eagerly responded with hope and boundless expectations.

Bella did not hear the doorbell over the noise of the vacuum cleaner, but on such a warm early July day, the front door was open.

"Mrs. McLeod," Mary called through the screen door. The only response was the drone of the vacuum cleaner.

"Mrs. McLeod!" she shouted more loudly.

At this, Bella switched off the vacuum and went to the door. There she found a young lady waiting with such a beaming smile on her lovely face that Bella thought, *She looks like she knows me! Now, who can it be?*

"You don't recognize me!"

Bella was puzzled. There really was something familiar about her. Was it her eyes? Where had she seen that impish smile before? She stepped out onto the porch. "I know I've seen you someplace before, my dear, but—" And then it came to her!

"Mary!" Bella exclaimed. "What? Where? How?" Words failed her.

Mary laughed and hugged her in a happy embrace. "It's been almost ten years, Mrs. McLeod, but you look just as I remember you."

"Your grandfather . . . he said nothing about you coming to visit." Bella was stunned! The lass she recalled, all arms and legs and pigtails had turned, in the blink of an eye, into this beautiful young woman! She needed a cup of tea!

An hour flew by as they sat in the kitchen, Bella full of questions about Mary, and Mary full of questions about Hawkins. They laughed away another hour reviving fond memories: of Hawkins doing a jig with two left feet, of Mary pounding a drum in the rail yard, and so it went until Mary rose to leave.

"Will you be back when Will's here?" Bella asked.

"I wish I could, Mrs. McLeod, but my plane leaves in just a few hours. I'm on my way to my first job." She could see that Bella was disappointed. "But it's not far away . . . at least not as far as British Columbia, and I'll be back. Perhaps next time, Hawkins will be here."

"Oh, I think she'll be back," Bella later said to herself. "The dear child! She hasn't forgotten Hawkins, I can see that. They were as close as two peas in a pod when they were children. What a joy it would be if they fell in love!"

At which point, she had visions of a little Mary and a little Hawkins doted on by loving great-grandparents!

Where had the time gone?

Chapter 2

FOLLOWING COMPLETION OF his training at the Art Students League, Hawkins decided not to remain in New York City. Life in Greenwich Village had been full of interest, and though tempted to remain with friends who had rented a loft for apartment and studio, he felt an urge for change. For some, the city with its museums, libraries, and theaters was an essential nutritive and liberating environment, but Hawkins longed for natural vistas, solitude to contemplate his artistic options, and the scents of country air.

This plan was less ambitious, almost deplorably lazy compared to those of some of his classmates. However, his friends felt his decision was in keeping with his quiet, amiable disposition.

A classmate, soon to accompany his fiancée to Paris, offered him the purchase of an older Chevy pickup truck, a bit run-down in appearance. So opportunely did this suit his plan of meandering home along the New England coast that he bought it. In his mind's eye, he saw small villages, picturesque coves where fishermen unloaded their daily catch, and wharves which displayed tide-stained and seaweed-coated piles at low tide. Such an experience would be novel and exciting, for his few previous trips home had been fast and direct, hitchhiking inland through the potato fields of Maine.

He longed to experience the Maine coast, that mecca for the romantic painters and poets of a bygone era. Their genius greatly affected him. He was spellbound by glowing dawns and sunsets, surf and figures frozen forever in a moment of time yet dynamic and full of life. Hawkins was a dreamer who daydreamed of a utopia where all was beauty, charm, and inner peace.

Dear Folks,

Knowing that you are both well, I'll not be heading home directly. The fiancé of one of the girls who is going on to Paris to study sold me his truck rather than storing it in Hoboken. After several years in the city, the idea of being footloose, sketching and painting out of doors strongly appeals to me. My roommate Pag and I will spend the summer traveling up the coast at our leisure. Hopefully, I'll have some watercolors to show you when I return. Of course, I'll write frequently and let you know where I am and what I'm doing. God bless you both.

Hawkins

"You're more wishful than I am, Hawkins," said his roommate Tony Pagliano, known to his friends as Pag. "You think we're going to find the kind of places Winslow Homer found long before we were born. I suppose they're still there but privately owned and plastered with warnings to Keep Out!

"I'll bet most of our time will be spent in a stampeding herd of trucks and cars, breathing exhaust fumes and spending a lot of time at toll booths and red lights . . . nothing to look at but places to spend money. For guys like us the so-called coast is a delusion . . . maybe a rare postcard scene if it's framed right." Hawkins smiled, believing not a word and convinced Pag didn't either. As pessimistic as he sounded at times, no real pessimist could draw the beauty out of metal, stone, and clay as Pag was capable of doing.

"Crabby genius!" he retorted.

Pag was a black-haired, swarthy complected, muscular sculptor with soft brown eyes which contrasted with the firm set of his chin. Though his nature was fiery, his speech profane, and his opinions intemperate, he would not harm any helpless thing. Despite his passionate often fierce rhetoric, he had the most tender of hearts.

His political philosophy was easily grasped. Its central devils were what he called the privateers, the term by which he designated that anonymous cabal who hide behind the dual fig leaves of politicians and journalists and, as he put it, "run the country." He saw them as dishonest, hypocritical thieves, pirates from the home port of Wall Street, sanctioned by laws of their own making. "The privateers bankroll their congressional lackeys who tax hell out of us and dump the money into their own cash cow, the so-called defense budget . . ." ran one of Pag's recurrent themes.

"They talk about government waste, meaning the pittance of 'we the people's' tax dollars spent on 'we the people.' The rest of 'we the people's' taxes is a political giveaway of public funds to private pockets via fantastically profitable waste: guns, bombs, warplanes . . . you name it! Stuff that does nobody any good. While, of course, giving themselves tremendous tax breaks.

"They pump a lot of their immoral profits into their propaganda servants. Not a sliver of unspun, undistorted truth ever gets through their iron curtain of propaganda. TV, radio, newspapers, and magazines keep us peons narcotized and ignorant—ripped off but enthusiastic. 'Boobus Americanus'

H. L. Mencken called us, upon whom no one ever lost money by underestimating our tastes.

"They spend huge sums on the services of congressional whores behind whose skirts they can hide while they pull the strings and rip the people off worse and worse. It's a vicious spiral, the biggest screw-job in history!"

Hawkins liked the generous, kindhearted fellow and had learned to turn a courteous but deaf ear to his christlike social commentary. Pag was an intelligent, sensitive, skilled, and inspired sculptor whose lofty artistic aspirations were in no way degraded by his low opinion of the "money changers" looting the human race. Hawkins' unconcern about matters social and political vexed and amazed Pag but oddly calmed his oft times turbulent exasperation. Pag ranted, and Hawkins listened, but they never argued. Oddly, they were the best of friends. They sincerely thought highly of one another, and each retorted spiritedly to anyone who spoke slightingly of one friend within the other's hearing.

Hawkins found Pag's summary characterization of the Maine coast not entirely unwarranted: an irresistible summertime attraction for many people, the province of entrepreneurs seeking to garner as much cash as vacation- minded tourists could be persuaded to part with. Nevertheless, it felt good to be out of the city proper though the traffic was often as congested and frustrating.

"What did I tell you? Hell . . . ! From where we are right now, there is no ocean in sight. What isn't business frontage, oil refineries, power plants, or marinas is probably owned by rich privateers who don't like trespassers. Oh, yeah . . . there are public beaches, but they're damned few. Just look how few green spots there are on the map. All I can see are Reid State Park and Acadia National Park, and they're probably packed with people . . . hardly the stuff for great art!" Pag fumed as they sat sweltering on Route 1 in a long line of scarcely moving cars and trucks, waiting to cross the Kennebec River at Bath, Maine. "People, people, people, cars, trucks, and commercial scab . . . some paradise! Just look at some of those license plates: Vacation Land, Live Free or Die! They're so fatuous, I don't know whether to laugh or cry."

"This isn't what I had in mind, Pag. I'm as disappointed as you are," said Hawkins as he pointed to a small green area on the map. "Why don't we head for this state park? It's not very far. Maybe we can find a place to nap, then drive all night and try to get beyond this heavy traffic."

They parked the truck in a sunbaked gravel lot, followed the *Rosa rugosa* lined wooden walkway to the beach, and picked their way cautiously down to the water between towels, blankets, bodies, and beach umbrellas. Only here and there on the long beach were there groups of bathers hardy enough to endure the frigid water. At intervals, some young man, woman, or child dashed into the gentle surf, flinging himself momentarily into the water then beat a rapid retreat to the sun-warmed sand. The people on the hot beach, sunning themselves on gaudy towels or shaded by colorful umbrellas, were joyous and numerous. Walking barefoot in the cold, gentle waves so refreshed the spirits of Hawkins and Pag that the vexing traffic jams were soon forgotten.

Pag noticed an elderly couple hastily preparing to relinquish a picnic spot under the dark pines which edged the beach and said, "Let's go claim that picnic table! It's shaded. We can spread out our sleeping bags and get some rest."

Hawkins fetched their sleeping bags from the truck, and they spread them in the cool shade under the trees. How good it felt to stretch out; he sighed with pleasure.

"Jesus Christ! Something's biting the hell out of me!" immediately exclaimed Pag jumping to his feet. "My god! Just look at these mosquitos! I'm afraid to take a good breath. I'll inhale the bastards. Run, Hawkins! They'll eat us alive!"

"They're almost as bad here as they are on Prince Edward Island," Hawkins cried, hastily bundling up his sleeping bag.

Once out of the trees, a light breeze blew away the voracious stragglers that had followed them. The truck was an oven, but the heat soothed the myriad punctures which covered their exposed skin.

Hawkins drove to the tiny, nearby fishing village of Five Islands, where on a deck overhanging the water, they ate lobster on paper plates and drank beer from cans, along with a crowd of happy tourists. Since there were no unoccupied table seats, they leaned against the railing and used it as their table.

Hawkins looked at Pag, and they began to laugh so heartily Hawkins beat on Pag's back to keep him from choking on the beer and the lobster, which he was in the act of swallowing. Both young men gave way to mirth so uncontrollable they bent over, beating their fists on the railing, with tears rolling down their cheeks.

"Vanquished by salt marsh mosquitos!" Hawkins was scarcely able to utter the words.

"We retreated just in time," replied Pag, gasping for breath. "Can you see it . . . ? Two men, chalk white, wrinkled as prunes, sucked dry, bloodless . . . coming down onto the beach . . . people scattering, panicked . . . Hahaha."

"Politicians rush through bill," replied Hawkins, "ban ghosts and vampires from all state parks . . . lauded in editorials."

Vexation vented in mirth loses its sting; they felt better and spent what remained of the afternoon and the long summer twilight in the village sketching lobstermen, their boats, and dwellings.

After the tourists had departed and sunset began to paint the sky in radiant pastels, the cool sea breeze ushered in a delightful evening. For several hours, they slept as soundly as they could while cramped in the truck to avoid the mosquitos. Hawkins, the first to awaken, stood by the truck stretching his stiff legs and gazing with pleasure upon the lobster boats bobbing at their moorings in the moonlit water. *I'll sketch that tomorrow,* he thought. *A composition in shades and tints of blue, capturing the moonlight and the shadow depths, and the mystery of being alone in the predawn by the lilting sea   It really hasn't been such a bad day after all!*

They drove through the remainder of the hours of darkness, passing through the deserted streets of sleeping towns and shared the road with only occasional headlights until the eastern sky heralded the soon-to-rise sun. Details of the slumbering, dew-wet landscape gradually emerged out of the darkness. The moon set in the west, behind rising morning mists. Pag yawned and said, "If they're like me, people fall into a deep sleep just before dawn. Leonardo da Vinci was right! We do have the world all to ourselves when everyone else is asleep. Okay, he didn't say just that, but he liked being alone." He extended and flexed his stiff arms and yawned again. "I wonder if we can find someplace to stretch our legs and get some coffee!"

They reached the more northern coast of Maine later in the forenoon and drove down an interesting byway pointing in the direction of the ocean, seeking some deserted spot where they might set up their tent and linger to see, feel, and paint.

The weed-overgrown dirt road they stumbled upon by chance and along which they slowly traveled wound through the cool shade of a forest of patriarchal oaks and conifers. The height of the weeds in the roadway made it unlikely that it had been used in recent time. Nearly a mile further on, the forest gave way to an expansive, overgrown field beyond which lay the ocean.

A surprised and delighted Hawkins parked beneath an aged, lofty oak, which spread its expansive boughs over the truck, and gazed with fascination upon an ancient, deserted, weather-beaten house and barn. The dim rumble of surf could be heard a long way off. Cloud shadows moved across the wide, boulder-strewn, green and sandy meadow, where wild blueberry bushes flourished. Silence, broken only by the lapping of distant waves, gave the scene a dimension of peace and tranquility. A half mile east, the silver offing shone beyond a line of dark green conifers, which to the eye, separated the field from the sea.

The dark forest, the expansive green meadow, and deserted dwelling captivated Hawkins. Was it the silence, a sense of trespassing on ruins left by the dead? Whatever the feeling was, whatever provoked it, whatever it disturbed, lay so deep within him that it was overwhelming and mysterious. He recalled Howard Carter, 1922 in the Valley of the Kings of Egypt, his disturbing emotions evoked upon entering the tomb of King Tutankhamen, sealed three thousand years before; "the shadows move but the dark is never quite uplifted."[1] How powerfully those words resonated within Hawkins as he gazed, pondering the abandoned dwelling they had stumbled upon.

The prospect before him evoked an impression of wildness and tranquility, that nature had recaptured something which had once known the hand of man but knew it no longer. It was stunning, momentous, a moment which influenced him more than he suspected.

He and Pag headed toward the sea in silence, neither of them wishing to disturb the pervading peace and found themselves on a headland which terminated in a massive rock buttress pushing out into the restless moving sea. On both sides, the rocky, tree-lined coast stretched as far as they could see. The only sign of human habitation, a few miles to the north, was a white church steeple rising above the trees.

The meadow ended in a thick line of centuries-old, stunted, wind-twisted pines, modestly taller than a man, the interlacing branches of which barred their way. As they pushed the scratching, clinging branches aside, a shower of irritating dead needles fell on their necks and down their collars until at last they stood upon the edge of a steep granite cliff. Below them the ebb tide waves broke and slid onto a beach composed of immense rocks of which some were partially and others completely covered in fine to gravely sand, making a flattened, slightly sloping beach perhaps five to six yards in width.

"Will you look at that!" gasped Pag. "It's a sheer drop of thirty, forty, maybe even fifty feet where we're standing!"

"There's water behind those rocks sticking out down there." Hawkins pointed to an outcropping ledge about five yards below them. "Which means waves must come up nearly that far at high tide."

"Awesome!" Pag replied. "What happens if you're on that beach when the tide comes in?"

"I don't know," said Hawkins. "We must come back later and find out!" Shortly after they returned from their initial jaunt and had set up their tent,

Pag crawled in and promptly fell asleep. Hawkins, however, was too curious

to be sleepy. Who had lived here? How old was the house? Why had it been abandoned and when? His foot struck something as he stepped into the grass. It was a sign: "For Sale. Leo LaChance. Hemlock Harbor." Perhaps he would look up Mr. LaChance; he would know, at least, when it was last lived in and probably more.

Hawkins went first to the barn, pulled open the door, stepped onto a floor of hardpacked clay, and inhaled the aroma of aged wood and the remains of sun-dried hay. He counted wooden stanchions for six cattle. Opposite the stanchions, a piece of the wall was rotted through, letting in outside light, but aside from that damage, the lumber had defied the destructive effects of time and was amber hued and grained with age. Across his mind flitted the pleasing image of a room paneled with such boards aglow in warm firelight, a snug refuge from biting wind and blowing snow.

Making a circuit of the barn before proceeding to the house, he came upon a mound of weeds which abutted the region of decay. *It's the remnant of a manure pile*, he thought, *which explains that bit of rot.*

To Hawkins' eye, features of the aged house, the unadorned outer walls and small upper story windows, were typical of early eighteenth-century New England farmhouses. White chalky dust, the residue of weathered paint or white wash, adhered to his fingers when he poked and rubbed the clapboards, and he found the wood to be remarkably dry and strong. Steps of granite slabs, worn smooth by the feet of many generations, led to a securely fastened oak door. Two chimneys of weathered brick stood at each end of the slate-shingled roof.

He then proceeded toward a group of large cedar trees some hundred yards to the south of the house. As he pushed toward this grove through tough, high weeds, lush in the summer sun, his foot struck something solid and unyielding. Tearing away the entangling growth, he uncovered a rusty, pitted section of cast iron fence, an ornamental picket typical of those which enclose, to this day, many family burial grounds throughout New England. His keen eye discerned a handful of other rusted pickets, largely obscured by weeds and lying almost flat upon the ground, which suggested a rectangular pattern abutting the more distant grove of those botanical emblems of mortality, the centuries-old cedars. A few steps farther and Hawkins stood amid the remains of headstones. It was a sobering sight. Soft, weatherworn, red stone, and gray slate slabs, some broken and tumbled down, all bearing epitaphs of long-forgotten folk, protruded through the entangling weeds. As far as he could then tell, not one remained erect and intact, but overgrowth rendered this uncertain.

Despite its neglect and disrepair, this hushed, solitary, abandoned graveyard impressed Hawkins as a place of mute stateliness caressed by the hand of time.

One large boulder, its graven epitaph obscured by tenacious lichen and inch-thick tendrils of an indomitable climbing rose vine, clad with giant vicious and tearing thorns, stood against the lofty cedars, a silent, ponderous monument of the past.

In Hawkins's reverie the present rolled away, ephemerally replaced by some now-forgotten time, a time when this deserted homestead had known the sweat of toil, the joy of love, and the sorrow of death. He gazed across the vast field which had known the hand of men long dead, where they had once planted crops of corn and winter squash and had swept their scythes through fields of hay.

He found a stout stick and, with it, having approached as near as he was able through the almost impenetrable thorns, scratched away a bit of the tenacious plants coating the boulder's face. It was hard work, but he eventually made out the family name of "Gibbs." That discovery at least provided him a provisional name for the uninhabited farm: the Gibbs' Place.

In the evening when the tide was at the flood, Hawkins and Pag returned to observe the height of the water: how near to the top of the cliff it rose and what danger lurked there for the unwary. Waves approached the shore in rolling silver gray swells which, when the energy of their momentum was abruptly stopped by the cliff, violently exploded a few feet below the rocky outcrop into geysers of spray, which reached the dripping conifers. The sound of the breaking waves made speech impossible. How high raging surf would rise against the cliff in a storm-driven sea, they had yet to find out, but calm sea or not, that precipitous edge was a precarious, potentially deadly place.

Beams of the newly risen moon, shining toward them across a lonesome sea, struck a chord in the depths of Hawkins' soul, convincing him fate had led him to this place. Though he knew not why, he felt certain if he cast aside whatever was beckoning him, he would wish with all his heart he had not.

Chapter 3

A LONELY SPECK of shipboard light, endless miles out on a sea of ink, made the pitch-dark, moonless vault beneath the stars an awful and awesome vastness, across the depths of which momentarily etched startling, random meteoric streaks. The starry background, hardly visible in light-polluted urbanity, overpowered the minds of both Hawkins and Pag. To them, it reduced man the arrogant, man the hub of his blundering egocentric delusions, king and pauper alike, to puny specks of consciousness. The Gibbs plateau had dissolved into this void. A campfire of red coals, the shadowy forms of two men and a tent, the moonless sky and the rolling murmur of the sea were suspended at the edge of the quicksand of impenetrable night.

A chill sea breeze began gently, persistently, unremittingly to make the fire flare and the shadows of the two men dance on the tent.

"Pag," said Hawkins as they huddled by the campfire in their winter jackets, seeking protection from this cold summer night by the sea, "do you have an odd feeling about this place?"

"What kind of feeling?" Pag asked, fully aware of the moonless night so densely black beyond the glow of the fire. "You mean spooky? Hell, yes! Especially on nights like this!"

"Not spooky." Hawkins was pensive. "A feeling as though we're living in close contact with the past, like time may have absentmindedly tipped us someplace where we don't belong."

Pag slowly filled then lighted his pipe. "Now that you've brought it up, there is something. I don't know if it's what you mean, but I get a funny feeling at times, like something might walk out of the house and scare the hell out of me."

Hawkins laughed. Pag's straightforward, often profane, figurative mode of expression amused him. He was neither subtle nor diplomatic; his words expressed precisely what was in his mind, whose rough guilelessness endeared him to Hawkins.

"I get a similar feeling, that somebody might be just beyond the dim light of the fire. Centuries seem to melt away here at night." Hawkins became whimsically melodramatic. "Something ghostly might come stomping up from the barn and lay a cold hand on your shoulder."

"Stop it, Hawkins! You're making my flesh creep!" A screech owl hooted its rasping scream from the depths of the forest. "Mother of god! What's that?" exclaimed Pag.

"It's a banshee calling from the house," joked Hawkins. "Why don't you go see what it wants."

"Banshee be damned!" said Pag, moving closer to the fire, in no mood for pleasantries. "When we go to town tomorrow and see other people, I'll feel a lot better just knowing there are some around."

Dawn looked for Pag the following morning but found only his sleeping bag which enclosed some concealed object from which escaped an occasional snore. Hawkins had risen in the frigid predawn and lighted a blazing fire to warm the bone-chilling air. The heat of the fire and a mug of hot coffee swept away the night's cobwebs and restored his senses. The old house and barn, the burial ground, forest, and overgrown plateau ending in a sea cliff, the sea of burnished gold—all, discarding the sable robe of night, captivated his eye and mind in the radiant light of the rising sun. He stood beneath the aged, massive oak tree, staring dreamlike at the Gibbs' house. Images of bygone days sauntered through his head: an old man leaving the house to tend cows in the barn, smoke lazily floating from the chimney, children swinging from the very limbs above his head.

It's run-down and neglected, he thought, *but it's still a magnificent old house, apparently as solid, or nearly so, as the day it was built. There are people who dream of quiet, peaceful places on an isolated, rocky ocean coastline like this. I'm glad we found it.* He picked up the realtor's sign he had stumbled over in the weeds and tossed it into the back of the truck, then wandered into the forest behind the house and eventually wound back to the overgrown road-path leading to the house. Sections of tumbledown stone walls, bordering what had once been fields, were visible among century-old oaks and hemlocks.

How many generations did it take to build those walls? he wondered. *I suppose one generation cleared an area, sledged out the rocks, and dumped them at the edge. The next generation extended the area and did the same thing with the rocks. With every generation, the fields and the walls expanded. What an immense amount of labor! I wonder, why, after all that work, the fields were abandoned once again to the forest?*

On his return his mind still dwelt on the generations that had been born and had died in the old house.

"What would you think," Hawkins said to the big sculptor, who was shivering by the fire with a steaming cup of coffee in his large hands, "about staying here?"

"How long? I'm getting tired of living cramped up in the tent." "Say . . . for the rest of the summer . . . in the house."

Pag looked at him and smiled. Hawkins was pleasantly surprised by the

look in his eyes.

"You like the idea, don't you?"

"Yes, now that you ask, I do! It's what we were looking for, and now we've found it, it doesn't make much sense to go away and leave it."

"I'll see the real estate agent when we're in town and see if it's for rent," said Hawkins, considering the money he had saved to begin his career; but they had to board some place! From an artistic viewpoint, this temporary location was as ideal as they could reasonably desire; the prospect felt good, it felt right!

The people of Hemlock Harbor, mainly fishermen and farmers, were thrifty by inclination and necessity. The most recent of the farms in the vicinity of Hemlock Harbor dated from around the time of the Civil War, and many were much older. They were not fancy places: a weathered house, a ramshackle barn, rusty machinery, a line of clothes drying in the breeze, a few chickens scratching about. The barns, time and weather stained to a grayish hue, leaned away from the north wind, and the barbed wire fences hung slack and rusty. A snow-covered lobster boat sat in most yards during the winter, and lobster traps were stacked by the barn. Men set out to sea at sunrise during spring, summer, and fall, spent hours tending traps and nets, returned to work the farm, then out to sea again in the evening. It was work for hardy men who would not willingly have led any other kind of life in any other place.

The buildings of the town, located on Main Street, were old. The newest, now close to fifty years old, was a gas station built in 1939. In addition to the grocery, drug, and clothing stores, there were a small post office, an antique shop, the Wicked Good Café, and a newspaper office.

Hawkins and Pag stopped in the post office to inquire about renting a delivery box. The aged building was small, divided into two sections by a partition which held the postboxes and the counter. The postmistress was a vivacious black girl bantering with a small group of locals gathered about the counter. "I'm not the postmaster." She smiled. "My dad is. He'll be back in a moment." Her father was a surprisingly tall, well-proportioned, black man with some obvious non-African ancestors. Being from the city, Pag and Hawkins saw nothing unusual in a black postmaster on the Maine coast, not the reaction the man expected from strangers and which led them into conversation.

Like many men of extraordinary physical strength, Howard Desmond, postmaster, was gentle and soft-spoken. His daughter Sandra was a charming young lady, who possessed not only the qualities of her father but the vivacity and beauty of youth.

Hawkins learned that Howard's family had lived in or near Hemlock Harbor for well over a hundred years. Howard did not know how long ago they had settled here. "But it was before the Civil War, and according to family legend, based on a rusted slave anklet inscribed in Spanish and handed down in the family for generations, it's more than likely I'm descended from an escaped slave from the Caribbean," said Howard. He gazed at Hawkins and Pag with a look in his eyes as though his train of thought was suddenly disrupted and confused when Hawkins described where they thought of settling for the summer. "As a boy," he began, "I have a vague memory of standing on that cliff overlooking the sea . . . something I've not thought of for years. It's given me a queer shiver." A quick smile reassured them the emotive memory was short-lived. This comprised virtually all that Howard remembered at the moment about the peninsula they had stumbled upon. "The reliability of any of it," he said, "is highly questionable."

Hawkins thanked him for the information, which captivated his interest, reliable or not. "If we're lucky and do move into the house, would you visit us and bring Sandra?" he asked, wishing to better know this man and perhaps paint his fascinating daughter. With a congenial smile, Howard assured them that it would be a pleasure for both of them.

Pag and he then wandered along to the wharf at the end of Main Street, where a small fleet of fishing boats were moored. The tide being out, a few rowboats sat on a plain of mud and sand. The wharf, which extended into the water even at low tide, had at the far end an unpainted, weather-beaten building where fishermen stored their gear. Attached to it by a ramp was a floating dock which rose and fell with the tide. Pag and Hawkins descended to the dock where a lobsterman was crating his catch.

Pag extended his leg from the landward end of the dock and touched his foot on the mud and, finding it firm, stepped out onto it.

"Bettah tell your friend not ta go too fah," the man said to Hawkins. "Tide's due in."

Hawkins thought of the cliff back at the Gibbs' place. "What's the tide like?" he asked.

"Fundy tides ah deep as you can see on the pilin's," the man answered, pointing to the twelve-foot span of sea stain on the posts. "And roll in fairly fast, couple o' feet an hour. You can be cut off if yo' don't watch out."

"What do you mean?"

"Don't get caught out on land you gotta get to by crossin' the tidal flat," replied the man, "unless you wanna get wet gettin' back." He paused and looked amused at Pag. "Bettah call your friend 'cause heah she comes, and he's no boots on."

Hawkins saw a sizable wave rolling past the rocky breakwater and into the harbor mouth. "Pag!" he called. "Get back on the dock! Quick!"

Pag ran back and jumped onto the dock. "What's the matter?" "Just wait and see!" said the man.

Soon the dock began to gently pitch and roll on the incoming waves as it

slowly but not unperceptively rose higher and higher.

"Jesus!" gasped Pag, kneeling on the wet planks. "What's happening?"

The man laughed. "Tide's on the way in."

Pag enjoyed what to him was a novel experience, the sensation of being tossed gently about by lapping waves.

"That's impressive! I want to come back near high tide and feel that again!" Pag said excitedly.

"If you do," warned the man, "make sure a good Nor'easter ain't blowin'! The wind'l wash watah right ovah this whahf and into the shack. It's not a good place to be then, nor a safe one neethah."

They thanked the man for his warning and advice and turned back to town to find Leo LaChance. Walking back up Main Street, they admired the white frame congregational church which sat on the hill west of town, the steeple of which could be seen from the place they now called home.

Forty years ago, Leo LaChance had converted the parlor of his colonial-era home into an office and fastened a sign which read "Leo LaChance, Realtor. Built 1856." to the front of his neat white house. It was a quaint, old- fashioned office with a faded carpet on the floor of wide pine boards, an aged wooden desk, and two large wicker chairs. Behind the desk, Leo LaChance sat reading an outdated magazine by the light of a large ornate china lamp. He was an elderly man with thin white hair and a large white mustache and whose wire-rimmed glasses were sliding off his nose. His striped shirt was loosely stuffed into a pair of faded corduroy trousers held up by washed-out pink suspenders, which had been red when new. He did not hear Hawkins enter but looked up when he placed his hands on the desk.

He took a long look at Hawkins, apparently liked what he saw, pushed his glasses back up his nose, and said, "Have a seat, young man! What can I do for you?"

Hawkins sat in one of the wicker chairs, stretched his long legs before him, placed his arms on the wide armrests, and glanced quickly around the room. He saw faded wallpaper of a bygone era, shelves on which were stacked papers yellowed with age, a print of Abraham Lincoln, and several by Currier and Ives; it was an old room that looked its age and had the faint aroma that went with it.

Hawkins wanted to learn anything this old man could tell him about what he called the Gibbs' place. Leo scratched his head. "Never heard of it."

Hawkins described the location. Leo thought a bit. "That's the old Dobbins' home," he said and then proceeded to tell what he knew about it.

"Old Mrs. Dobbins lived there all of twenty years ago," he began. "The husband died about ten years before, then the widow lived there until she passed on. Nobody's lived there since. Everything went to the wife's younger sister. She lives in Howarton over in the next county."

"Does she still own it?" Hawkins asked.

"Ayah, Jemima Stowe's a spry eighty and still goin' strong." "Is the house for rent?" asked Hawkins.

"Nope. Jemima's tired of our winters. She wants to sell out and go to Florida, and she's waited a good while," Leo said, implying she would readily accept the first reasonable offer.

Leo noted the disappointed look on Hawkins' face. "She's not asking that much."

Hawkins was momentarily stunned. Was he willing to part with the money he had managed to save, the money for which he had foregone many of the pleasures of student life? The words were out of his mouth before he could stop them: "How much?"

"Well, let's see . . . The buildings ain't worth much: no indoor plumbing, no running water, and no electricity . . . say two hundred dollars an acre for the land and twenty thousand for the buildings. That would be forty thousand dollars."

Hawkins thought the price was reasonable, maybe even a bargain, not that he knew what property was worth so far north. A down payment would not deplete his entire savings, but what of the repairs?

He left with the key to the house in his pocket.

Exploring the house was an adventure. The large parlor would make an ideal studio in which both Hawkins and Pag could work comfortably. It had a large fireplace, and there was a pump in the old-fashioned kitchen.

Pag pounded on the walls, pronounced them solid, and stomped up the steep narrow stairs. "Neither of us can stand straight up here," he yelled down to Hawkins, "and the roof leaks. There are watermarks on the ceiling."

Hawkins was in the cellar and yelled back, "We can't stand up down here either. We'll just have to be careful!"

"What do you think?" asked Hawkins when they had completed their inspection.

"We'd need a ladder to patch the roof," answered Pag, "a lot of firewood for heat and cooking, and a couple of beds."

"It needs a lot of work," Hawkins said happily, "but we wouldn't want to change it too drastically and then be sorry we'd destroyed the spirit of the old place. After all, we'd be buying two hundred years or more with this property and wouldn't want to lose them. Are you discouraged?"

"How about you?" Pag replied.

"It means a couple of years of hard work and rough living, but I'm all for it!" Hawkins waited for Pag's expected negative response.

"By god, it's a challenge!" said Pag enthusiastically grasping Hawkins' hand. "Let's do it!"

Word spread that two artists had bought the old Dobbins' place, and townsfolk wondered what two fancy New Yorkers would do with it. The secondhand pickup truck and two tanned and muscular young men in soiled work clothes quickly revised their attitude. Mainers were skeptical of people "from away," especially when they bought a big piece of land and moved in. "They come here because they like Maine, but as soon as they're here, they want to make it like the place they came from," was a universal complaint. Neither Hawkins nor Pag noticed their chilly reception. Soon the townsfolk began to notice that "they keep pretty much to themselves and don't bother anybody" and "they work hard, weren't born with silver spoons in their mouths" which gradually changed to "they ain't so bad" which was the highest praise they had for outsiders.

George and Martha Cottager were an older couple, whose home lay between the small peninsula, of which the entirety consisted of the Gibbs' place, and the town of Hemlock Harbor. The Cottagers might be said to be their closest neighbors, as the crow flies, although separated from them several miles by road. George and his wife had retired to Maine several years before "from away," meaning, in regional dialect, from out of the state, and though they had lived on the coast for several years, found that epithetical phrase to be a permanent but not prejudicial attribute.

George, a pleasant, clean shaven, gentleman of scholarly appearance, was their first visitor. Hawkins thought he might be the age his own father would have been had he lived. Knowing they had friendly neighbors pleased Pag and himself exceedingly. Heartened by his courteous interest in them, they readily entered into pleasant conversation.

"Incidentally, it doesn't matter how long ago you moved here from away," said George with a grin. "You and we shall always be quaint foreigners. That term really doesn't mean anything. It's only a label which helps local people define your identity to people whom you haven't met yet. The people are friendly, and I'm sure you'll like them as much as we do."

Their smiles and intelligent faces won George's good feeling and respect. He liked these two hardy newcomers at once and had no doubt of their becoming intimate friends.

Pag was surprised that George and his wife Martha had retired to Maine. "Retired here?" exclaimed Pag. "I thought the first thing New Englanders

did when they retired was to head south!"

George laughed. "If I'm not interrupting your work and if you really want to know why we came here, I'll tell you."

"I'm ready for a break," Pag said. "The sun is damned hot up on that roof, and the shade of this old oak is just what I need."

"Martha and I," George began, "met and fell in love while attending Chamberlain College, which is on the coast not far from here, and so naturally we have a powerful sentimental attachment to this bit of coastline. Martha's roommate, Matty Dawson, returned to Chamberlain to teach, which is another very strong tie to the area. And I really think you'll find, after a time, the sea and the shore lay hold of you, and you'll never really be happy away from it.

"You will like Matty. Though she's semiretired from teaching and research at Chamberlain, she is very active in preserving Maine's seacoast and forests, an indefatigable fighter in a noble cause—and I think, you're both the kind of people she's happy to know. Martha will see to it you meet and get to know one another.

"We had other reasons as well for returning here. Martha and I are a couple of nostalgic diehards who wanted to take a step back in time to make a change in our lives, which somehow were picking up distressing speed and momentum. We wanted time for reflection and relaxation.

"Perhaps I should describe us as unrealistic dreamers. We know we emotionally equate 'the good old days' with our childhood memories, and our parents' lives were a lot more arduous than we imagine, but we persist in our delusions nevertheless."

"Go on," Hawkins said, "this old place has cast a spell on us. There are moments when I'd like to take a long step backwards and try to understand what it was like then myself."

George was pleasantly surprised; perhaps, these new neighbors, young as they are, might share his and his friend Lilly Williams' interest in local history.

"When Martha and I were children," he continued, "there were only half as many people in the country as there are today. Life was slower and simpler. Milk and ice were delivered in horse-drawn wagons, and farmers still plowed with a team. Before there were so many automobiles and trucks, people mingled more—they used trains, trolley cars, and sidewalks. They mingled, mixed, knew each other. It gave them a sense of community.

"Before a hierarchy of political bureaucracies took over people's affairs, citizens were proud of their local school, their library, and their municipal park because they all belonged to them. They were, in fact, theirs, and they felt a fond responsibility for them. It was a time of 'rugged community-ism,' if I may coin a phrase. A time when Americans felt that they could do things for themselves, before that became somehow 'communistic.'

"All that has vanished, of course, but we missed it. Most of our vacations had been spent in downeast Maine, and we liked it. Hemlock Harbor seemed as close as we would come to what we were looking for, so here we are."

"Has it been all that you expected?" queried Hawkins.

"Not entirely," George responded with a note of exasperation in his voice. "But that's another matter best left to Matty. And," he said, shaking hands with Pag and Hawkins, "a beautiful summer day is no time for politics and philosophy, particularly when you're putting on a new roof. I've kept you from work long enough, so I'll be off. Martha and I won't bother you while the weather is nice. You've got too much to do before snow flies, but expect us then. We'll have you to a nice Sunday dinner when you can meet my wife, my niece, and Matty."

"He's a nice man!" said Pag after George drove off.

"You're right!' replied Hawkins, regretting that he had not asked if George Cottager and Howard Desmond were friends.

Chapter 4

ONE COULD TELL at once the Williams' farm was different in character from those worked by the other families in Hemlock Harbor. Labor on the farm of Earl Williams was performed by hired help, the residence was elegantly maintained, the barn was trim and tidy, and it was the only farm in Hemlock Harbor with a swimming pool. The white freshly painted appearance of the buildings and carpetlike lawn gave the farm a neat and pleasing aspect. Within the white paling of the paddock grazed curried saddle horses whose coats glistened in the sun.

Two children, a son Wiley and, a decade later, a daughter Lilly, had been born to Earl and Esther Williams. In middle age Esther was still a strikingly handsome woman, intelligent, refined, a tranquil swan who glided calmly unperturbed through life. With a tolerance which bordered on indifference, she was an agreeable and cheerful lady. Those who knew her were sincerely fond of her. Her husband and her son, neither of whom was churlish or unkind, were less caring and attentive than she deserved, but this caused her little concern.

Earl was an intelligent, portly, and genial man whose businesses usually kept him away during the week because his newspaper was printed in Bangor, the office of the Maine Association of Forest Product Companies was in Augusta, and his TV and radio station were in Portland. But, unless prevented by pressing circumstances, he looked forward to spending weekends in Hemlock Harbor. The editorial office of the newspaper, nominally controlled by both Earl and his son, was, however, under Wiley's sole command and located in the the *Dirigo Vigilance* building on Main Street in Hemlock Harbor. Though Hemlock Harbor was essentially Earl's convivial weekend retreat, Wiley spent most nights there.

When he retired, Earl would probably be made a local magistrate or justice of the peace, which prospect strongly appealed to him. He would make an outstandingly common sort of judge, an upholder of preferential laws while devoid of any real sense of justice, unaware of his indulgence of the rich and his indifference to the poor. The sort whose public respect for the Constitution and the Bill of Rights belied his subconscious scorn.

As CEO of the Maine Association of Forest Product Companies, he was primarily concerned with statehouse lobbying and public relations. He and his colleagues in business and politics formed a homogeneous group; no individual was notably different in thought or action from any other. He provided cleverly crafted though specious arguments for those politicians who needed them . . . like a gag writer peddling jokes to funny men. His arguments were plausible if critically unexamined, pertinent past events twisted or excluded, and countervailing facts disregarded or distorted.

In short, he was a naturally gifted lawyer though he had never set foot in law school. His genius for deception, of inestimable financial and influential value, was in constant demand.

However, Earl, voluntarily, no longer retained sole ownership of his media outlets. He had conferred a quarter of his holdings to Wiley when the latter graduated from college. Williams and his son were worthy chips from the same block and, on matters of importance, never seriously disagreed. Business trips, which they enjoyed in the company of well-to-do clients, seldom took father and son farther than Washington, D.C. Most of their time was spent in Bangor, Augusta, and Portland with occasional jaunts to Boston and New York.

Wiley lacked virtually nothing: suavity, money, power, position, and prestige were his birthright. No one called him handsome: his features were too irregular, his eyes too washed out and close together, his brow too low; but his ingratiating charm effaced any marked awareness of his somewhat simian appearance. The alumni office of his Ivy League alma mater most gratefully acknowledged his generosity and flattered him, whenever occasion presented, by ranking him among their most illustrious graduates. His costume of tweed jacket, blue linen shirt with button-down collar, school tie and smooth, brown leather oxfords was flawlessly conventional Ivy League garb. At the age of thirty-four, he sat on the boards of two banks, a hospital, a country club, and the local school district.

As editor, publisher, and co-owner of the statewide newspaper the *Dirigo Vigilance,* his influence was courted by all incumbent and would-be office holders. No one doubted, though he might help make a man, he needed no help in breaking him. His genius for advocacy on behalf of allies was legendary and for merciless, pernicious denigration of opponents, greatly feared. As Abraham Lincoln astutely observed, there are those who prove by telling the truth, what they cannot prove by telling the whole truth, and Wiley Williams was second to no one in that fraternity. Wiley cared nothing for *truth.* His power derived from mastery of the art of persuasion. To his father's genius for deceit, he had added powerful tools of his own: evocation of groundless fears, induction of bandwagon enthusiasms, slander rendered in an artful manner so difficult and expensive to prove, and pitiless ridicule. He was a virtuoso.

Wiley stared grimly at a paper lying before him. As autocratic owner and editor of the *Dirigo Vigilance,* he only selected personnel for employment on the paper with whom he was philosophically comfortable. He graciously provided any "associates" uncomfortable with his notion of "proper news" the immediate freedom to seek more congenial employment. His well-paid assistants submitted all dubious matters for his authoritative approval. Such a matter was now before him.

At 4:00 a.m., his cousin's loutish son Wallace, eighteen and drunk, had sped through a red light in Bangor, collided with a battered, old sedan grinding across an intersection and killed a migrant worker, his wife, and young daughter. At 5:00 a.m., Wally had appeared before Judge J. Williamson Cockalorum. The judge found him guilty of vehicular homicide, sentenced him to six months in prison, suspended the sentence, and sent him home in the police car that had brought him.

Wiley's task was to shield the judge from any suspicion that wealth and power had influenced his action. He scribbled a note to the section chief:

> Judge sentences local youth to prison for fatal early morning auto accident. Deceased   cited by police for operating vehicle with multiple serious violations of state safety laws. Employer says, "He should have known better, but he was obstinate and careless." Family of youth grateful and happy that he survived in spite of severe injuries. Police plan to inspect intersection traffic lights for proper operation. Take it from there; expand on these themes. No one is likely to give a damn about the victims anyway.

Wiley's sister Lilly, ten years his junior, was the maverick of the Williams family and shared none of Earl or Wiley's propensities. She was emphatically ethical, honest and virtuous, oblivious to the dishonesty of her father and brother.

There had been another maverick on the mother's side, but Uncle Ben had been killed more than fifty years before Lilly was born. When great- grandfather Norman was alive, many were the tales he had to tell of his uncle. They interested no one except a little, blond-haired girl in pigtails. She knew that her great-great-great-uncle Ben had been a friend of Jack London, that he had been an inveterate socialist, lumberjack, sailor, and jack-of-all-trades, mauled by "goon squads," and had been in jail. That little girl climbed trees, rode horses without a saddle, and fancied that some of Uncle Ben's blood ran in her veins; she could feel it. Even when she had grown and become an expert dealer in antiquities, she felt it most strongly whenever Wiley was around.

Lilly had a womanly yet wiry, athletic figure and a face which none of Wiley's associates found attractive. Her mouth was a bit too wide, her bright hazel eyes a bit too skeptical, her nose a bit too pugnacious, and her hair, worn pulled back, a bit too severe. Her offensive sin, mentioned only in whispers among his friends, was her innocent tactlessness in wounding their pride. They were shocked by her occasionally skeptical retorts to their hoary maxims. She had caused too many burned fingers to be considered an attractive flame despite her familial assets. Earl and Wiley thought she had too much of a mind of her own for the country club and were secretly glad she seldom went there.

Someday a man would come along who did find her beautiful and would cherish all the things about her which her father and brother found irritatingly unladylike. He would be well worth waiting for, of that she had no doubt. She also knew when he did appear, she would readily recognize his qualities as similar to her own.

Lilly had a strong affection for early American antiques, not only for the artifacts themselves, but for the culture of the people who made them. A historian by training, she took keen interest in the events of the times in which they were crafted. Her book, published while she was still in college, *Authenticating New England Antiques: 1640 to 1780*, was a highly praised classic. Among her clients were the country's major museums.

Lilly was drawn to Mary Ayrshire at their first meeting when Mary had joined the staff of the *Dirigo Vigilance* in the capacity of editorial assistant and part-time reporter. Now three months later, each sensing forthright honesty and generosity in the other, a sturdy bond of mutual friendship had formed between them. Mary's slight accent, a combination of Canadian intonation and Scottish idiom, unnoticeable to most people, delighted Lilly. They both had undaunted verve and a courage born of innocence, which led them where angels feared to tread.

Mary, a recent immigrant, was eager to learn all she could about her new surroundings while Lilly was delighted by the Saint Andrew Society's Highland Games which took place in August at Thomas Point

Beach, a seaside park nearby the egregiously polluting Brunswick Naval Air Station. There she heard and saw her first authentic, fully kilted, bagpipe bands and Mary's dancing skill. The games brought Hawkins to prominence in Mary's thoughts though she said nothing of him: how she wondered where he was and if they were destined ever to meet again.

Since the shops on Main Street were closed on Sundays and few people passed through town, Hawkins chose a Sunday morning in early October to make a watercolor sketch of the quaint, local antique shop. He neither knew nor cared to whom it belonged but did admire their taste. It was a memorable sunny, tranquil morning, with the frosty daybreak air now warmed and the leaves in full autumn color. Dressed in a bulky, gray sweater and stained tan trousers, he set up his easel across the deserted street.

The shop belonged to Lilly Williams, but Mary had developed such a keen amateur interest in antiques, Lilly had given her a key to the shop where she was free to browse and study as she wished at any time. She often arrived at closing time, and Lilly stayed, if wanted, in order to guide and help her. Mary loved the shop and the happy hours spent there among the aged artifacts.

This brisk autumn Sunday, Mary, seated at a desk examining a vase, checking it in various books and catalogues, happened to glance up and saw a stranger at work across the street. His features were obscured in the shadow of a disreputable hat. Noticing the easel, the realization that he was painting this shop flitted across her mind. As she retrieved another book from the shelf, she thought a portrait of Lilly's shop would be rather nice. Absorbed in the task at hand she worked on, all thoughts of the artist forgotten until weary and needing respite from the task, she placed her elbows on the desk, cradled her pretty face in her hands and gazed vacantly at Hawkins, her mind still on the vase.

Gradually she began to look at him more attentively; his slouched hat made her smile. He stopped painting, relighted his pipe, and crossed over for a closer look at something on display in the window. Mary was embarrassed; if she moved, he might notice her, might even think she was . . . was what? Spying? She sat very still! Hawkins, quite unaware that anyone was in the shop, leisurely smoked his pipe, stretched, saw his reflection in the glass, tipped his hat, smiled, bowed to himself, and said, "Hello, young feller. Care to buy a painting by an unknown artist?" and then laughed heartily as he knocked ashes from his pipe. Mary was delighted by this unexpected revelation of self-effacing drollery. She noted his warm green eyes . . . the frank ingenuousness so evident in his face and fancied herself playfully pulling off that silly hat. There was something about him; had she seen him before? No, she was quite certain that she had not.

Presently, Hawkins went back to work; she was relieved, feeling sure he had not seen her. Her interest was aroused, a handsome young artist, casually dressed, with a sense of humor. She must meet him! Finished for now with the vase, she walked out the door, taking no notice of Hawkins. Assuming an air of preoccupation with business (she might be the owner leaving her shop; nothing strange about that). She turned her back to Hawkins, jingled her keys, perhaps had difficulty finding the right one, jingled them again, and at length, locked the shop door.

With feigned surprise, she noticed an artist, gazed momentarily at him, and was about to walk off. No, she couldn't do that.

Hawkins smiled.

Now she could nonchalantly walk over and see his work. It would be rude not to.

Hawkins drew in his breath, thinking how beautiful she was. What lovely, long brown hair and dressed so informally in jeans and a light jacket, but such a serious expression! He gathered his wits and assumed a serious expression too. Stunned by the unexpected approach of a lovely girl, he was rendered dumb. *Think of something to say! Think of something to say!* went through his mind, but nothing worth saying did come to mind!

Hawkins cleared his throat, pulled the hat over his eyes and muttered, "Hello."

Mary turned to the painting and pretended to study it. Her hands in her jacket pockets fumbled the keys, and she blurted, "It's very good!" Then she waited until the blush she felt receded, incidentally giving Hawkins time to recover himself.

"It's only a sketch," he said, hoping his nervousness did not show. "I'll do it in oils back at my studio." Back at my studio! He had no studio, just an easel set up in the parlor where he and Pag had begun to work; he was shamed by the pretension.

"I don't mean that," he said sheepishly. "I don't have a real studio."

Mary turned laughing and said, "I didn't think so, not with a hat like that!" And with a sudden impulse, she reached up and pulled it off.

"Hawkins!" she gasped. "You're Hawkins Shortreed!" Hawkins was struck dumb with amazement. "You don't remember me, do you?"

Hawkins's mind jumped to New York City; nothing came to mind! "Think!" she said archly. "You can't have forgotten the train yard in

Halifax!"

"Mary!" he exclaimed. "What are you doing here?"

"If you can't say you're glad to see me, I won't tell you!"

"Glad to see you! After all these years! The surprise has blown my wits clear away!" He hardly believed his eyes. "I'm overjoyed to see you!"

These childhood friends, boy and girl yesterday, man and woman today, having met suddenly and without warning were delighted with each other. An ancient Chinese philosopher once said, "Happiness to a gorgeous butterfly is the nectar of an exquisitely beautiful flower," an apt poetic evocation of the emotions excited in Mary and Hawkins by their unexpected meeting in Hemlock Harbor. Words flowed, laughter and joy poured forth, and time flew by.

Hawkins learned, with a twinge of disappointment, Mary was staying that weekend with Lilly Williams in the home of the richest man in the county and was expected back shortly for dinner. He knew who they were, for who in Hemlock Harbor did not!

Neither wanted an end to this meeting, but Mary had to leave.

"As our grandfathers would say," Hawkins said, extending his hand. "And here's a hand, my trusty friend, and gie's a hand o' thine!"

Mary looked surprised and delighted, held out her hand, saying, "For auld lang syne?"

"Yes," he said, still holding her hand, "for it has been a long, long time."

Mary looked into his eyes and answered, "I know." She hesitated and then went on, "You could see me back to the Williams' home!"

Hawkins had never been comfortable in the company of materialists. As children, he and Mary had often lain on their backs, side by side, gazing into a clear blue or star-filled sky, amazed and dumbfounded by the mystery of consciousness and the beauty of infinite nature. They lacked the power to speak of such spiritual moments, which lodged forever in their hearts and minds. As adults, though each knew it not about the other, their sensitive natures remained unaltered. However, each had begun to learn that many people were more worldly than themselves. Hawkins was torn between his desire to accompany Mary and aversion. He failed to understand the lust for money and power but surmised sublimity would never grace the hearts of such men. Meeting a Williams would spoil this splendid day.

"I'd really like to, Mary," he said, hoping not to offend her, "but I can't. We would probably meet some of your friends, and somehow, I don't want that. It would be difficult for me. Their world is so different from mine, and I don't want to feel that difference, especially just now."

"Oh, Hawkins, you'll never change! Please stay the way you are forever!" Remembrance of those days of youth in Halifax suddenly returned and overwhelmed her. Mary had matured into a sensitive, perceptive, romantic woman with a heart so like that of Hawkins, they beat as one. The sky belonged to her, that immense canvas filled with enormous, towering clouds of the purest white: sweet clouds which made her wistful, angry clouds which excited her. The sea and the earth belonged to her; her senses, her emotional self ever sought the beauty, mystery, and texture of life.

"Look at me! This sweater, these pants, even this hat," which he donned anew, "they speak for themselves. My way of life, I am what I am." He paused unsure what to say next.

"You're Popeye, the sailor man!" she replied. "Well, Popeye, then I'll tell you where you can find me, if and when you want to," she said in a happy, jaunty manner and gave him the names of George and Martha.

It was a day of wonders! "George didn't say he had a young lady staying with him. He only mentioned his wife and a niece whom I thought was closer to their age. But he did say he'd be back for Pag and me when the snow began to fly. Those were his exact words, more or less. Snow be hanged! I'll not wait that long to see you again!"

"I'll be glad to see you, Hawkins," she said gently, laying her hand on his arm. "Let it be soon!"

He watched her drive away in her friend's car, packed up his materials, and started home. He walked slowly to the truck, his mind filled with thoughts of sweet, lovely Mary. Two more congruous, harmonious souls were never better met; possibly both might have sensed it or perhaps had only wished it, for there was no way either could do more at present than guess and fervently hope.

Mary drove to the wharf and parked. "Why am I feeling this way?" she asked herself. "He's just an old friend I knew as a girl . . . but I'm lying to myself! That lanky artist, that dear, gentle man? I can't get him out of my head." She smiled wistfully gazing out over the harbor, not seeing it, "or my heart."

Would auld acquaintance be forgotten? The gods themselves scratched their heads in perplexity and knew not whether they had absentmindedly made two from one or one from two.

Chapter 5

HAWKINS COULD NOT see the home of George and Martha Cottager looking north from where he stood in the meadow at the edge of the cliff after his hasty, cold, saltwater bath. The house was lost among the trees, but mornings had turned colder, and a wispy patch of smoke indicated its location at a line of flight distance of about a mile. It comforted him to know Mary was so close. The mystery of the confluence of their two lives, the slim probability of their reunion, awed him. Nothing, he vowed, must ever sunder that miracle. Was it merely chance or something greater, something beyond the power of understanding? He was aware of a sense of mystery, a deep thankfulness, an ineffable, baffling, certainty about something he could not fathom. A strong need to see her today overpowered him. Yet he was disconcerted about having waited so long to visit her, but repairing the house, readying it as best they could for winter, left him and Pag totally exhausted at day's end. After their evening meal and a last pipe of the day, they nodded and barely crawled into their sleeping bags before they were sound asleep.

His feelings toward Mary rose and fell like the tides importuned by the moon. There were periods when he felt secure and comfortable in their companionship, but at other times, sweet desire sprang upon him as unexpectedly as alarming fogs spring without warning on the unwary mariner. There were moments when he longed to hold her in his arms, to gaze into her limpid, smiling eyes, to whisper words of enduring love and to kiss her enticing lips! Today, his longing for her rose within him like the powerful sea dashing against the cliff on which he stood. Inner conflict assailed him. What end would be served by abandoning restraint and declaring his love for her? He must hold in check the overpowering adoration which there was no hope of manfully and honorably resolving? A possible marriage, were she willing, was beyond his means. Where could they live? What would they live on? The conundrum so numbed his brain, he thought of abandoning his proposed visit, but love was too powerful an opponent in that contest with indecision. He shaved, had Pag trim his locks as best he could, then donned hand-washed clothes which were dried in sunshine and sea air, pulled his sweater over his head and was ready.

Waiting until they might reasonably be expected to have arisen and breakfasted, his impatience to see Mary could be restrained no longer. He had just parked the truck in the wide stone drive before a large log-style home when Mary, even more lovely than she appeared at their first meeting, approached across the lawn. "When I woke up this morning," she said in gay welcome, "I knew you'd be here." A brief spontaneous embrace surprised them both.

He forced a gay and trite response to hide the swirling giddiness he felt. "Had I brought my bagpipes, would you have brought your drum?" They laughed, the mood lightened, and all was well.

"Let's get inside where there's a nice fire!" Mary surprised him by taking his hand and gently squeezing it. He was thrilled and returned the squeeze, and they both laughed again, their mirth a bit more nervous and embarrassed than before. Nevertheless, neither relinquished the other's hand.

"Uncle George says that Indian summer is over, and it will get colder and colder, probably colder than Halifax since the Gulf Stream is farther away. I think that's exciting!"

George and Hawkins renewed their acquaintance, and he was introduced to Mary's Aunt Martha, whose merry eyes gave away the kind and happy heart which lay beneath her confident, matter-of-fact manner. Hawkins liked her at once.

They settled themselves around the fireplace in the spacious living room, and Mary delighted them with her childhood memories of Halifax. An embarrassed Hawkins had little to say when Mary described his awkward dancing. When description of their musical practice among shuffling freight cars brought tears of laughter to the eyes of George and Martha, they both joined in and laughed heartily at themselves.

"If Mary's drum arrives," Martha spoke excitedly, "you must give us a rousing concert of Scottish martial music!"

"Well," mused Hawkins, "if you insist, I'll play sometime at the Gibbs' place when the wind is right. Our practice days were no doubt awful for folk, but we did progress a bit beyond them. My grandfather spoke longingly of the faraway sound of the bagpipe 'wafting over the hills and braes.' My playing may please you too, at a distance. I understand you've seen Mary dance at the games, so you know how graceful and precise she is."

Martha and George, having heard the pipes at the games, did not demure at a long distance concert. Love of the instrument, independent of culture, family, history, and legend might come of hearing it on a sea breeze. Mary was certain it would.

George looked at Hawkins momentarily as though he had a question for him which he thought better of.

After a light lunch, Mary suggested she show Hawkins about the Cottagers' property, especially their fine view of the harbor. They were walking across the lawn when Martha called, "George, come here to the window!"

She clasped his hand and nodded her head toward Mary and Hawkins, who were just entering the woodland path holding each other's hand. She smiled knowingly at him.

"That may not mean what it did when we were young," George remarked. Martha gave an audible sigh of exasperation, which George readily understood; sometimes Martha had no need for words. "But," he quickly added, "I'd not be sorry if it did. He's a nice young fellow."

Martha said no more; she had seen the joy and admiration in Mary's eyes and knew what it meant! She took her cup of tea and curled up in her chair with a crossword puzzle. *Men!* she thought, mildly vexed; but perhaps she recalled the first time she and George held hands, for she glanced fondly at him as he reached unaware for a book.

"I'm sorry we didn't continue our correspondence when you moved away," declared Hawkins. "We forgot about each other when new people, new surroundings, and new activities entered our lives."

"Yes, you're right, Hawkins. At that age, childhood memories are easily overlaid as the momentum of life picks up. But . . . however temporarily far from mind they may be, something happens, and they spring back to life."

"What was it like being at college?" asked Hawkins.

"Probably much duller than it was being in a world famous art school in New York City."

"It didn't seem to matter to me how famous the school was or how large the city. The museums were grand, and we spent many hours drawing and painting there. The store of knowledge, the problems solved, the techniques of masters . . . nothing could equal that . . . but as they say, 'the proof of the pudding' you know . . . what I will do with it is what will count."

"Oh, how well I know what you mean!" Mary replied as they exited the woodland and entered upon the lovely cove. "I wonder if I will be able to write about what I can see in my mind, to give life to characters real only to me, bring to life events only I can see unfolding. Well, as you say, we'll see by 'the proof of the pudding.'"

"Did you know," Mary asked demurely, "that I once had a crush on you?" "No, I didn't! And I hope you didn't know I had one on you!"

They laughed, but their merriness was tinged by sorrow that words of love

which they would have been overjoyed to say and to hear were neither said nor heard.

A crimson autumn sunset was nearly upon them when Mary and Hawkins strolled back down the path. For nearly four hours they had relived for each other the years they had been apart. Though they had left relative strangers, they returned, friendship renewed, as close as they had been as children.

"Mary," Hawkins said in the fullness of happy reunion. "I feel like I've been reunited with a dear friend who means so much to me," he was too frightened to speak of *love,* to speak of that which appeared hopeless. Wisdom quelled expression of his aching love for her. "It's made me very happy."

What Mary thought she did not say, but a smile both happy and somewhat arch crossed her lips. "Friend indeed, Hawkins Shortreed!" she said to herself. "We'll see about that!"

Martha prepared a warm supper. When they had finished and were again gathered before the fire, Hawkins said, "Your home is very comfortable. I hope the Gibbs' place will be neat and cheery like this someday."

"The Gibbs' place . . . that's the second time you've called it by that name. May I ask why you call it the Gibbs' place?" asked George with evident interest. "Have you heard it called so?"

"No, it's just a name. I call it that for no better reason than I found it on a headstone in the old graveyard."

"Hawkins, would you be interested in a somewhat vague story which might concern your new home?"

"Yes, I would!" replied Hawkins. "Anything about the Gibbs' place is important to me."

"Well, it may be only a coincidence, but that name figures in something Martha and I overheard," George began.

"On a wild stormy morning last spring, we were having breakfast at the Wicked Good Café. The wind and rain were furious, and the fog on the harbor was so thick, no boats had gone out. Two men in sou'westers came in and sat in the next booth. We couldn't help overhearing their conversation— you know how they talk there, everybody knows everybody else.

"'Must 'a been a storm like this when that ship was wrecked someplace around here in the old days,' said one.

"'Ayah,' said the other. 'Wish I knew where it happened. I'd go lookin' for that treasure!'

"'They say the place belonged to somebody named Gibbs, but nobody knows where it was,' his friend replied. 'Only Gibbs I know is Archy. He lives inland an' don't have a clue where it could be.'

"That's all that was said, but it intrigued me because of my interest in local history."

"Uncle George is quite the expert," said Mary. "People from the historical society regularly consult him."

"My blushes," said George. "It's just that, being retired, I have more time to devote to it than most. Out of curiosity, I went to the Maritime Museum to see if there were any records of shipwrecks along this coast. They put me in touch with a man in Boston interested in maritime history who was very willing to help, but we didn't have anything to really go on. If there had been a wreck, when did it happen? Now that I know where it might have happened, it gives me a place to start. Searching old deeds, I can find out when the property went from a Gibbs to someone else and get a most recent possible date at least."

"Do you think," asked Hawkins, "there's anything to the story?"

"I don't know," George said with a pleased smile. "It may well be apocryphal, something to yarn about on long winter nights. At any rate, it will give me something to do."

"How exciting!" Mary exclaimed. "If it has anything to do with money or treasure, Wiley is sure to know something about it and may have mentioned it to Lilly. I'll ask her."

At length, the subject of Hawkins' artwork came up.

"This is an out-of-the-way place for artists," Martha remarked. "We have a few in the summer, but none that live here year 'round so far as I know. Won't it be lonesome for you professionally?"

"I live with a sculptor," Hawkins replied. "No one would be lonely with Pag around. Once we have electricity, he'll go down to Newark and bring up his welder and cutting torch. And oh, yes, his stereo. Between Italian opera and banging metal, we won't lack entertainment."

"Good heavens! Can you work with all that noise?"

"He'll do his work in clay in our studio, of sorts, which we've set up," Hawkins said reassuringly. "After we repair it and run electricity to it, he plans to do his metal and stone work in the barn."

"Before the leaves are down," George interposed, "I hope you'll find time to visit Old Woods. You might find it inspiring."

"This is the first I've heard about it," said Hawkins. "What is it?"

"To the west of Hemlock Harbor," George began, "there are a hundred thousand acres of old growth timber that belong to the State of Maine. Martha and I go there off and on during the summer to enjoy its unsurpassed beauty and tranquility. It's not virgin forest. It was lumbered off in the 1880s but has regrown. Of course, there are no patriarchal oaks and maples, but the trees have grown to an imposing height. It's an impressive forest."

When it came time for Hawkins to leave, he thanked them for a day which meant a great deal to him and shook hands with Martha and George and Mary. His hand was on the door when he turned and said, "Would you like to show me Old Woods tomorrow, Mary?"

"That would be very nice," she said, forgiving the handshake when she wished he'd given her another brotherly hug.

"Early?"

"At the crack of dawn!"

Mists still lingered in the hollows of the Old Woods Forest when Mary and Hawkins arrived. It was still cold beneath the trees, now in their full autumn glory, and Mary slid both hands into the opposite sleeves of the cotton pullover which she wore over a flannel shirt. She knew the sun now lighting the treetops would soon dissipate the mist and take away the chill. Birds flitted from tree to tree, seeking food wherever they could find it for their long flight south; gray squirrels rummaged among the fallen leaves in search of acorns to hoard for the barren days ahead; diminutive red squirrels twitched their tails, screeching staccato indignation from the lower branches.

Mary envied Hawkins' bulky sweater. "Is that your only sweater, Hawkins? I haven't seen you without it."

"It's my favorite. My mother knitted it for my dad before they were killed. It's a bit large, but I'm glad it is. It doesn't cling like some sweaters—the elbows haven't worn through, and it's warm and comfortable. When it wears out, I'll put it away as a keepsake."

Mary's slight pique at having Hawkins shake her hand the night before when she had wished to bury herself in his sweater and nestle against his breast evaporated with this unconscious display of sentiment. He was still the same old Hawkins! She determined to knit herself a sweater to match his. It would be a bond between them, not much of a bond, if she were honest with herself, but it gladdened her heart. She shook her hands free of the pullover's sleeves and grasped Hawkins' hand.

The sun rose in the sky. Fair-weather cumulus clouds began appearing over the plowed fields lying beyond the forest boundaries; ponds and streams rippled and glistened, reflecting the blue sky.

"What a lovely place!" she said joyfully. The gentle sound of rustling leaves seemed to accentuate the silence of the forest. Nature banished the hustle of town and the irksome nuisances of everyday life. "I feel at this moment that I'm an integral part of the forest and its peacefulness!"

"I feel it too," Hawkins responded, "an atavistic hypnotic spell, that we're part of the fabric of nature."

"I feel an aura akin to it," Mary whispered, "when I'm away from people and see a village or farm in the distance. People may be working the land, tending cows, or harvesting the ocean, but there must be silence."

"Yes," Hawkins added. "Let a truck or airplane come on the scene, and it's spoiled. The world is too much with us."

"But," Mary said sadly, "we might be about to lose this lovely oasis." Hawkins looked at her with surprise. "Lose it! What do you mean?"

"It can wait. This is not the time or place. I refuse to let anything spoil the magic. I'll tell you about it, but not today. Today is special." And so it was.

They wandered the forest trails for several pleasant hours before they returned to Hawkins' truck. Mary sighed as she sank wearily into her seat. The sun was positioned just below the treetops, and shadows were lengthening when they reached the Cottagers.

"I'll come over to your place soon and tell you what I know about Old Woods," Mary said as she gave Hawkins a kiss on the cheek, slid from the truck, and hurried into the house.

Chapter 6

LUMBER AND PAPER companies, with home offices located outside the state of Maine, own almost half of the state's total landmass and dominate the state legislature. The organization which had raised the money in 1888 to buy Old Woods State Forest, or rather the previously lumbered off acreage upon which the forest had regrown, had donated it to the State of Maine with the understanding that it would be a public resource, forever protected from exploitation: a place of refuge for all species, not excluding the human one.

Maine, scooped and scraped by glaciers, mountainous and rocky, once had four outstanding natural resources: its seacoast fishery, its forests, fine granite, and primeval beauty. All these were now rendered to degraded vestiges by human prodigality. These, which might have been husbanded, had been pitilessly mined to virtual extinction; this left its working people "a hard row to hoe" to earn a living.

For the residents of Hemlock Harbor, earning a living meant independent, dangerous, often unpredictable, harvesting of the ocean and farming rocky soil in a short growing season. The environmental vagaries, the difficulty of making a living, paradoxically intensified their love of this, their rugged home and fostered a keen sense of humor which mocked self-pity in hilarious ridicule.

The lumberjacks of yore, once essential to the corporations that claimed ownership of the state's forests in the days when Old Woods was purchased, had now been largely replaced by machines. Those who had followed in their father's footsteps were in less demand for work that was arduous, dangerous, and poorly paid: work which allowed people to live in trailers, to go without health insurance or dental care, to face winter layoffs, to do without retirement, to live as best they could in hand-to-mouth insecurity. In short, people now had to depend on low-paying jobs doled out by businesses to suit corporate needs.

Conservation could not but be regarded as a threat to these latter-day lumberjacks living under such conditions. If Old Woods entered their thoughts at all, it was as a question of how people might benefit from it: perhaps as a tourist attraction, perhaps as a source of timber. The question was, what did tourists want? Or, more ominously, what did business want from it?

The word "jobs" was a potent but fictitious talisman in Maine, an empty charm which politicians harped on, which businesses seeking largesse from the state treasury promised, and the media cynically lauded. As meaningful jobs that paid a living wage with long-term stability terminating in a decent retirement became nonexistent, the talisman hypnotized the desperate unemployed.

Politicians jangled it more vigorously, businesses beat the drum louder, the media lied more egregiously, the old trick of the mythic carrot before the stupid mule. Workers grasped at it with a desperate belief like that which drove them to gamble some of what little money they had on the minuscule chance of winning the state's "Megabucks Lottery," and who could blame them?

The Great Amalgamated Pulp and Hardwood Company wanted Old Woods State Forest's timber and meant to have it, not only to have it but to have it as cheaply as the timber it logged from federal national forests, which also facetiously . . . belonged to the people!

The Conservation Group, a nonprofit organization dedicated to "preserving and enhancing Maine's environment and guiding the responsible development thereof" included among its founders the Great Amalgamated Pulp and Hardwood Company and the Maine Association of Forest Product Companies. The day-to-day organization and operation to achieve the objectives of this civic enterprise were left in the hands of Earl and Wiley Williams.

The headquarters of the Conservation Group was located in an industrial park in an inconspicuous and peripheral location convenient to Augusta, the state capital. This isolated campus of small manufacturers, warehouses, and trucking firms provided requisite privacy and anonymity. The building itself was unimposing; its facade of brick and concrete blended inconspicuously with neighboring structures. The shrub-bordered walk, the trimmed front lawn, and the gravel parking area, which lay behind the building and was completely shielded from the road, gave it an ordinary, inconspicuous, almost deserted appearance. From a vividly visible pole in the front lawn, the American flag and a black MIA-POW flag clearly proclaimed not only the organization's political persuasion, which its radical members termed "conservative," but its avid exploitation of military mythology. There was usually little visible activity in the building during the day. It did not catch the eye. It did not stand out.

A conference room and two offices separated by a hallway occupied the ground floor to the rear of the reception area, where an austere, middle-aged lady seated at a desk near the front entrance greeted any unexpected stranger, usually someone seeking directions, and answered the telephone. A door marked Administration at the rear of the hallway led to a foyer, where a locked door guarded the entrance to the upper story and a glass-paneled doorway exited to the parking area.

Two gentlemen, of genial and confidential mien, made only occasional use of their offices; for most of their time was spent entertaining their assiduously cultivated statehouse "friends." Smiles and goodwill characterized such a profitable collusion, which dealt with underhanded and probably illegal rewards, attendant upon legislative support for a current policy of the Conservation Group.

An unforgivable blunder, severely looked down upon, was to refer to these collegial gentlemen as lobbyists; for to their hypocritical "friends," they were essentially respected expert "educational representatives" of that lofty "conservative conservation think tank," the Conservation Group.

Meetings of the Conservation Group occurred ad hoc in this Conservation Group building. At such times, elegant, expensive automobiles occupied the rear parking area, unseen by even the most keenly observant passerby.

Not long after Mary's employment on the *Dirigo Vigilance*, such a gathering, which made valuable use of her skill at shorthand, occurred to devise a plan for the acquisition of Old Woods' timber.

As she had promised, Mary went to the Gibbs' homestead to disclose to Hawkins all she had learned at that meeting of the threat to Old Woods. Pag and Hawkins listened eagerly to her account of the conspiratorial gathering of members of the Conservation Group.

According to Mary, Earl Williams, typifying an amiable but smug attitude of superiority founded upon wealth and power, sat in a chair at the head of an expansive table in the conference room, smoking a cigar and sipping coffee; Wiley stood by the door greeting men in suits as expensive as his own as they entered. The visitors mingled amiably, providing themselves in a refined manner with coffee and pastry, before taking their seats. Assuming that customary intimidating, accusatory expression cultivated by business executives, they trifled with the pencils and notepads provided. Wiley's demeanor, smiling and hospitable, marked him as chairman.

"Gentlemen, feel free to take notes as we go along," Wiley began. "Use them during the meeting, but put them in this receptacle when you leave." He held up a waste basket. "They will be burned! We don't want anything possibly incriminating to leave the room. Mary," he said, indicating the only lady present, "will take everything down in shorthand. Back at the paper we'll edit it, after which the shorthand notes will be shredded!

"I would like to introduce, to anyone who doesn't know them, three of my friends and trusted consultants. First, Senator Mike Perry of the Maine State Legislature." An elderly, portly, smoothly shaven man with small eyes and large jowls patted his head to reassure himself his hairpiece was secure, smiled broadly and waved his hand.

"Next to him, Butch Flint of the FBI." Butch Flint, a young man with an innocent, ingenuous face, nodded.

"Lastly, Gus Gold. Gus is with the state police and is responsible for keeping those 'tree huggers' off our lands." Gold, a bald, thin man with lifeless, gray eyes and a mouth seldom burdened with a smile, raised his coffee cup.

"These guys are on our side! They are one of us! Mike knows all the state legislators, which ones are with us and the rare maverick who needs to be educated. Butch has dossiers on the men and women most active in all the so- called conservation groups, and Gus knows where and when we need him. I vouch for them without any reservation. You can trust them!

"Old Woods State Forest is the reason we're here, and I'll let LeRoy Carlson get us started."

LeRoy Carlson, president of and major stockholder of the Great Amalgamated Pulp and Hardwood Company, home office in New Jersey, tapped his pencil on the end of his large nose. After a moment of thought, he began.

"We, meaning the company, want the timber! We don't want the land, just the timber. The question is how are we to get it? We've been through the process of obtaining timbering permits countless times, but two things make this permit a bit different: the timber lies outside our holdings in the north woods, and it's in a state forest. Selling the project to the state legislature won't be difficult, as we know, provided we can make it appear to be in the public interest."

"I think," said a man from Dow, Stubble, and Crumb Advertising, "jobs are our chief selling point. Loggers can see their jobs are drying up as the timber dwindles with clear-cutting, and they're worried.

Holding out the prospect of jobs to them is like dangling raw meat in front of a hungry tiger, state forest or not!"

"I agree," replied Carlson, "but with our machinery, there won't be very many jobs."

"You don't specify how many jobs," Mike Perry added. "We let the papers allude to 'many' jobs and to how much money the project will add to the economy."

"How much money will it add?" asked the lawyer representing the Byam and Dyam Paper Company.

"You estimate the value of the timber, what the company will make from it," answered the man from Dow, Stuble and Crumb, "and inflate it by a few million."

"That money goes out of state," a corporate lawyer responded. "Will the people fall for that?"

"That's my job," said Wiley. "We use that figure. The governor uses it. Everyone we quote, every argument we present uses it. There will be analyses which dispute it, but we don't print them. We don't use their figures. Their only hope of reaching the public is a press release which we don't print as is. We refer to it but use it against them. In our hands they show up as unreliable, overzealous, hair-brained enthusiasts who put a turtle or a bird ahead of jobs for workers and who are against putting money into the hands of working people."

"How do we handle the legislators?" again queried the corporate lawyer. It was his first meeting. The others present were indulgent; it took a couple of meetings to get a man up to speed.

"In a few words," Perry said, "money and intimidation! Not bribes." He smiled sardonically. "That's corrupt! Politicians know who owns the media, and people vote the way the media tell them to. Remember Nixon and McGovern? We call it propaganda—they call it news! If they do what big business wants, then people like Wiley market their image in such an attractive package their election is assured. If not, then it's thumbs down at the polls. That's intimidation! Our millions go to buy them the TV exposure that makes them celebrities and gets people to the polls. After all, an election festival looks pretty paltry if no one shows up."

"We like that," said a representative of the Association of Broadcasters of which Wiley was an influential member.

"There may be a lot of irate people when this proposal is made public," persisted the corporate lawyer. "They could tie us up in court or collect enough signatures to put it up for a referendum vote. We have to be prepared for that!"

Mike Perry looked at the lawyer, realized he did not know him, and thought some assurance was in order.

"Let's take the referendum!" he began. "First of all, it would be worded so most people, thinking they were voting for it, would actually be voting against it. The governor will schedule the vote in the dead of winter when most people prefer to stay home. Wiley will see to it they don't know or care much about it anyway."

"The legislators will have to come out clean!" added the lawyer.

"Do you know of any dirty legislators?" asked Perry. "I don't! There haven't been any since our side gained monopoly over the press, radio, and TV. Unless, of course, they stray too far from us. Not dirty, just wrongheaded. That will do well enough for the public."

"Okay," said the lawyer, "politicians don't show up dirty. But can they be persuaded to give away public property, like timber?"

"Bear with me, gentlemen!" Mike Perry continued indulgently. "This young fellow is sharp but naive. However, we all started out that way. He deserves a bit of education left out of law school, so here goes:

"There are plenty of examples of public property being given away: mining in the national parks, grazing on the public lands, publicly paid for water supplied to agribusiness, lumbering in the national forests, all at token prices, all paid for by middle-class taxpayers, but let me use one closer to home!

"Every day, there are miles of bumper-to-bumper cars on the interstates, people commuting to and from work. It's so stupid. Why do they do it? Because there is no alternative, no public transportation. But do they care? Do any of them consider what it costs them to own and operate a car? Not in my experience!

"What happened to the railroads and the trolley cars?" He paused to take a sip of coffee. "They see miles and miles of rusty rails and miles and miles of highways. Do they ever connect the two? Never!

"Back in the fifties, we businessmen, led by General Motors, which decimated the trolley lines, decided trucks would replace trains.[2] Of course, that left the public virtually bereft of public surface transportation and dependent on cars. You can guess our motives! No trains meant 'good riddance' to powerful railroad unions, a fabulous market for lots of trucks, a bonanza for oil companies, tons of tar and concrete and fortunes to be made paving, a lot of cars to be sold to a lot of drivers, with nothing to do but inhale each other's exhaust fumes and listen to what we feed them on their radios, auto supply stores, two to the block. So we handed out money, subsidies for trucks instead of railroads. The results have been a businessman's bonanza!

"But trucks need roads!" Perry continued. "How did the trucking companies get their roads?" He looked about the table. Did the younger men remember? "The Interstate Highway System was built for them! And it didn't cost them a dime! How? By saying it was needed for national defense and national security, to shuffle missiles around   Hahaha!

"The Interstate Highway System was engineered solely for the trucking industry. The next time you come to an area under repair, look at the thickness of the damaged reinforced concrete blocks that are sawn out. It may take a few inches of Tarmac or concrete to support automobiles, but it takes concrete measured in feet to hold up loaded monster trucks, and the public foots the bill both for its construction and for repairing the damage the behemoths cause. Have you seen how the trucks slide under the bridges? You've never heard of a truck being stuck on an interstate and never will. It was designed for trucks, and when one is widened, it's because the trucking companies want it wider.

"People love the interstates, which is just as well since they paid for them. Do they ever ask why the interstates are not parkways from which trucks are excluded or why the trucking industry doesn't have to build its own roads or rest areas and doesn't pay its honest proportional share of the cost for upkeep and repair for the damage they cause?

"My point is this: it's immoral, it's crooked. If the people knew all the facts, if they knew how businessmen and politicians fleece them, there would be a lot of dirty politicians and a lot of dirty businessmen too. But they don't know, so we're heroes! They only know what people like Wiley tell them. They think what we want them to think. We can do anything we want! The people are putty in our hands!

"Yes, we will have opposition: Common Cause, Ralph Nader, nature lovers. But you won't see any of them on TV, and you won't read about them. We censor them into oblivion. They can't reach the public! We have all the power!"

The men around the table were delightfully enthralled; one could read the utmost satisfaction in their faces.

"We have de facto control of government, state and federal. The judiciary is packed with our men from the Supreme Court on down, the military protects our overseas investments. The FBI, the National Guard, the state police, and the drug police take care of any domestic troublemakers."

At this the man from Keystone and Lockem Private Prison Company smiled with pleasure.

"We can do a lot of things immediately. Others take planning and time, and this is one of them."

"Mike has given us a good review of some things we need to keep in mind," Wiley said with an encouraging smile. "We have power, we know that, but now we have to plan how we're going to use it."

The remainder of the day was spent delegating tasks. The responsibility for public persuasion went to Wiley and to the other men representing broadcasters and advertisers. Senator Perry, along with the newly initiated lawyer, assumed the task of coordinating the policy with the state legislators. Butch Flint and Gus Gold volunteered to handle any popular opposition.

Hawkins was silent when Mary had finished. She was deeply moved by his despondent expression.

"Oh, Hawkins," she said wearily, "I feel so dirty. It's obvious why Wiley needed someone who could take shorthand notes. He couldn't risk recording such meetings and have a secretary type it up—there would be too many chances of it leaking out. He took my notes before we left the room, dictated sanitized minutes, and sat there while I typed the edited version in his office. There is no other factual record of what went on."

She began to cry. "I'm disgusted and ashamed of myself, but there's nothing I can do. You know that neither of us comes from money. I've got to stay in that job until I can get away!"

Hawkins took her hand and looked steadily into her eyes. "You must not go away! You're their Achilles' heel. If anything can stop their disgraceful plot, it depends on you!"

He put his arm about her shoulders and patted her eyes with his handkerchief.

She rested her head on his shoulder and said with relief, "Dear Hawkins, you never change. Inside you're still the same honest, affectionate boy I looked up to in Halifax. "But," she added sheepishly, "we must be careful. Wiley is so powerful. I could be blacklisted for life and not only in journalism! I don't know what he could do to you, and I don't want to risk hurting you. As underhanded as it sounds, we must be careful to keep everything to ourselves!"

"I understand," Hawkins replied soothingly. "It's not the way Grandpa said the game is played. He never mentioned cheaters, but I know what you say is right. Cheaters must be exposed, but we must wait until we can do it effectively. We're a team, and we'll bide our time, hard as that may be!"

Mary threw her arms around his neck, and they held each other close. "Damn the bastards," Pag swore. "My grandfather was right! Capitalists

are 'nature's mistake' . . . they're Frankensteins!"

Hours after Mary's disclosure, Hawkins experienced an epiphany, a moment of sudden intuitive understanding, the beginning of an understanding would be more correct. What was happening to Mary did not fit into the circumscribed experience of his life. Was he blind to some evil and chicanery affecting his life too? Perhaps everyone's life? The impulses which drove him, the forces which directed his thoughts and actions, were uncomplicated: to paint the beauties of his goddess Nature, to dream, to follow a straight road doing no one harm. Please God or the devil, he was not sure now of the nature of fate. Could he lead a happy and useful life with such men in control?

Epiphany! Men such as those in the Conservation Group were not like Will. They were driven by evil motives and abetted by lesser men only too willing to do their bidding. Was it the realization or its ubiquity which stunned him? He learned early what many take years to learn and many more never learn. "They, in God's image?" The arrogant idea nauseated him! He slumped in the chair where Pag found him holding his head, elbows on his knees, eyes on the floor.

This was not the Hawkins he knew! What had happened? What was wrong with him? Why didn't the sound of the opening and closing door cause him to look up?

"Hawkins, old fellow, are you sleeping?" he asked in a low voice.

"No," he replied, "I'm not asleep. In fact, I think I'm waking up in a way and not quite sure how I feel. To find Mary, my dear friend for whom I feel such affection, in such a situation where she suffers is unbearable . . . and I don't know what to do!"

Pag was politically naive but not quite as naive as Hawkins. His boyhood in the Ironbound section of Newark, New Jersey, what he had seen and experienced, had long made him wonder about Hawkins and caused him to be frustrated by his friend's almost childlike conception of reality. Pag was, as they say, streetwise, which was an unexpected but efficacious remedy for Hawkins' soul sickness.

"I'll be back soon, Hawkins. I think I may know what has happened and a simple way to open your eyes."

Hawkins heard the truck depart, but it was a long time before Pag returned with a bundle from the supermarket in Seal Point. What a strange collection of objects he placed on their rustic table: bottles of various vitamins and lotions, and of all things, boxes of crackers.

"Okay, my friend . . . here beginneth the lesson. Get the ruler, pencil, and paper!" After Hawkins had done as requested, they pulled chairs to the table and began to open Pag's purchases.

"Let's start with this little bottle of jock itch medicine, in a box half an inch longer than the bottle. Notice how the bottle's label covers up the liquid so you can't see what's inside? Now, tip it on its side. See how full the bottle is? That's right . . . it's half full! Open these vitamin bottles! That's right, more than two-thirds full of worthless cotton wool . . . the bottle, three times too big! Why? Okay, now measure the box of saltines, then take out the contents, and measure them. Do the same thing with the graham crackers!"

When the measuring and calculations had been done, they found more than a quarter of the volume of the saltine box and greater than a third of the graham cracker box were empty.

"They need that airspace to prevent damage," said Hawkins.

"How does that prevent damage? It gives more room for the contents to move, bump around, and shatter. The real purpose is to make the package look like you're getting more than you are."

"So what?" Hawkins was puzzled.

"Look, Hawkins!" Pag was exasperated. "What do you buy, the package or what's in it? Dammit! Oh, you think you know what's in it, but that's all . . . all you get to see is the pretty, fraudulent, and deceptive packaging. The actual contents are artfully concealed. Open your eyes, man! The package is the only thing you can buy! Why is that? Who creates the packages? Who sells them? Liars, scoundrels, Republicans, Democrats, TV demagogues— anybody who whores for corporate dough, that's who! As they say in Newark, 'You can't shine shit,' but you sure as hell can put it in an attractive package! Can't you see it's universal?

"You're a bright guy. Instead of swallowing the cartloads of bullshit that are dumped on you, think! Stop being a blind, believing ass! You can see now what Mary's up against, can't you? She's bumbled into being a lackey of the legal Mafia, the bullshitters whose business it is to sell you a nice package, to pull the wool over your eyes, steal your money, stab you in the back, and come out kings of the mountain . . . all powerful, owning everything that they have no moral right to own . . . so powerful that people like Mary either do what they want her to do or starve. That's power! Power depends on the strongest of all social forces, fiction. Give it any other name you like: propaganda, public relations—it's still fiction, not truth, lies." He stopped for breath.

"Old Woods doesn't belong to them! God didn't make trees, water, metals, oil, land, or any other natural resource to be owned and monopolized by anybody! Especially the greedy bastards, the ones who make the laws to suit themselves . . . who make you and me pay for a fascist military so they can steal from the poor on God's earth, so they can sit on their fat asses and count their loot! Who make *their* private property precisely what should belong to everyone?

"Don't get me wrong—I'm not talking about personal property. I have nothing against personal property: a person's home or car, any of the things he's worked for and prides himself on. But Old Woods is no one's personal property!

"Poor Mary is part of a packaging fraud, packaging a giveaway of public property, wrapping it up in make-believe baloney. Not because she believes it's for anyone's good other than the likes of Wiley, but because she has to make a living. She's confused, ashamed, and helpless. Okay, knight errant, if you want to live with yourself, you better start thinking damned hard about what you're going to do about it!"

Hawkins did begin to think about it. This time, Pag's rage, his explanation of Mary's plight, was not in vain. "Diego Rivera" Pagliano had made a dent in the consciousness of the dreamer. If an objective of education is to inspire reflection or to launch a few students on the road to enlightenment or to ruffle the tranquility of ignorance, Pag had succeeded better than he knew; for Hawkins felt indignation and misgiving and now realized one cannot always trust that one's opponent is worthy and honorable.

Chapter 7

AT THE GIBBS' place, the early winter sun shone cold and pallid through the dull leaden clouds. The forest was shorn of leaves. The graveyard blended with the meadow under a blanket of snow. Bleak and brooding was the steel- gray ocean; no lobster boats were to be seen in such weather. A nor'easter was brewing; one could feel it in one's bones . . . snow—maybe two or three feet likely. A sprinkle of flakes began to fall in the afternoon, and by four o'clock, the last light of day, not even headlights could be seen through the dense, eye-smothering, windblown sheets of snow. The long winter night had begun; the frigid north wind howled down the chimney and moaned like souls in torment as it swirled around the corners of the house. By morning snow would lie hip deep, and the two young men would need to get about on the snowshoes they had providentially purchased at LeVerdier's Drugstore, just in case.

"Another day, another snowstorm," Pag said scornfully, taking a moment to put potatoes to boil on the wood-burning range. "Damned, if I'm not beginning to feel like an Eskimo."

"Eskimo!" Hawkins replied laughing. "How many Eskimos have a nice cozy house like this, a warm fire, and lantern light? They live in igloos without sunlight half the year."

"I guess you're right, Hawkins. I feel like an Eskimo living in a nice cozy house . . . during the day anyway. At night it might as well be an igloo—it gets so damned cold!"

"Keep your mind on the game! You're in check. And while you're figuring out what to do about it, I'll throw another log on the fire."

Pag watched Hawkins stoke the fire. "Who was that guy who froze to death in the Yukon and came back to life when someone put him in a stove to cremate him?"

"I know who you mean. Sam McGee, I think, but I'm not really sure.

Why?"

"Well, if you find me frozen in bed some morning, try it—I might surprise you!"

"Do you want to be done rare or medium?" Hawkins quipped. "Well done!" replied Pag. "Even unto charcoal."

Poor Pag! Temperature in the house plummeted at night when the fire died

out. Every winter morning found him swathed in his bed blankets, starting a fire in the stove, putting the coffee on to perk. He cursed the frozen milk but blessed the day they had the foresight to run an extension cord from the meter post to put a light bulb by the pump to keep it from freezing.

One morning later that January, when the road through the forest had become rutted by the wheels of their truck, passable though bumpy, George Cottager arrived unexpectedly. Hawkins cleaned his brushes, and the room was filled with the aroma of turpentine. Creating a stunning clay model of a horse at one-fifth normal scale, Pag continued working on his realization of a dynamic equestrian drawing by Leonardo da Vinci. Though wan sunshine slightly warmed the floorboards, George retained his parka. When spring, blessed spring, arrived and they were on sale, Hawkins and Pag had finally agreed they really must buy a good woodstove.

Hawkins was delighted and eagerly expectant to learn what George had to tell of his discoveries about the legendary shipwreck. Pag yawned; it was his ardent suspicion speculations about a mythic shipwreck were a frivolous waste of time.

"I was able to find the date when your property ceased belonging to a Gibbs," he said. "In 1831, the title went to Eliza Dobbins, born Eliza Gibbs. Apparently there were no living male heirs when the owner died, and it went to the female line. Thereafter, it stayed in the Dobbins family until the last surviving couple died childless. Then it went to a surviving sister, and then to you."

"That transfer of the owner's name took place about a hundred and fifty years ago," Hawkins noted with surprise. "No wonder the association with the name Gibbs died out."

"Exactly!" George resumed. "I asked my friend in Boston for a list of ships lost any place off the eastern seaboard of Maine or New Brunswick prior to 1831, but there were still too many.

"I did hit pay dirt on another tack however!" he said with a triumphant smile and stopped to fill his pipe. "I posted a query in our historical society newsletter asking for any information about a possible shipwreck off our immediate coast anytime in the eighteenth century. Though it was unlikely to yield any hard-and-fast information, I did receive several responses which all referred to variations on the story handed down among fishermen of which I told you. I learned nothing more than I knew already. But last week, I received a phone call from a Caleb Potter. He's a friendly and intelligent fellow in his nineties, housebound with arthritis. He asked if I'd like to come down and see what he'd found. Of course, I went at once.

"It was a fortunate day for me in two respects: I made a very interesting friend, and when I arrived, he had already laid out an old and fascinating manuscript for me and had the most absorbing tale to go with it.

"The Reverend Ezekiel Stearns, he told me, had been a Tory minister in Hemlock Harbor in the turbulent days before the Revolution. Sometime around 1776, an irate patriot mob confiscated his property, sent him packing to Canada, and burned down his church. Why his diary was saved is anyone's guess, for I doubt if anyone in the mob could read or write—which perhaps explains it. They probably had no idea what it was. Whatever the reason, it's been passed down in Potter's family ever since.

"The pages were brown with age, and the ink is badly faded, but Potter had carefully gone through it using a large magnifying lens and had found a pertinent entry from 1761. That year, Reverend Stearns learned from a parishioner that a ship had been wrecked on the rocks off the property of one Abner Gibbs."

The effect of this news was stunning! Even Pag was speechless for a moment. "Go on, George!" Hawkins exclaimed as George rose to knock the ashes from his pipe into the fireplace. "For goodness sake, don't leave us in suspense! What else did it say?"

"That's all it said," George replied with evident disappointment. "The page had torn, and the rest is missing. But what more needed to be said?"

He became animated and emphatic in a scholarly manner, "Finding that entry, the fact that it was recorded at all and preserved for over two hundred years is an incredible miracle!"

"That's interesting," Pag said, turning back to his clay model, "but what of it? So a ship was sunk. Is that important?"

"It might be," Hawkins answered, embarrassed to mention a possible treasure. The idea was too fanciful to be taken seriously. "Should I tell Pag?" Hawkins asked himself. "Would he thank me if he's bitten by the bug of seeking treasure and it comes to naught?" He decided to let events unfold and tell their own story. Mary's excited enthusiasm was enough for the time being. She enjoyed it and, most importantly, would keep any mention of it from Wiley's ears.

"Thank you," he said softly as George wrapped a scarf about the neck of his parka preparing to leave, "for all your effort and this fascinating corroboration of the shipwreck. If, by any chance, I find anything which adds to the unfolding mystery, you'll be the first to know."

"By the way," George confided to Hawkins at the door, "if you do, keep it to yourself. Mary told her friend Lilly Williams the tale which Martha and I overheard, and she in turn asked Wiley if he knew anything about it. He showed up at our house asking for particulars . . . wanted a story for his paper or so he said. From what I've heard from Mary, I don't trust that scoundrel! You should have seen his greedy eyes light up at the mention of treasure. You don't need his impudent nose poking over your shoulder!"

The following week and the next went by, and Mary had heard nothing from Hawkins concerning George's discovery. Had she done so, it would undoubtedly have given her mood, compounded of irritation and self- loathing, a bit of a silver lining. When she next entered the shop as Lilly was closing for the day, Mary was not her exuberant self. Her lackluster expression alone was evidence that she was not there to talk about antiques; she had something on her mind.

"Had a bad day?" Lilly inquired.

"Not an unusual one," Mary answered, "but my job is . . . well, frustrating."

"What's happened to upset you?" Lilly asked sympathetically.

"It's the job," she replied. "I'm not pleased with what I do."

"What do you mean? What do you do that upsets you?"

"Oh, Lilly, someday soon I'll unburden myself completely, but right now I'm burning with shame because I lie and don't know what to do about it. I lie!"

The answer surprised Lilly. "You, lie? I refuse to believe that! Tell me what you mean!"

"Wiley is your brother. This can't go beyond us or I'll be finished at the paper!"

"I understand that, Mary. We're friends. Say what you want to—get it off your mind!"

"Lilly, what do you see as a journalist's responsibility?"

"Why, I guess, it's to inform the public."

"Inform the public with what? The truth?"

"Maybe you'd better tell me. What is the truth as a journalist sees it?"

"Nothing profound," Mary answered. "Lawyers have a pretty good working definition: 'the truth, the whole truth, and nothing but the truth.' Meaning, I take it, who, what, where, and when, the facts and nothing but the facts."

"That sounds pretty straightforward to me."

"I would be very happy doing just that, but I can't."

"Perhaps an instance would help me to understand why you can't," said Lilly, sorry to see Mary so vexed and discouraged.

"Are you sure you want to hear me complain?"

"That's what friends are for."

"Each year," Mary began, "the high school invites interested townspeople to come in as guest speakers one day a week during the last six weeks of the fall semester. They spend an hour on topics the school doesn't cover: sex education, what this or that profession is like, and so on. It's informal, and the kids choose anything they like.

"This year, a man from a local credit union did a good job on the cost of credit. That's important! The kids will all use credit. What will it cost them? How should they shop for it? That's all he wanted to tell them.

"It's not very difficult—just something no one ever thinks about. Even some of the teachers sat in. I thought that it was newsworthy and wrote an article extolling the wisdom of the school in offering what it calls 'minicourses' and featuring the one on credit. It was one of the best pieces I'd done, and I was very proud of it. Days went by, but it never appeared in the paper.

"I asked Wiley about it. It came down to the fact that statewide, the bankers, the auto dealers, and credit card merchants didn't like it. 'They are our advertisers, advertisers pay our salaries. Where would we be without them, etc., etc.'

"And that's not all! Wiley is on the school board, and the cost of credit won't be offered again. It's not a big issue in itself, but it's typical. We can't report facts. We have no choice but to project the picture that things are as they should be, they couldn't be any better and definitely shouldn't be changed. And that's not true! There are a lot of things going on which could stand a good dose of sunshine, but if any reporter touches on them, he finds out management, namely Wiley, has misgivings about his responsibility and hints maybe he would be happier on a big city paper. Perhaps he's right."

Lilly was surprised. This couldn't be the way it was on the *New York Times*! She read it every day, confident that she was getting "all the news that's fit to print!" But a doubt now slipped into her mind.

"I do see how frustrating that must be, but is that everything on your mind?" Lilly asked.

"No," Mary answered dejectedly, "I haven't seen Hawkins for an age."

"Well," Lilly said gaily, "we can at least do something about that! You've mentioned him from time to time, but I've never met him. If you'd like to introduce us, we can pay him a visit."

Lilly was delighted to see Mary's mood brighten at once. "That's a grand idea! Tomorrow is Saturday. Are you free in the afternoon?"

A warm, low pressure trough had settled over the Gulf of Maine, ushering in the annual "January thaw" and showed no sign of leaving in the near future. Through fog and misting rain Lilly drove toward the Gibbs' place down the road through the woods which had now turned to muddy slush. She became ever more apprehensive the mud and slush striking the car's underbelly warned of the possibly of getting stuck.

"It will be pitch-black when we drive back out this muddy, godforsaken lane. Great heavens! What is that?" she cried bringing the car to a sudden halt.

An unperturbed cow moose stood in the headlights, looking listlessly in their direction.

"Nice!" Lilly said scornfully. "She could stand there all afternoon and all night."

"Try the horn!" Mary suggested. Lilly leaned on the horn to no effect.

"Now what! I can't back out. It's almost a mile. I'm afraid we'd slip off the road and end up stuck, and until she moves, we can't go forward."

There they sat, wondering what to do for what seemed to them an age.

"She has nice eyes," Mary noticed.

"Yes, she does," Lilly agreed.

Headlights approached from the opposite direction. Hawkins, having heard the horn, edged his truck toward the moose, which languidly turned her head, looked at the truck, looked back at the car, then slowly ambled off into the fog and what had now become dim, gray darkness.

They were not far from the house. Hawkins backed the truck, and Lilly followed.

At first no one got out of the car, which puzzled Hawkins. Even more puzzling were the peals of feminine glee issuing from within. "Who are they?" he wondered. "I don't recognize that car."

At that point Mary got out of the passenger side, came around to the driver's door, and tugged at a young blonde woman, both in the throes of uncontrollable laughter.

"What's the matter?" Hawkins asked in a loud voice.

"Oh, Hawkins, don't ask!" Mary replied gasping for breath. "It's too ridiculous, and we're so relieved. We couldn't figure out a way to get that moose to move. I can just see the headline: 'Maidens in distress rescued from stoical moose by gallant artist,'" and again gave way to her sense of the ridiculous.

Spontaneous mirth is contagious; grinning broadly, Hawkins went to Lilly and said, "Hello! I'm Hawkins. And you are?"

Lilly sniffed and wiped her eyes. "Hello, Hawkins, I'm Lilly."

"Now that we all know one another," he said, extending his hand, "let's shake hands and get out of this slush and drizzle!"

Pag was visibly impressed by Lilly and insisted on starting the wood-fired range to prepare cocoa for, as he put it, "the girls." Lilly heard the squeak of the hand pump and went into the kitchen to look. Pag, a bit bemused by Lilly, had forgotten to prime the pump but eventually drew water, filled an iron kettle, and set it to heat on the range.

"How rustic and quaint," Lilly said admiringly. "A nineteenth century kitchen actually in use. I must come back with my camera! I'll bring a period dress for you. A photo done in sepia will be charming in the shop."

"A dress for who?" a startled Pag ejaculated. "You're thinking of putting a picture of me in a dress in your store? No, lady, I don't think so!"

Hawkins' guffaw made Pag blush at which Mary and Lilly gave vent to mirth which rose within them like bubbles in champagne.

"A blushing communist!" Hawkins jested. "Now I've seen everything!"

"A communist!" Mary and Lilly gasped in disbelief.

"Yeah, my grandfather was a Hollywood screenwriter in the fifties who got busted and blacklisted by the McCarthyites."

Mary and Lilly stared at him, startled amazement written on their faces.

Pag was irked. "Look, comrades," he said satirically, "nothing's perfect! Power hungry devils are the same the world over—it's human nature! Stalin wasn't any worse than Kennedy and Johnson. Look what they did to the Vietnamese!"

He felt uneasy at the silence which followed this utterance.

"Look," he said, irked by their reaction, "'communist' means 'community,' and I have a hell of a lot more respect for a philosophy that puts community good ahead of a bunch of grab-everything-for-themselves capitalists who make themselves filthy rich on other people's taxes."

Still they said nothing.

"Okay," he said conciliatorily, "it was my way of thumbing my nose at the bastards who ruined my grandfather."

"He's a fiery fellow," Hawkins said with fraternal kindness, "but only a nominal communist. He's proud of his membership card but never paid any dues, and they dropped him. I'm afraid it's just symbolic—his way of rebelling."

"That's not entirely true," Pag rejoined. "I don't like other people urging me to do anything I haven't thought of doing myself. I'm not a joiner! So I'm not a communist today, but Marxism strongly appeals to me. It's such a sensible and humane philosophy, I think Jesus Christ would be a Marxist today!"

He sounds like my uncle Ben, thought Lilly, *and very, very different from Dad and Wiley.*

Pag looked crestfallen.

"But he has nice eyes," Lilly remarked with a roguish smile.

She and Mary looked at each other and relapsed. The goddess of mirth and glee had unquestionably captured their hearts that day; they laughed without restraint.

Regardless of the weather, it had become a joyous late-winter evening and brightened for them all what had been a dismally gray day. But the rain, the fog, the drive out on a pitch-black path through the woods, and perchance another moose worried Lilly who was anxious to depart. This fear was allayed when Hawkins said, "No problem, just follow me!"

As they were leaving, Lilly turned to Pag and said, "We were stopped by a moose on our way here. Do you know what kind of a moose it was?"

"A bull moose?" Pag ventured.

"A Marxist moose!" Lilly said with a mischievous smile.

"Oh," grunted Pag.

"We could tell by its nice eyes."

Though this point eluded Pag, it was a promising start to a warm and lasting friendship.

Chapter 8

"MUD SEASON" USHERS in every Maine springtime. The shallow earth surface thaws during the day and refreezes at night. Early seasonal rain upon the surface of frost-frozen soil converts it into boot-clotting mud by day which refreezes into irregular patterns of mud-ice by night.

Toward the end of this insipid, gray-brown interlude, when the South Lighthouse horn moaned regularly through pea soup fog, Hawkins chose to explore the forlorn burial ground. Fog and the tenacious web of soggy, winter-killed weeds, clinging to the wrecked graves like a soaked and tattered shroud, induced in Hawkins a somber mood. The large boulder, set against the dismal rank of dripping cedars, drew him toward it.

A barrier of wild rose canes, armed with piercing and ripping thorns, surrounded the mighty rock. Hawkins grasped and pulled while stoutly resisting canes painfully embraced him, clawing and cutting like living demons. With considerable effort the granite surface facing the house was freed of them but still remained obscured by tenacious moss and lichen. Villainous rose vines clung to his trousers; his nails now ragged, his shirt now torn and bloodstained,

Hawkins saw vague carving on the boulder face begin to emerge. Were these indistinct letters which he glimpsed? His breath came quick and shallow; his mind swam; icy fingers raised gooseflesh on his neck and spine. He leaned against the rock, letting the cold stone restore his equilibrium, wishing someone were with him to share what he was experiencing, someone more detached to steady and reassure him! Was he watched by something or someone? He turned a searching gaze on the dark recesses of the cedar grove.

A lone, vertical wisp of fog separated from the gray mass silently sliding across the plateau and wafted ghostlike, disappearing into the cedar depths. "Imagination!" he scoffed, wiping beads of cold sweat from his brow as he set back to work, scrubbing the rough rock until drops of sea mist dripped from a word now distinctly wrenched from the forgotten past . . . the name "Abner." He felt stunned. That lonesome eerie place on a bleak afternoon gave Hawkins the illusion that a funeral which had occurred more than two centuries before had just taken place, an illusion of mourners recently departed, leaving this lonesome monument to endure through time as though two hundred years had suddenly disappeared from the ground on which he stood!

Reason was restored as he shivered in the wet atmosphere, his clothes torn and his legs imprisoned in strong thorny canes. He hastily extricated himself and returned to the house where he washed, wrapped himself in a blanket, and settled before the fire. He must think! Abner died in 1761. Wasn't that the year of the shipwreck in the old diary? George heard the fishermen talk about a treasure. They were right about the wreck. Could they also have been right about a treasure?

Was it nonsense? What sort of a legend would it be without a treasure of some sort, and yet, why would one shipwreck out of many be memorialized in a legend at all? Surely, there must have been many wrecks. What was there about this particular one which made it special?

He shook off the oppressive mood induced by his experiences in the graveyard and resolved to clean more of the headstone next day.

The morrow dawned as gray and wet as the day before, but Hawkins now proceeded to the graveyard with a bucket of sudsy water and a floor brush. Getting to the rock was still a nuisance. He would burn those thorny roses as soon as the weather dried them out! It took less time with the suds and brush to clean the whole front of the rock. There he found:

Obadiah Gibbs   Ruth Gibbs
1680-1723   1683-1730
Abner Gibbs
Born June 22, 1703
Died September 19, 1761

LET NONE FORGET
In truth let all ye
Befriend each lost
Outcast wanderer.

And a shallow vertical gouge at the base of the rock.

Jotting down this epitaph, he hastened to the Cottager home. The inscribed verse and a seemingly irrelevant mark at the bottom of the stone puzzled him. He would let George make what he could of them.

"Well, well, well," George responded on learning of Hawkins' discovery. "That's interesting! A historical mystery unfolds. I'm intrigued! We know there was a wreck and where it occurred. Perhaps I can hunt up additional data: where she was from, what she was carrying, and so forth. Wouldn't that be fascinating?"

"Yes," exclaimed Mary, "and it might truly have carried a treasure!"

"Don't set your heart on it," George said, smiling. "The treasure is probably apocryphal, added to make a fireside tale more engaging and romantic."

"I'm going to imagine a treasure anyway!" Mary replied. "Will you take me back and show me the grave, Hawkins?"

"Of course, but you had better put on your Wellington boots. It's pretty muddy."

"They're in the mudroom; so I'll get them on our way through."

Hawkins parked the truck, and by the dim daylight remaining, they made their sloppy way to the graveyard. Its appearance, which had become even more forlorn as the day waned, did not detract from the romantic vision Mary entertained. She noted the few visible arrow-headed pickets of the iron fence rusted, thrown down and almost totally obscured by entangling dead weeds. The gate lay moldering by broken posts from which it had once swung. The conventional headstones had toppled from their bases and fractured into disjointed fragments, but the massive rock stood untouched by time. Below the names of Obadiah and Ruth Gibbs, Mary read with a sense of reverent awe:

LET NONE FORGET
In truth let all ye
Befriend each lost
Outcast wanderer.

"That's strange." Mary seemed puzzled. "Why 'In truth'? Why not 'in kindness,' say, or just leave out 'In truth'? It's as though the word 'truth' had some important meaning. Does it mean divine truth?"

"That's the way I read it," said Hawkins, "but I wondered about it too."

"What's that slitlike scratch just above those thorn bushes?" Mary asked.

"I don't know. Probably a mark used to set the boulder where they wanted it. You can see its crude and was probably covered by dirt which has settled over the years."

"Yes, I can't think of a better reason," Mary agreed.

When she returned home, she wrote down the epitaph and made a sketch of the grave which included the scratch.

Mud season drew to an end; the days grew longer; the world turned greener; and the bane of Maine, its biting black flies, hatched.

"Hawkins, I think we should get to work on the barn," Pag announced one morning. "Any rotten boards on the side with the hole will have to be removed. We'll also need a woodshed to keep our fuel dry. If we find boards for one, maybe there will be enough for both. Let's keep it in mind."

After protecting themselves with insect repellent, they began early on a Sunday morning to restore the barn. Both were eager to work out of doors after the long winter.

"The first thing we have to do is get rid of that weed-covered mound up against the rotten boards," Hawkins suggested. "It's too irregular and dangerous to set a ladder on."

Armed with shovels and a wooden wheelbarrow with an iron wheel, which Pag had picked up at a local yard sale, they began to dig. An hour later, they stopped, so absorbed by what they had discovered, they did not hear a car pull up in front of the house.

When Mary called to them, Hawkins said to Pag, "Let me tell her about it first, then we can show her."

"Okay! I'm going to clean up if the tide's out." Pag looked at Hawkins. "You're a mess. Want to come along?"

"Not just yet. Make sure the rope's still secure in case the tide turns while you're down there!"

Hawkins then hastened to intercept Mary. A rustic log bench, discovered in the root cellar, sat under the oak, and to this he headed, calling out, "Let's sit on the bench. I've something to tell you."

When they were seated, he asked her if she recalled the possible treasure.

"Of course, I do! Have you found it?" she gasped excitedly, looking at Hawkins' mud-covered clothes.

"No," he answered, "but I think we should follow George's advice and keep what we do find out to ourselves. I'll tell you why.

"Pag and I began getting ready to restore the barn this morning. The first thing we had to do was clear the weeds around it so we'd have room to work. There was a large mound of earth needing removal, and we began with that. When we were down to solid earth, my shovel struck what I thought was a stone, but it wasn't. It was a slate slab with something scratched on it." He paused to wipe his muddy hands and to light his pipe.

Mary noted a tremor of excitement in his fingers and impatience got the better of her. "Oh, hurry, Hawkins! What was scratched on it?"

"A shiver went through me when I wiped the dirt away." He stopped, recalling his astonishment. Mary waited breathlessly. "On it was scratched 'Drowned man unknown to us. Laid to rest April 14, 1761.'"

Mary gasped with amazement!

"We kept digging." His mouth was so dry that he had difficulty swallowing.

"What then?" Mary eagerly grasped his arm, her eyes sparkling with excitement.

"Not very far down, we dug up pieces of bone!"

"Bone!" cried Mary.

"We spent the rest of the time carefully removing dirt and screening it. There were a lot of bones. I should say pieces of bones because they were pretty well decomposed. Then we found part of a skull!"

"A human skull?"

"I'm sure it is, considering what was on the slate."

"What have you done with them?" she asked.

"I'll have to notify the coroner. Unfortunately, I'm afraid it will make the news. I don't know if it's somehow connected with the Gibbs' grave, but to ease my mind, I'll cover the boulder with a heavy canvas tarpaulin. The dates are too close. Abner or someone buries a drowned man on April 14, and then Abner himself dies on September 19 of the same year. It could well start someone thinking about the legendary wreck at the Gibbs' place and the supposed treasure. I say someone, but it could be many, and we would be the focus of a gold rush, not an appealing prospect."

"What does it mean?" Mary was excited. Her thoughts too flew instantly from this discovery to Abner Gibbs' grave. "Could it have anything to do with that enigmatic epitaph?"

"I don't know. But it might, which is why, I think, we must be careful of our secret. Maybe the body we found was from the shipwreck." He hesitated then said in a firm voice, "And maybe there was a treasure."

Hawkins looked intently at Mary. "Our mysterious treasure may turn out to be nothing. But just in case, I think that no one but us should know anything about it. What do you think?"

"I know that you have a reason, Hawkins! What is it?"

Hawkins looked embarrassed. "I've lost whatever good sense I had. I believe there's a chance there really is a treasure, and I want to find it. To whomever asks questions tending in that direction, I think we should say we know only what the coroner tells us. Does that bother you?"

"Not in the least!" Mary smiled reassuringly. "It's our business and no one else's. We have every right to keep it to ourselves."

Hawkins was right about the discovery being news. The coroner notified Wiley, who sent his most experienced editor to personally gather the story, which then went out on a syndicated news service. A TV crew showed up by helicopter the next morning, and it was announced to the world that evening. Hawkins and Pag had wisely departed before anyone connected them with the discovery and avoided being asked awkward questions. The coroner was delighted to handle that task and basked in his instant ephemeral notoriety.

One of the first people at the site was Wiley Williams himself. His cunning mind suspected an ancient burial could well imply more, and if it did, he wanted to know of it! He returned later in the evening and introduced himself in an affable, offhand manner as the editor and publisher of the *Dirigo Vigilance.*

"I imagine you were surprised to find a body behind your barn," he said after shaking hands with Hawkins. "Why didn't you let the coroner handle it as soon as you had uncovered the slate?"

"I should have done that, but it could have been a prank. Anyone could have put the slate there on a Halloween years ago. Until I found part of the skull, I didn't really know if it was a grave or not.

"Besides," he said, knowing that if Wiley scented money, Mary's job would be secure as long as he suspected she might know something, "there might have been something else in the grave beside bones."

He noted the crafty glint which sprang into Wiley's eyes.

"Was there?"

"If there was or is, I haven't found it," Hawkins answered. "You're welcome to dig around if you like, but the coroner has already dug a hole big enough to bury a young moose. If he has found anything, he hasn't told me about it."

"Well, if anything should turn up," Wiley said, getting into his car, "be sure and let me know. It's news, and we pay well for that."

Hawkins was glad to see him depart. Wiley did not favorably impress him. That he and Lilly were brother and sister amazed him; no two people could be less alike.

The disinterring of a skeleton from an unaccountable grave over two hundred years old lured scores of curiosity seekers. Not content with seeing only the hole by the barn, they scoured the graveyard, took picnics into the fields, and wandered dangerously close to the cliff edge.

There seemed no end to the number of unwanted visitors and no limit to their impudence. Hawkins discovered two women in the upper story of the house. Pieces of the rotten barn boards were torn off for souvenirs. Pag saw an intrepid older man even used their rope to descend to the beach. Hawkins' good nature allowed the visitors to wander at will, but the house doors were locked, and he removed the rope at the cliff edge. Signs warning of the cliff and of the dangerous tide had to be put up along the ocean verge to protect him from a lawsuit in case anyone was injured. The number of visitors shrank to a handful after a week, and after two more weeks, there were none.

When the burial was no longer sensational and no more curious visitors arrived, Hawkins prepared to pursue his search for evidence of a shipwreck. He purchased two snorkeling masks, one for himself and the other for Mary if she cared to use it.

"Low tide's at four o'clock Saturday, Mary. At that time, the water should be shallow enough to allow us sufficient light to see items on the bottom. Care to come along?"

"Care to come along! You know nothing could keep me away!"

On Saturday, they walked to a place on the cliff where natural footholds enabled them to descend safely and walked along the beach. Hawkins had replaced the rope on the cliff top and had dropped it over the edge at the place where they would swim, both to mark the spot and to provide a means of escape should they forget the time and be threatened by rising water.

"The water is very cold, Mary. You may find it unbearable," Hawkins said as they approached the place where the rope dangled down the cliff.

"I know," she said, "that's why I brought these huge towels to wrap up in."

They stepped into the icy water and quickly withdrew. Hawkins then fearlessly rushed in and rose shivering. He knew from experience he would get used to it, but if he stayed too long, warming up would be very painful as though his body were pierced by a thousand searing needles.

Mary stepped into the water then hurriedly retreated to the warm, sandy beach. "The ocean's not this cold in Nova Scotia!" she called to him.

The seafloor fell sharply, and Hawkins swam only a few yards from shore before the water was deep enough to float a large ship. He placed the mask over his face and scanned the bottom. Between large rocks sand and pebbles were swept gently to and fro by the motion of the sea. Something covered with barnacles and seaweed, apparently wedged between two large rocks and protruding several inches out of the sand, caught his eye. He surfaced, inhaled deeply and dove for a closer look. He touched it; and beneath the adherent mussels, barnacles, and seaweed, felt rusted metal. He surfaced again, sucked in as much air as he could, and again swam down to it. On this dive he felt a large encrusted ring on top of a shaft buried in sand and gravel, clawed away some mussels attached to it, and saw two large links firmly rusted to it.

He emerged from the water and wrapped himself in a towel.

"Did you see anything?" Mary asked, alive with curiosity.

"I did," he said through his uncontrollably chattering teeth. "I think it's the end of an anchor."

"A fishing boat anchor?"

"I don't think so. It's too big. It's three, maybe four inches in diameter, and the chain links are bigger than any I've seen around here."

He had not been in the water very long but was very cold. "I'll rent a wet suit and try again when the sun is high and the tide is low. The light will be better, and the sun, hot enough to warm me up for several dives."

His words of good and wise intention fell on deaf ears.

"I must have a look," Mary said, diving into the gentle waves. "It's like ice," she screamed in a quivering voice, "but here goes!" She pulled the mask over her face and disappeared.

Hawkins plunged in after her, swam to the anchor, and beckoned her. She felt it, briefly ran her fingers over the links, zoomed to the surface, scrambled onto the beach, and wrapped herself in her towel.

"I saw it!" she cried. "I felt it! A ship wouldn't have sailed away and left its anchor. It must be from the wreck!"

Shivering on the verge of hypothermia, they could say no more until the sun had warmed them enough to move. Hawkins began to help her up the rope, but in a moment she scaled the cliff with ease. Hawkins turned his head to swat a horsefly and saw an expensive boat round the peninsula from the direction of Hemlock Harbor. He hastened up the cliff, pulled up the rope, and they hurried toward the house.

A fire was quickly lighted, and they warmed their chilled bodies before it. Mary dressed in the small upstairs room where she had left her clothing, and with difficulty Hawkins got a cotton undershirt over his resisting skin and put on his sweater.

"I need a warm drink! How about you?" asked Hawkins.

"Tea, please," she said.

"Pag, old fellow," pleaded Hawkins, "will you put the kettle on for us? We're frozen!"

"What have you two been up to?" asked Pag.

"I could see that you were absorbed in your work when we came in," Hawkins said apologetically. "Don't let us interrupt you further right now. I'll tell you about it later."

Pag returned to his task, and they pulled two chairs close to the crackling fire.

"Let's say there was a wreck, and the body was on the ship," Mary quietly began, almost whispering. "We have five things now: the wreck, the body, the slate, the puzzling epitaph, and now the anchor. Are they somehow connected? Can we think of anything that might connect them?"

"I wonder," said Hawkins softly, "what happened to the things in this house when it was put up for sale: the furniture, the clothes, any old records? They might hold some clue."

"Perhaps the real estate man knows where they went," Lilly suggested. "That's an idea! I'll ask him."

"I'm excited about this, Hawkins, very excited. If it turns out to be a fizzle, I'll really be let down!"

He smiled and touched her arm. "Let's not allow ourselves to get carried away. If we keep it a game, we'll enjoy it no matter how it turns out." He then told her about the coincidental appearance of the boat.

Mary knew of only one boat which was not a working vessel in Hemlock Harbor, and that belonged to Wiley Williams.

Chapter 9

A COLD WIND blew in off the ocean, rolling thick, raw fog over the land. Nothing could be seen outside the windows but the dull gray mass pressing against them. Such days are not rare on the Maine Coast even at the height of summer. Hawkins sat warming himself before the wood blazing in the massive fireplace, his creativity temporarily snuffed out by the depressing weather. He felt no motivation either to paint or to work at restoring the barn. Over the fire, a rusted and corroded hook held his pot of morning coffee. Absentmindedly using a stick of wood to swing it toward him, he heard a car pull up before the house. Wondering if it were Mary, his somber mood vanished as he rose to open the door.

Mary, Lilly, George Cottager, and a tall, thin lady stepped from the car. Matilda Dawson was the archetypical female activist: tweed suit, horn- rimmed glasses, low-heeled oxfords, and self-assuredness—a semiretired biology professor active in several organizations attempting to preserve what remained of Maine's natural environment.

"I met Matty when she came to visit Aunt Martha last week," Mary said after Matty and Hawkins were introduced. "She and Aunt

Martha were classmates at Chamberlain College, and she has some distressing news about Old Woods."

When they were settled before the fire, Hawkins expressed surprise they were out so early on such an unpleasant morning.

Mary turned to Hawkins and laid her hand on his arm. "I hope you don't mind, Hawkins. This doesn't concern you directly, but I need you to stand by me. I haven't kept the plan on Old Woods a secret from you, and now there's something more to tell, and I wanted you to hear it."

Hawkins understood how Mary courageously jeopardized her job by violating Wiley's demand for absolute secrecy about anything which transpired in the Conservation Group. She needed him, his concern, his support! He laid his hand firmly on hers, which said more powerfully than words that he sensed her anxiety, that come what may, he pledged to her his unwavering fidelity.

Lilly's eye caught this gesture and envied its tenderness and strength, for she too would have found comfort in having a champion, someone who cared enough to help her bear the shame of being Earl's daughter and Wiley's sister.

"You may think it treacherous of me to have told the four of you and Pag what I was warned to keep secret." Mary looked imploringly at them. "but someone had to know! I couldn't keep it secret and live with myself!"

"Don't fret about it, Mary," Matty said. "We've known for a long time the so-called Conservation Group is anything but. What is alarming is that they have their sights set on Old Woods, which brings me to the reason I'm here." She turned to Hawkins.

"Do you know several days ago, Senator Perry introduced a bill that would give Old Woods' timber to the Great Amalgamated Pulp and Hardwood Company?"

"No!" Lilly and Hawkins replied with angry disbelief.

"Mary wants me to tell you and Lilly about the public hearing he sprang on us the day before yesterday." Matty then spoke directly to Lilly.

"I'm afraid that what I now have to say will be offensive to you, my dear. I'm sorry."

"I know what you're going to tell us is the truth, Matty," Lilly said quietly. "I know something about what goes on at the Conservation Group and how my brother and my father are mixed up in it. I'm shamed by it, but I can't stand by and see Old Woods destroyed!"

Just then, Pag came down the stairs yawning, his dark locks disheveled and with a beard of several days duration.

Mary introduced him to Matty, but his attention was fixed on Lilly. She was not herself; she looked worried and ill at ease.

"Have you heard what Matty's been saying?" Hawkins asked.

"Yup," he said, yawning and reaching for the coffee pot.

"Do you want to hear the rest?"

"Nope!"

"Why not?"

Pag looked affably at Lilly; he had to say something. "It's none of my business, but I'm going to say it anyway! Lilly, from what I've heard about your father and brother, they are a couple of shits." Lilly gasped. "But you're not like them, and I don't think they give a good goddamn what you're like! Hell, they're too selfish to care. Do you think family loyalty, particularly loyalty to you, would stand in their way? I know it wouldn't! The way I see it, you've the right to stand on your own two feet and to do what you know you have to do." He smiled warmly at her. "If they love you, they'll respect that right."

"I second that!" said Hawkins.

"So do I!" said Mary, Matty, and George.

"One for all and all for one," quipped Pag.

"I don't know anything about this Old Woods," Pag went on. "I've never seen it, but it's the same dreary old story over and over again: privateers, capitalist plunderers plotting to screw the people. Damn 'em—they're always at it!"

Lilly laughed with profound relief and said, "I'll take this Marxist moose with the nice eyes to see the woods if he likes."

Pag turned his soft dark eyes on Lilly, the hint of a smile on his swarthy face. *She's rich, she's pretty, and she's spunky!* he thought to himself, *I like that!*

Lilly wished he wouldn't stare so then gave a start, for Pag winked at her and smiled. That Uncle Ben feeling . . . what brought it on?

"Who could resist such a charming invitation," he said in a kindly tone. "Give me time to wake up and get ready, and we can be off."

Lilly returned his wink, noticing for the first time the muscular arms and strong hands of a sculptor, and smiled in return. She had wished for a champion; perhaps she had found one.

Matty felt a sense of relief. Whoever this fellow was, he lightened everyone's mood. Was it his informality, his careless lack of self-importance? No matter! Gloom turned to smiles, and a jovial, more confident mood prevailed. Even she felt happier and could go on with a lighter heart.

"I must get back to Augusta as soon as I can; so I'll be as brief as possible and, with George's help, try to give you the gist of the committee hearing," Matty began.

"Earl Williams, CEO of the Maine Association of Forest Product Companies, tactically preempted the morning and a good part of the afternoon." She took a small notebook from her handbag. "Let me see what I can make of it. Bear with me, Lilly! I tend to get sarcastic—it vents my indignation. I don't wish to hurt you, my dear, just give me a kick if I go too far.

"He began his testimony," she said, consulting her notes, "though oration would be a more accurate term, by regurgitating the doctrinal cant of the vacuous economic benefits the forest companies bestow on Maine, the usual garbage. Bless their generous hearts! Let's see . . . oh, yes . . . . Jobs for workers, workers spend what they earn, that's good for local business, more tax revenue, etc., etc. No mention of the fact the millions of dollars the companies will make from the trees, which we the people have grown, will go out of state! Like all good propagandists, he puffed up a fiction to look like a valid argument and avoided the reality of theft from the people."

"No significant cross-examination by the committee followed, by the way," added George, "just rhetorical stuff to make Williams' responses look good. They smiled and nodded their satisfaction with his answers. You'd think he was Jesus Christ spoon-feeding his disciples!"

Matty could not help herself. She was angry and began to show it.

"Then this pompous windbag delivered a panegyric on the benevolence of the companies, especially the Great Amalgamated Pulp and Hardwood Company. After they have lumbered off Old Woods, the company will create a one-hundred-acre park where all the dear woodland creatures can live happily between hunting seasons and the dreamy nature lovers, wander in rapt delight. The committee loved that, more smiles and nods! No pertinent questions about erosion, stream pollution, or how animals now roaming on a hundred thousand acres were going to live in one-tenth of a percent of the space!"

"Didn't anyone on the committee ask how many jobs would be left in ninety-nine thousand, nine hundred acres of stumps and weeds?" Hawkins asked. "Or how many tourists would be attracted to such a wilderness?"

"Not one!" said Matty. "Those of us in opposition were not given the opportunity to testify until about nine at night, and he was long gone by then."

"What else did he have to say?" Lilly asked.

"When we got back after lunch," Matty resumed, "he went on about all the state and federal agencies whose regulations the companies must comply with and how admirable their compliance record was. 'Strict regulations' and 'unblemished compliance' were the words he used. Of course, all the agencies he cited are headed by businessmen. The companies have been 'deregulated,' and no one checks to see whether any remaining regulations, which look good on paper, are, in fact, complied with."

"Yeah," said Pag, "the company's say-so is good enough. Agencies like the DEP go after little guys who can't afford to defend themselves—it makes them look good! They don't touch the big guys!"

"The next person," George continued while Matty caught her breath, "was John Ableson, speaking for the state forestry commission. It was heartbreaking! I've known John for years. He's a dedicated conservationist, a birder, a hiker. He lives outdoors and loves Old Woods as much as we do. It must have destroyed all his self-esteem to read aloud each of the reasons, concocted without proof, why the commission determined clear-cutting Old Woods was in the public interest: It would be a healthier forest, access roads would be constructed, wildlife would not only flourish but increase, the new crop of trees would provide another 'harvest,' the so-called park would be a valuable economic public asset—every one a bold-faced lie!"

"There were plenty of questions from the committee after that, all put to him in a grim accusatory manner." Matty continued with lightly veiled sarcasm. "Essentially, what the committee did was ask him to repeat what he had already said. The politicians were setting up their defense. The record would show how diligently they had pursued the issue. If the public ever felt betrayed, it wouldn't be their fault. They had relied on the best state authority. What more could they do?"

"I called John this morning," George added, "to tell him we understood he either had to lie or lose his job. His wife answered the phone. She didn't know where he was. She started to cry and told me what a wretched night he had. She was worried!

"Matty and I promised to stop and see him after we leave here, which is why we're anxious to get back to Augusta."

They could tell by the look on Matty's face she was worried. To force an honest man to dishonor himself was cruel and cold hearted! Could he bear the self-reproach? What if he couldn't? "Keep a stout heart, Matty," George consoled her. "John wouldn't do anything more drastic than resign if he could, but he can't—he's too close to retirement age."

"There isn't much more to tell," Matty went on. "After a break for supper, they opened the hearing to the public. I suspect the Conservation Group had put together a coterie of logger families. The wives did all the talking and were very affecting. Life is hard for those folk! They're poor and go into debt just to scrape by. They're so desperate for jobs! You can't help feeling sorry for them. Their forefathers had good jobs when it took a two-man saw to cut down a tree. Then along came the chain saw, which probably didn't diminish the number of jobs but did wipe out a lot more trees. Now a monstrous 'forest harvester' drives in, grabs a tree in its jaws, saws it down, runs it through its maw, taking off the limbs, and deposits a finished log onto a waiting truck. They 'clear cut' a forest like mowing a hay field, and it doesn't take many men to do it.

"The men see the forests disappearing and their jobs along with them. The only course they see open is to cut down everything that's left.

"After that the few reporters left. By the time I and others had a chance to speak, the place was nearly empty."

"The guys who work in the woods," said Pag, "are just peons caught in the web of corruption spun by big business greed. They call it 'the bottom line,' but that's only a euphemism for maximizing executive greed and foisting shoddy goods on the public. We're all caught in the web—the country's caught in it, and the corporate spiders are draining our blood!"

"But some of us, and unfortunately we're not many," George replied nodding. "Will fight back as long as we draw breath!"

"This threat to Old Woods is staggering! Can anything be done about it?" Hawkins asked.

"Not very much, I'm afraid," Matty replied. "Old Woods is largely hardwood of which there isn't much left in Maine, which is why the Great Amalgamated Pulp and Hardwood Company wants it. It's our David against their Goliath. We have some facts, a little money, a small membership, and a mailing list, but that's about all. On the other side, Goliath, the Conservation Group, that 'think tank' of corporate conspirators, has unlimited money and power."

"This is the first time I've really thought at all about the woods," Hawkins said. "I took it for granted they've always been here and they always would be. I'm dumbfounded!"

"It's a dreary old story," continued Matty with a world-weary note in her voice. "The legislature is stacked with a majority of big business 'toadies and humbugs' who do whatever they're told to do. Big business owns the media, and we're locked out. We can't reach the public. We are, as they say, 'marginal,' meaning invisible, nonexistent. Oh, we send out mailings, but that's just preaching to the choir."

"Our problem is pernicious television!" George said emphatically. "The social consequences of that phenomenon have been so profound, I could spend all day on the subject and barely scratch the surface.

"The basic problem is the airwaves are deregulated to the extent they're now privately 'owned' and not, in fact, under effective public supervision to ensure they serve the public welfare. The communications corporations present basically only one end of a social spectrum, that of the rich class which includes, of course, those who own the corporations. Social, political, and environmental news has been reduced to an embarrassing and pretentious sham."

Matty and he had obviously discussed and analyzed this matter at length over the years. She continued where George had left off. "As time went by, the people were also incrementally deprived of informed debate on public issues which a viable democratic society depends on."

"Yes," said George, "and when the corporations fully realized what power they wielded, they cut off meaningful debate entirely. How? And by whom? Arbitrarily and by corporate myrmidons we euphemistically call government. A small percentage of people still continue to vote, but for what? One of two minor variations of the aggressive rich class? It's ludicrous!"

"What do the rich want?" Matty asked rhetorically. "Total political control for themselves, unopposed by the rest of us, and by god, they've gotten it. When the people remonstrate, the police crush them. That's democracy in ashes!

"Wisdom, anathema to infallible totalitarians, had to be censored so people would stop thinking because they'd have nothing to think about. Wise and honest people who cared about our social, political, and environmental issues were gagged, censored, and blacklisted because they gave people plenty to think about. They were replaced with clever, fatuities, well oiled with corporate money."

"I find symptomatic of public ignorance," said George, "the cessation of people discussing issues over the back fence in the evening and instead spending their evenings passively sitting glued to 'the box.' Neighborly differences of opinion have given way to pitiful mental oblivion, atrophy of thought, the natural result of insidious, unstimulating trivia, and the glorification of intellectual frauds, whom money has made into celebrities."

"It was the death knell of the republic," said Matty on the verge of tears, angry and frustrated at being checkmated by incredibly rich, dishonest corporate businessmen.

"The brains of the majority of people," quipped George, "wired, so to speak, to their TV, swallow the propaganda spewed out by the likes of Fatty Rushbottom, hook, line, and sinker. They're so deluded, so sure they know what's going on and so wrongheaded, they aren't remotely aware of what their folly is costing them!"

"But we're too damned dumb," said Matty, "to stop banging our heads against a brick wall! We present our case to legislators. They listen, some even encourage us, but nothing happens. When it's a bill which puts money into the pockets of the rich and defrauds the people, the result is a forgone conclusion. That's the way things will be handled concerning Old Woods. Any voting will take place late on a Friday night, and it will be by secret ballot. No one will know who voted for or against it. On Monday, the media will report it as a big win for the people."

"I can hardly believe what you're saying. It's so dastardly undemocratic!" Lilly's indignation was evident. "But surely, something can be done. Something must be done!"

"When the bill giving away the timber in Old Woods is passed, we'll go to court and try to block it," Matty said without much enthusiasm.

"That sounds hopeful!" Hawkins said. "They're going to give away property which belongs to the public in which the people have invested a lot of money."

"Don't be too confident," Matty said, recalling past defeats. "If we're successful in court, which is doubtful, they will appeal and appeal until they get what they want. They have the money it takes to do that, and we don't."

Hawkins was disturbed. "What happened to government 'of the people, by the people, and for the people'?"

"That was Lincoln's ideal, rhetorical definition of a republic. Did it ever really apply? Maybe in a limited way. When there were real newspapers, the kind where editors got shot and presses were dumped in the river, the people had a chance," Matty said, laughing. "There was diversity—at least some real social, economic, and environmental information got through to the people.

"The rich have always made war on the classes below them. Adam Smith summed it up in *The Wealth of Nations*: 'the evil maxim of the masters of men: All for ourselves!' To subvert a democracy, the people must be deluded by propaganda. That's the job of the media, and they have always done it very well. Democracy is fast becoming a myth. The United States has always been essentially plutocratic. Now it's government of the corporations, by the corporations, and for the corporations, with a gigantic military force to back them up. It's tragic, but that's the way it is!"

"Good god!" ejaculated Lilly, "But there are organizations like Common Cause and Public Citizen and magazines like the *Progressive* which have the interests of the public at heart!"

"There will always be a few people who can't be fooled," Matty went on, a mixture of discouragement and defiance written on her face, "but corporate businessmen know they can fool enough of the people, enough of the time to get what they want. I'm afraid things, as bad as they are, will have to get much worse before people are forced to wake up. But even if they do, what can they change? I saw a bumper sticker which summed it up: 'If voting could change anything, it would be illegal.' Sure, it's ironic, but as long as there are only two political parties and big business controls them both, nothing can change in our electoral system of 'winner takes all.'

"To get back to Old Woods . . . we might try getting enough signatures on a referendum petition to oppose its being lumbered off. Even here we're stymied. Security police throw us out of mall parking lots, even the parking lots at local supermarkets. Since the Supreme Court gave corporations the right of free speech, they can prohibit anyone else's on their premises. Nearly every place people get together today is private property. Going door-to-door is one way to reach people, but that's a problem. Usually, a babysitter or a child answers the door: mom and pop are both working to make ends meet. Most of our time is wasted, but we persevere.

"We might try to find a rich donor who wants to save Old Woods, but that's not likely to happen.

"We could have informative handouts printed, but distributing them is difficult. We can't afford postage, and we run into the same problem distributing them which makes getting petition signatures so difficult. It's damned frustrating, but we cannot do nothing!"

"Do you think," Hawkins asked, "if you spoke at the colleges, there would be any student response? It might help if they knew of Old Woods and what might happen to it."

"We've been working on that," replied Matty, "Philistinism has already claimed most of them, but a few still have ideals and hope. But our opponents also try to sway them with their specious arguments. The most we can do is to raise important questions, give them honest facts, and urge them to reason their way to the truth."

The gloomy weather outside matched the disappointed mood within. They looked at one another profoundly discouraged.

Mary had listened attentively to what Matty had to say and now said, almost to herself, "I'm glad I told you what I have. Even though it doesn't help, it has eased my conscience."

"It looks like we are going to lose Old Woods," Hawkins sadly stated.

"Yes, we probably are," Matty agreed. "I think we should be prepared for that. But we won't lose it without a fight! We're not many, we're not rich, our weapons are weak, but we are tough! We'll mobilize protests and hope to gain some public support that way, but short of mayhem, arson, or murder, the media will ignore them. If it comes to that, you can be sure blame and censure will be laid at our door."

Lilly was stunned by this revelation of perfidy involving her father and her brother. She knew their instincts were selfish, they were, after all, businessmen, but she had never realized the scope of their cupidity.

"To the ramparts, comrades!" quipped Pag. "I'll fling paintbrushes and chisels at their gunship helicopters. Do you think they'd do to Maine what they did to Vietnam? Dammit! I know they would!"

"Look," cried Lilly. "The sun is breaking through, it's going to be a beautiful day! Come on, Pag . . . let's be off!"

"Oh, Hawkins, let's go too!" Mary exclaimed. "A picnic in Old Woods before it becomes 'Old Stumps.'"

Matty smiled. Youth! Indeed a happy, zestful time when the future beckons with hope and boundless expectations!

Chapter 10

THOUGH OLD WOODS was not a virgin forest, the winding entrance road meandered gracefully through mature woodland. Overhead, the boughs of ash and maple trees bordering the road arched and intertwined in a canopy of living, shimmering green through which showered golden sunlight. Morning fog, with which dawn had festooned the low-lying vales, was now blowing away on a light southern breeze. The lively interplay of brilliant light and deeply shadowed depths accentuated the forest's cathedral-like expansiveness on this luxuriously warm morning.

Lilly parked before a restored white farmhouse, which now housed the Ranger Station, from which point it appeared most striking against the massed, dark foliage of the forest. Hawkins and Pag stretched their legs with pleasure after the lengthy drive.

"So quiet," Pag almost whispered as he stepped onto the lush lawn. "Until this moment, I didn't realize how I blot out the incessant surf . . . it's lovely! This is balm for the heart and a refreshing restorative to the mind, a refuge for my creative soul overburdened by petty cares." He smiled. "Like restoring a house and barn!" He turned a tranquil gaze upon Lilly which told her more eloquently than words how affected and impressed he was by the tangible peace and solitude of this haven.

"This place is so lovely and peaceful, so deserving of peoples' care and respect," sighed Mary as they trod the soft earth of the trail which wandered through the trees. "Why, oh, why can't it stay as it is forever? It's difficult not to cry, feeling such serenity and knowing that it is soon to be destroyed."

"Man and nature," added the exasperated Pag, "cheated and betrayed by scurrilous, money-hungry pirates who don't give a damn about the repellent vapidness they leave behind when they're dead. I'd say good riddance to them, one and all, but that would be useless. There is a ready army of younger, plundering boors standing cloned at their heels and a younger one at theirs, ad infinitum. There is no hope for the sensible protection of nature unless some catastrophe wipes homo capitalist, the despoiler-for-profit, the all-consuming monster, from the face of the earth?

"Man," he mused, "the destroyer, the money changing thief, the murderer of beauty and serene life, admires his crime just as all criminals do, dotes on it, bloated with self-love, and regards himself as cast in the image of God, hah! What hubris!"

Old Woods so deeply affected Pag, he put into intemperate prose the frustration and the anger they all felt. The forest struck a lyric arpeggio on the harp of his romantic soul. Such sublime creation evoked both his wholehearted admiration and an intense anger, that such a senseless tragedy was about to unfold.

He then spoke more to himself than to his companions, his voice as low and gentle as a sunset breeze. "Does this overwhelming peace, this stirring magnificence, flow from the hand of God? It matters not, no other metaphor will do! My spirit exalts in this arboreal cathedral. But money-mad men will blow it away for generations." He thought of something he never expected to recall in his life, the Psalm 23. "'The valley of death,'" he concluded, "is man's handiwork, not God's!"

A wave of empathy swept over Lilly. She felt as Pag felt, and the thoughts he expressed astonished her. There was more to this amiable

Marxist moose, this *ugly duckling*, than she had yet suspected. Were they two *ugly ducklings*? "Damned right!" she said to herself, not shocked in the least by her spontaneous profanity.

Hawkins looked at her, startled to see her glowing blush.

They all knew the end was coming but recoiled from the thought and said nothing more, for Pag and Mary had put into words the awe and indignation they shared. Their angry impotence and the certain futility of their efforts were an outrage to their sensibilities and reason. All the talk in the world would not impede the criminality of those who conspire to enact and execute unjust laws or the propaganda industry's power to persuade people to folly. Where must such folly lead? Where else but to disaster!

They came to a stream shimmering in the golden sunlight, streaming through leafy boughs and spanned by irregularly placed stepping stones, some too far apart for a lady's stride.

A startled deer bolted away as Pag flung off his sandals, splashed in, waded to where Lilly stood hesitant to cross, and offered her his hand. With a timid smile, she took his outstretched hand and jumped from stone to stone. Losing her balance on the last stone, she fell against Pag then righted herself. When they stood on the opposite bank, he did not release her hand, nor did she withdraw it.

"I think," Mary whispered to Hawkins, "it would be kind if we left them alone for a while."

"There is something on this side," Hawkins called to them, "Mary wants to show me. You go on, and we'll catch up with you later or meet you at the car."

Lilly and Pag, hand in hand, were soon lost to view.

"I've never seen Pag like this," Hawkins said, turning to Mary, "is he angry or happy, sad or just a little crazy?"

"Oh, Hawkins," Mary spoke with subdued mirth, gently taking Hawkins' hand, "I think they're falling in love!"

Hawkins nodded; the same thought had occurred to him. Lilly was just the girl for Pag, but it was so incongruous! Pag was poor—his character, diametrically opposed to that of her father and her brother. He dared not think where it would lead!

Mary read his thoughts. "Love will find a way!" she whispered reassuringly, "it always does!"

Pag's gay exuberance vanished as he and Lilly strolled alone together.

"Pag," Lilly asked, "what are you thinking about?"

After a prolonged silence, Pag replied, grasping for words which eluded him, "It's so damned wrong! This wonderful place to be destroyed by venal 'privateers' . . . the 'bottom line' . . . bucks in their pockets and beauty destroyed . . . it cuts like a knife! What in hell gives them the right? What's wrong with people?"

"Oh, Pag, don't think about it today," Lilly pleaded. "Let's pretend, just for today, Old Woods will always be here!"

"I feel so out of place, Lilly, so out of step. Our popular culture: comic book fantasy called drama, the crazy jungle clangs and castrato sopranos wailing out popular music, the 'divine rights' of capitalists which includes trashing everything for profit. It's so painful . . . so tasteless . . . suffocating . . . hopeless!"

"I know," Lilly said. "There was a time when men with heart gloried in nature, praised her in lofty works of art. Romantic art! Magnificent music, paintings, poetry, literature. I see that culture, real culture, as a great wave that swelled for centuries, endured through the eighteenth and nineteenth, then fizzled out in tin-pot television of the mid-twentieth. What we crave in the arts, the glory of classical music, the rhapsody of poetry, soul-stirring literature, must be sought in the past. Why? What's the matter with us that we have become so barbaric? Is it the inevitable end of a culture driven by greed, the lust for luxury and power . . . and deliberate lying?"

Pag looked at her with intense interest. "Then that's why you're so taken with antiques?"

She returned his gaze, "Yes, it's my escape. Just holding things, beautiful things, made by real people doing real things, takes me back in time. It's my fairyland."

"It was the Industrial Revolution," Pag declared, "and it did in more than antiques—it did in sentiment! I mean real sentiment, not unctuous soap opera crap or patriotic buncombe but the wisdom of the heart, as Pascal put it. I think that's what Dickens tried to convey in *Hard Times,* man yoked to a machine instead of pulling hemp with his hard-up buddies in the poorhouse . . . fragmentation . . . isolation."

"You're quite the philosopher, Pag," Lilly said encouragingly.

"Yeah, a seat-of-the-pants philosopher pissed off at the abominable garbage shoved down our throats by the damned 'privateers.'"

A chill of horror ran down Lilly's spine as she suddenly saw her father and her brother, the way they ran their newspapers and television stations, as agents of a modern dark age, an age of ignorance in everything but science and of moral insensibility even in science. "Damnation!" she cried with tears in her eyes, "my father and brother are part and parcel of the evil we're talking about."

It dawned on her in a flash. The crass minds and cold hearts of such men, blind to everything beyond the limits of their 'money changing holes,' were a fountainhead of unlimited cruelty and deceit, absorbed by selfishness and a lust for power. They would cinder this hospitable speck floating in the cold, mindless void of space . . . mine it to extinction in their unholy greed for money! Blind to past and future, obsessed with opportunism, what was nature to such minds and hearts? "Oh, my god!" she cried.

"What is it?" Pag said with alarm.

"I've got to get out of here. I feel like I'm in a condemned cell with an innocent prisoner waiting for the executioner." Lilly began to cry. "This wonderful place going to the corporate guillotine by my father's and my brother's hands . . . I can't stand it!"

A chipmunk scurried by.

"'Ye wee timorous beastie, what a murmur in thy breasty,'" quoted Pag hoping to divert her thoughts by recalling one of Hawkins' favorite poems.

"That was about a mouse. Not about me!"

"I didn't mean you," Pag replied. "I meant the chipmunk."

Lilly looked at Pag, smiled and dried her tears. Pag took her hand; they turned and retraced their steps. It was time to leave. Knowing the fate which awaited Old Woods, they could not stay.

When they entered a glade shadowed beneath tall trees where the soil, mixed with decaying leaves, felt like a cushion beneath their feet, Pag abruptly halted. Lilly drew back before the fire she saw in his eyes.

"I want to do a piece that will memorialize this place as we see it today," Pag declared. *The Girlhood of Mother Nature*, a child touching the stars." He struggled to express himself. "The sky, the earth . . . to somehow bring my emotional vision to life."

"How wonderful!" Lilly exclaimed.

"And another," Pag rushed on, "of man, a monster in a three-piece suit, standing over a poison landfill, armed with a machine gun, gunning her down! Spilling her blood while she is strewing roses!"

"Oh, Pag," gasped Lilly, "if only you could turn your passionate anger into such a monument!"

"Yeah." Pag laughed at his intrepid folly. "It would take one hell of a big piece of marble. Where would I get such a block? And how could I buy it if I did?"

"You could do another Mount Rushmore!"

Pag laughed even harder. "That's great! I'd put Ronald 'when you've seen one redwood, you've seen them all' Reagan there in a three-piece suit!"

Mary and Hawkins were waiting in the parking area more somber than when they had parted from Lilly and Pag.

"Why," Hawkins wondered, "does a sentient mind and heart respond to unmolested nature: the starry heavens, earth and ocean, infinite sky, the charm of color and form?"

"Gifted people, artists, scholars, and scientists, sensitive to the mysteries of nature," Mary said with mounting indignation, "suffer from deliberate neglect and derision because scholarship and creativity are neither effortless nor guaranteed profitable."

Hawkins was surprised by Mary's insight. "You're right, Mary! Corporate sales and profits from pretty packages probably skyrocketed when human mental maturation was arrested at a despicably childish level. Ignorance, nationalism, and prejudice are preached in the national media pulpit by windbag mentors. Ergo, our pitiful culture . . . community facilities, too numerous to name, schools, museums, libraries, parks like Old Woods, crumbling and unfunded while useless military porkers suck up our taxes! It's madness to think Old Woods could survive in such a culture!" His attention was diverted by Lilly and Pag just returning to the parking lot. This conveniently left unsaid the great issue, "But . . . what's to be done about it?"

Lilly clung to Pag's arm as they returned to the car.

"Let's get out of here!" Pag said.

No one objected.

Although it was Lilly's car, Pag took the driver's seat. She handed him her keys and slid in close beside him. Despite their fears for Old Woods and the sadness of what might be a last farewell to this noble forest, a feeling of tender attachment had formed between Lilly and him that day.

Chapter 11

SLATE GRAY CLOUDS with charcoal underbellies, majestically melancholic, had covered the sky during the night. Fog banks rolled steadily in from the ocean, dense one moment, thin and wispy the next. A steady drizzle fell. Tomorrow or the next day, Mother Nature might shower the Gibbs' place with sunshine, but that day, she wept.

"I'm going to Howarton," Hawkins said to Pag, "and look up the lady who owned this house. Care to come along?"

"Might as well," answered Pag. "It's hard to get with it on days like this."

The road, after leaving Hemlock Harbor, ran through farmland, thence wended into forested hills on its way to the paper mill town of Howarton. The farms they passed were much alike, aged buildings which had received minimal maintenance over many decades. So too did the herds, pastures, and machinery convey the impression of neglect. Hawkins saw all this as perhaps the work of a solitary, overworked man, who had neither money, time, nor strength to do all that needed doing. Rural poverty was a way of life. How did they earn the little money they needed in order to survive? What sort of lives did they lead?

Ahead of them, an oncoming school bus stopped before a very small house sided with clapboards far from new, where laundry hung to dry on a small screened porch. In a driveway of tracks in the lawn of sorts, which needed mowing, stood a car of ancient vintage. Also stacked in the small front yard were thick logs, drying and waiting to be cut into proper stove length, the fuel for next winter's heat.

Two young girls, remarkable for the bright smiles which lighted their innocent faces, exited the bus. This very small house was obviously their very small home to which they now returned with obvious delight. A small dog wagging his tail in eager greeting ran to them and was lovingly picked up and fondled. Hawkins' heart went out to these charming children happy to return to their loved ones and their abode. They were well loved and well cared for in that very small home; of that he had no doubt, and they brought a ray of charismatic sunshine into the dreary overcast day. Though living in rural poverty, they, he knew, were happy. If they were lucky, their futures would be materially no poorer than their past, and a likely future awaited their own children. They would ask no more than that. "Honest poverty," said Burns, who knew it well, "a man's a man for a' that." How often Hawkins' grandfather had repeated that poem. However these dear, worthy people hung on to life, he honored them in his heart and hoped every blessing, every joy to be found in every such very small house would never be diminished.

A disturbing ambivalence now struck him. "These people are not in any way remotely connected with the destruction of Old Woods," he remarked to Pag, who also had been keenly observing the children. "I don't feel about them as I thought I would. I'm fond of them. I admire them. Whatever I could do to help them, if they wanted it, I would try my best to do."

In his socialist philosophy, Pag divined a major cause for their poverty. "Look at it this way, Hawkins," he began, "these people don't own the trees. Who does? And why? Because some king gave away land to his buddies, which rightfully belonged to the Indians!

"Hell," Pag declaimed, "men claiming ownership of what they have no moral right to own: airwaves, natural resources, labor . .

. you name it . . . propagates a corrupt feudal society based on the injustice of private property.

"These poor souls know only 'who,' candidate or party, they intend to vote for but not 'what' they're actually voting for, in terms of political actions, harmful bills introduced, and disastrous judicial appointments with damnable long-term consequences.

"They vote, or do not vote, in accordance with whatever trust they absorb from the persuasive, delusive PR of Wiley's for-profit media. Blindly trusting his contemptible propaganda, they elect Trojan horses of whom, knowing the likes of Wiley, they damn well know absolutely nothing germane.

"Once safely elected these, 'toadies and humbugs,' these eager servants of the rich, emerge like the Greeks at Troy. Do they perform as they promised? You bet . . . ha!

"Being deluged with crap, the likes of which the Williams' put on their radio and TV, how would these people ever know?"

Two little girls, a little dog, and a little house had made Hawkins as puzzled and confused as he had ever been.

"What's that god-awful stink?" Pag exclaimed with visible disgust when they were still several miles from their destination.

"I don't know," Hawkins replied, wrinkling his nose.

"Look at that stream on our right! The water looks like moldy pea soup!"

Entering the outskirts of town on the ill-paved, much-patched road, they saw the unpleasant, acrid smell belonged to the dirty, white smoke belching from the mill's smokestack. The mill itself was a baleful thing. It had a slapped together look like windowless shanty-like buildings piled side by side and one atop another, a dirty, ugly thing, with two large pipes: one polluting the air, the other polluting the water.

The houses of the dingy town looked like neglected offspring of the mill, whose occupants lacked the money and inspiration to tidy them up. The small supermarket, the drugstore, the gas station, even the post office, were grimy and in need of a good wash . . . not an attractive place at best . . . but on a dreary day, depressing.

"Where's this America the beautiful?" Pag asked in scornful rhetoric. "Is that what they call scabby places like this?"

"There are places like ours," Hawkins suggested.

"Yeah, there are a few places, I guess . . . something for postcards and travelogues." An eighteen-wheeler careened by, covering the windshield with muddy spray; roadside debris struck the glass.

"Damn those road-hogging, rubber-tired locomotives!" Pag swore indignantly. "It's impossible to get away from the bastards. They're everywhere! On every back road! The goddamn country is overrun with them! What in hell is the matter with this godforsaken country? Have the people no brains at all? Noise, commercial scab, nothing whatsoever to lift the spirit or bring light into the mind. Let's never leave the haven we've stumbled on, Hawkins, it's an island in a sea of commercial shit! Christ, this is an ugly country 'from sea to shining sea,' the land of too many ignorant brutes, too much rich man's self-serving bullshit as far as I can see! Damn little to inspire the soul of an artist."

Hawkins stopped at the gas station to ask where he could find Jemima Stowe. Inside, raucous music blared to a battered wood desk, several magazines with curled pages, and a cigarette machine, all heavily covered in dust and grime. He followed the music into the working bay, where he found two legs in grease-covered overalls and oily boots sticking out beneath a gaudy stock car. He knelt and yelled at whoever was under the car, not knowing if he could be heard over the noise of the radio. Apparently he was, for a young man with a happy face rolled out to speak to him.

"Do you know where Jemima Stowe lives?" he shouted.

"Ayah!" replied the youth. He appeared not yet twenty.

"I can't hear you!"

"Kneel down closah!"

Hawkins crouched down. The music was making his head ache.

"Where does she live?" he shouted again.

"Next street take a right . . . second house on the left."

Hawkins thanked him and left, got back in the truck, his ears still ringing, and followed the young man's directions.

As he approached the side door of the house (the front door was still sealed by a plastic sheet in lieu of a storm door), a small dog ran, snarling and barking at him. The dog was tied to a rope, which allowed him to just reach the concrete pad on which Hawkins stood. So long as he didn't take a misstep, he was safe. He rapped on the locked screen door; the wood frame bounced and rattled without making very much sound. An elderly lady, probably hearing the barking dog rather than his knock, stood back from the screen door, making it impossible to see her clearly.

"Does the dog bite?" Hawkins asked.

"Will if he gets a chance," the lady answered in a laconic drawl.

"I'm looking for Jemima Stowe."

"You've found her."

"May I come in?"

"What do you want?"

"I'd like to speak with you about the things from the Dobbins' house near Hemlock Harbor. I'm Hawkins Shortreed who, as you may recall, purchased it from you."

She opened the door, and Hawkins stepped in. What he saw was as bright and clean inside as the house was dull and dirty outside. The lady herself was plainly but neatly dressed, her white hair in a bun, her merry eyes twinkling behind wire-rimmed spectacles.

She seemed glad of company and offered him coffee, which he accepted. A half-filled pot sitting on an electric coffeemaker indicated that she probably did not live alone. She bade him sit at her kitchen table and waited for him to speak.

"Mr. Leo LaChance in Hemlock Harbor gave me your address. He thought you might have whatever was left in the old Dobbins' place when it was put up for sale."

"I did have some things but not much."

"Do you still have them?"

"No."

"Can you tell me what happened to them?"

"A young fella bought it all a while back."

"Does he live in Howarton?"

"No."

"Do you know his name or where he lives?"

"Ayah," she stopped, trying to recall it to mind. "Name's something like Wirey or Willy . . . can't remember his last name. Said he came from someplace I never heard of."

Hawkins was stunned and dismayed. It must have been Wiley using a false address. Perhaps Leo could tell him. What is he up to? Of what use would the things be to him?

"You all right?" Jemima asked, seeing the bewildered look on his face.

"Yes . . . yes, I'm okay! Can you tell me what things he bought?"

"There wasn't much: just a clock, some old books, and some useless glass thing, all dried up, to tell the weather."

"Was there a family Bible or any family records?" He was almost afraid to hear her reply.

"A Bible? No!"

Hawkins thanked her graciously for her hospitality and information.

"I'll write my name and address for you just in case anything was overlooked. You might think of something after I leave. It's unlikely, but I do wish you'd hold on to it just in case."

"I will, young man. I like your looks a lot better than that other fella. If I think of anything, I'll write to you." She shook hands and locked the screen door behind him.

Hawkins was puzzled. What use did Wiley have for the things from the house? What was he up to? What of his surveillance from the sea? He must have found something. He thought, *It's the only explanation! It tells us something too! There probably is something in the house or around the house, and it's valuable enough for Wiley to want it!*

Hawkins was deeply disappointed. Pag knew from his downcast expression something was wrong.

"Wait!" Jemima Stowe came racing to the truck. "I found this shoe box after I sold the junk to what's-his-name. It's goin' in the gahbage, but you can have it if you want it."

Hawkins thanked her and handed the box to Pag who opened it and partially extracted a worn satin garment with frills about the neck and cuffs.

"Probably some theatrical costume," responded Hawkins to Pag's description. "Just slide the box under the seat!"

"You know that I'm not a nosy person, Hawkins," Pag languidly opened conversation as the boredom of being confined in a monotonous motor vehicle began to plague him, "but why do you care if this lady has anything from our house or not?"

Hawkins was perplexed. It was an honest and straightforward question. There was nothing else for it but to confess his suspicion of treasure and bear Pag's humorous skepticism. How he wished that Mary were there to answer his question. Her enthusiastic belief was contagious as he well knew.

"Let me see if I can get things in a row," Hawkins replied. "Everything is supposition. There is no hard-and-fast evidence, but Mary and I have a suspicion there was once something of value in the house that may still be there."

Pag straightened up at once from a slumped position and gave Hawkins his complete attention. "Go on! I'm really interested. Start at the beginning and don't leave anything out. I'm all ears."

Hawkins told of the shipwreck legend and the supposed treasure. When he came to the lost identity of the location of the wreck and George's inference, it was possibly just off the coast of their property, Pag was enthralled.

"You don't mean to say that we have a mystery and a treasure hunt on our hands—that's terrific!"

Pag's enthusiasm caused Hawkins concern.

"Before I go on, let me ask for your secrecy. There are now seven of us who have an inkling of something being hidden, and unfortunately, one is Wiley Williams. When all we knew was there was a legend about a wreck and a treasure, Lilly asked Wiley if he had heard of it. After we found the skeleton, all of us, including Lilly, were convinced he would betray us. Don't ask me why! His greed is so overpowering, Lilly convinced us to keep anything we discovered strictly to ourselves."

"You can rely on me."

Hawkins smiled at Pag; no further reassurance was asked for or needed. Each knew he could implicitly rely on the other. Hawkins proceeded freely and with a light heart to share all he knew with his friend.

When Pag learned of the anchor, his expectations and his dreams were boundless. How could he tell Hawkins how Old Woods had affected Lilly and himself? His dreams at the moment totally absorbed him. With his share, and in his dreams, a boundless share it was, he would fight and save Old Woods for Lilly. Why he would do so was something which he failed to ask himself. He would do it for her; that's all there was to it. His dreams went no further, or so he believed, in spite of that gnawing something which whispered, "Lilly, Lilly, Lilly," until reality intruded upon his sweet illusions.

Chapter 12

WHEN WILEY SAW for himself the grave in which Hawkins and Pag had discovered skeletal remains, he recalled a question Lilly had put to him during the winter. Had he heard a local folktale having to do with a sunken ship and treasure? He had shrugged it off at the time, but this discovery put it in a new light. There might be something to it. There was something odd about Lilly's response when he brought it up again. She had forgotten about it, didn't know from whom Mary had heard it; Mary had not mentioned it again. Was she being purposely evasive? Mary Ayrshire was friendly with Shortreed. What did she know? Nothing more than anyone else, or so she said. Were they playing his game? If they were, he'd show them how a master operated.

A drowned man buried in an obscure grave meant the body was not that of a family member nor of a local seaman, for neither would have been unknown to the fishermen who discovered the body nor to the local farmers. The slate said it was a man who had drowned sometime in late March or early April. Whoever he was, he must have drowned within sight of land for the body to be recovered. But if there had been a wreck, then why only one body? Was he drowned?

Maybe, but there was no way to be certain. He could have met his death on land and his body dropped in the water.

Why had the body not been given over to the proper authorities? There must have been some reason why they buried the body without notifying anyone in an official capacity. Deep snow, a lame horse, illness in the family, distance, there were many ways to account for it. But had the death been reported? If so, there was a possibility of either a clue to the questionable treasure or an actual report of the treasure itself.

Judge Cockalorum owed him a favor; he'd have him search for any record of the death and make sure that whatever he might find was kept secret!

"Williamson," Wiley said with tones of goodwill, "I have a favor to ask. If you have the date of death, can you search for any record of it having been reported? You've surely been seeing the stories about the skeleton found near Hemlock Harbor. That's right, 1761. And Williamson, if you find anything, keep it to yourself!"

Several days later, Wiley was contemplating the fascinating question of treasure: what it might be, where it might be, and how he might get at it, when the telephone put an end to his airy musings. The call was from the judge.

"I think I've found a record about that matter you're interested in," he said, "but I'm not sure how newsworthy it is. Of course, any tidbits titillate the type of readers who are fascinated by such trivia. I can't say that it amounts to much, but here it is."

"Good work, Williamson!"

"The body was that of an old man apparently dressed in the clothing of a foreign gentleman. He was found dead and was buried at once because the weather had suddenly turned warm. I guess the Gulf Stream must have been pushed in toward the coast by a storm at sea. The heavy rain from the storm, along with the melting of the deep snow still on the ground, had washed out the bridge over Quenshukney Stream. There was an ill woman in the party, so they were forced to wait until the water went down before they could get a wagon across. Apparently this was what delayed them from getting to a magistrate. What with this holdup and a warm turn to the weather, I think it was probably a good thing they did bury him!

"There are two unusual items mentioned in the report. First, the face and hands of the body were dark as though they had been exposed to strong sunlight. He wasn't dressed as an English gentleman, so it's likely he was from someplace south of here! The other is that the body was not found on the beach. It was lodged behind a rock higher up, but the clothes were soaked. There had been rain at the time, and there had been some sort of an accident in the storm because parts of a fairly large ship were floating on the surface of the water. The surf was too dangerous to attempt launching a boat, and by the time it was safe to risk it, the debris had either sunk or been washed out to sea.

"One other item, probably of no importance, but a big black man, who spoke no English, mysteriously showed up and led them to the site of the wreck. He repeated something that sounded like 'Demon he' which they took for a superstitious reference to some demon. He left and was never seen again. The magistrate declared him a shipwreck victim and let the matter drop."

Wiley thought a moment then asked, "Williamson, who reported it? Did it say?"

"An Abner Gibbs."

Wiley, recalling the legend, said with a note of irrepressible excitement in his voice, "Williamson, I'm after bigger game than sensational news. Whatever you do, don't breathe a word of this to anyone."

He hung up and drew a deep breath. Everything fits: Lilly's question, the place, her connection, through Mary, with Shortreed, the skeleton! His cunning mind fixed on a rich man from the south with something valuable perhaps concealed on his body or possibly found in what remained of the ship, something which this Gibbs had robbed . . . . Treasure! His pulse quickened at the thought. What had he found and where was it? Was it still in the house? It might be gold, probably foreign gold coins.

Gibbs, he thought, *must have found gold on whatever remained of the ship.*

Speculation momentarily seized his imagination. "The man was undoubtedly a wealthy French or Spanish trader from the Caribbean, shipwrecked after possibly loading a shipment of guns at Boston for the French and Indians battling the British in Nova Scotia . . . and returning with a large payment in gold. Trying to barter with gold would have raised too many serious questions for Gibbs and would have landed him in serious trouble. What did he do with it? What could he have done with it? A hoard of French or Spanish gold coins of that era must be worth a fortune!"

Wiley had taken advantage of the time during which curiosity seekers were converging on Hawkins' property. Two women he had sent into the house found nothing noteworthy in any of the rooms. The rope at the cliff was suspicious, but Gus Gold had seen nothing remarkable when he had climbed down.

"Getting down was easy," Gus related to Wiley, "but getting up again was a different matter entirely. I thought my last moments were at hand, but believe me, when those waves started lapping the rock, I pulled on the rope for all I was worth. My pulse beat in my ears like a machine gun. I don't know how long I lay on that sandy grass before I could get on my legs, but it was getting on to late afternoon before I managed it. Never again will I get near that edge and look into that man-eating surf . . . what a nightmare!"

Bare rooms! Nothing left behind! What happened to all the things that were in the house when the old woman died?

He searched the back issues of his newspaper and found the obituary of the old lady who had died in the old ocean-side farm, now so important to him but in which his agents had found absolutely nothing of importance. But wait a minute; it did say that the entire contents of the farm were to be auctioned. Hurriedly he searched the classified section of the papers of the time and found the advertisement for the auction. It contained a list of farm implements, housekeeping tools and utensils, but no mention of any memorabilia. Why mention anything like that? It would not be of the slightest interest to the farmers or the fishermen of Hemlock Harbor. Wiley noted the name of the auctioneer and lost little time in traveling to see the man. What he wanted was any record of items which were sold and the names of the successful bidders if they were still available.

Sam Smith, the auctioneer, was found in a dusty warehouse, in which he housed furniture, tools, and equipment so numerous and various it was hopeless to identify or categorize them, except under the most general headings, and which also contained rows of chairs for the local curious and the bidders who would show up at the next public sale. In one corner of the hall, a battered old desk was placed at Wiley's disposal, and two mildewy cardboard boxes containing myriad unsorted decaying folders were on the floor beside it. Luckily, Smith had neglected destroying out-of-date records, and the boxes at least had the correct year crayoned on them.

Wiley was dismayed by the daunting task of searching through them in such a place; perhaps Smith would sell or rent them? Since he would do either, Wiley bought them. No one else would ever have access to them but himself. He returned with them to Hemlock Harbor, where he proceeded to put them into order at once, preparatory to investigating them at leisure. He carefully examined each packet of each auction held during the months marked on the boxes, each of which was luckily labeled with the estate name, looking for that of Dobbins.

There wasn't much to sell, mostly aged farm machinery, but he found what he wanted! "Assorted personal effects sold to Herman Brucklacher $2" along with a receipted bill to a Jemima Stowe for $42.25.

Mr. Brucklacher came forward to meet him in muddy boots, a small dairy farmer, his gray beard several days old, clothes dirty and unkempt. *What could someone like him want with personal effects of an old lady?* wondered Wiley. *More importantly, did he still have them?*

"I saved some of the things," Mr. Brucklacher replied, eyeing Wiley with suspicion. "Why do you want to know?" Could there be something in that box of old cooking recipes, letters, and bills, that crumbling old Bible, worth money?

"If you will let me see what there is"—Wiley had judged his man—"I may see something I want, and if I do I'll pay you well for it."

Mr. Brucklacher knew Wiley's sister was in the antique business and brought the box out to the front porch. Wiley spotted the Bible at once. "One hundred dollars for the lot," he offered. Mr. Brucklacher gazed on the box, unsure, maybe there was more here than he thought.

"A hundred fifty dollars is my final offer," said Wiley, setting his foot on the stairs feigning to depart. "It's a present for my sister. She'll enjoy going through it. What she sees in such old junk, I don't know, and frankly, I don't care to know. Take it or leave it because I have an appointment I'm late for already."

Mr. Brucklacher stuffed the money into the pocket of his overalls and trudged back to the barn. Wiley put the box in the trunk of his car.

Perseverance, cleverness, and extraordinary good luck put him in possession of the Gibbs' family Bible, and he planned to carefully search for clues though, at this time, he did not know exactly what it was he hoped to find!

Every evening for a month, working carefully lest the fragile pages be further damaged, Wiley went through the ink-faded handwritten family notes page by page unable to curb his driving momentum and found . . . nothing. He was dismayed, baffled but not defeated; whatever it was had to be there. Again he read every entry, persisting until he could make sense of every word, especially the dates. Still he found nothing!

"Something has to be here! I've missed it," he told himself. "Brown paper, faded ink, scratchy, misspelled words, abbreviations . . . I must have missed it!"

He began once again. Many were the nights he spent carefully, painstakingly poring again over the handwritten entries and this time scanning every page of Biblical text as well, looking for something, anything that had been added in ink, even a stain.

Then when he had spent more than another month on the task, he found a faint, faded ink mark which read "end" in the book of Jonah, chapter 2, next to verse three:

> For thou hadst cast me into the deep, in the midst of the seas; and the floods compassed   me about: all thy billows and thy waves passed over me.

And at the chapter end he found the following:

> Aprl 1761. Bdy of man on east medow clif. Hevy storm in night. Drest in silk or satn. Buryd by barn ere it putref'yd.

And then so cramped that it was barely legible, as though it had been added as a secret memo, he espied the symbol for the pound sterling. That was enough for Wiley. Pounds meant money; money meant treasure, treasure he meant to have at any cost!

Chapter 13

TOTALLY CONVINCED BY what he found in the Gibbs' family Bible that a treasure existed, Wiley was unable to restrain his cupidity. Visions of gold! Hoards of Spanish gold! His imagination blazed with legends of pirates and buried treasure. Wiley, the hardheaded, coldhearted, calculating, covetous business executive, burned to lay hands on it. He must have it, be the means fair or foul, but how? He knew no better source of advice on that question than Augustus Gold of the state police. Gus knew every rich man in the state who skirted the edges of the law or cleverly bent it as necessary. A quid pro quo promised to his intimate connections in state and federal government would arrange the imaginative interpretation of any law. He was an encyclopedia of mechanisms, means, and realities of subterranean power.

"Gus," Wiley began, "what I have to tell you can't go beyond us! Without going into the reasons, I strongly suspect a hoard of eighteenth century gold, probably coins, is hidden someplace on a piece of property. It's been there for over two hundred years, and no one has ever suspected it. The owner's renovating and poking around and might stumble on it. I want that property! How can I get it?"

Gus Gold inclined his bald head closer to Wiley; his normally cold gray eyes glinted through his spectacles with eager interest at the mention of gold. "I assume you've tried to buy it?"

"I sent a proxy with an offer to the realtor who handled the last sale, but the owner won't sell!"

Gold lighted a cigarette, closed his eyes, opened them, and gazed abstractedly through the window, drank some coffee, and remained thoughtful for a minute.

At length he said, "There is one way. You're probably not familiar with forfeiture,[3] so I'll give you a thumbnail sketch.

"Let's say the police find a marijuana cigarette in somebody's car. The car is guilty!"

"The car?" asked Wiley with surprise.

"Yes, the car! The police take the car by civil forfeiture and sell it or auction it off. Whatever money they get stays with the police. That's basically all there is to it."

Not many things astonished Wiley, but this news did.

"What about the owner of the car? Surely he would go to court to get it back!"

"He can try, but it won't do any good. The law is on our side. Oh, people have tried, but no one's succeeded. For example: police raided a house while no one was home because they suspected drugs. A previous owner was mixed up with drugs, but the present owners were entirely innocent. They lost everything: house, contents, and over $2,000 found on the premises. They went to court to get it back and lost.

"It's big business for us. About three quarters of our annual budget is obtained that way. We've taken yachts and businesses and . . . and evidence . . ." He did not finish, but Wiley understood his meaning. Evidence could be fabricated.

Wiley was fascinated. This was a powerful tool and a legal one, which he mentally added to his crafty armamentarium.

"Gus," he asked with keen interest, "are you saying you could confiscate the property I want and sell it to me?"

"It could be arranged," Gold responded, "one joint found on the premises is all it would take."

"But the owner doesn't smoke cigarettes. I'm positive there's no possibility of finding drugs of any kind."

"It could be anything illegal, for instance: an unregistered firearm or a large amount of cash he can't account for."

"This guy is clean! There isn't a possibility of finding anything illegal in his possession."

"It doesn't have anything to do with his possessions. He doesn't have to own it or even know about it. It's the property on which it's found that's guilty, not him—and who can say how it got there. Who even cares?"

"How can property be guilty of anything?" Wiley asked in disbelief.

"That's the law. It was originally meant to confiscate the property accumulated by criminals, but now it's anybody's property."

"Do you mean if a marijuana cigarette butt was thrown away by anybody, just lying on the ground, then that house, barn, and land is forfeit?"

"Exactly!"

"Suppose, just for argument," Wiley was still dubious, "I pass by in my car and throw the butt out the window. It lands on his property, you find it there, then the property is forfeited?"

"Precisely!"

"Let's say I do that. What then?"

"The feds have to be in on it in order to get their share of the loot. So we, a local constable, guys from the IRS and DEA make up a party. A dog sniffs out the butt and that's it. We take everything!"

"Suppose I tossed the butt. If I'm found out, what happens to me?"

"Nothing! We're not interested in people. Their property is valuable, not them, and that's what we want."

Wiley rose and paced the room. It was almost beyond belief, but Gold always knew what he was talking about. It would be a monstrous injustice; that didn't matter; but was it legal? He still had doubts.

"Gus, I don't doubt anything you've told me. Still, I want to run it by my attorney, just to be sure I'm not risking anything."

The following day, Wiley called lawyer Henrietta Panky to his office. She was a tall, thin woman of indeterminate age in a bright dress and a large floral hat who handled legal issues for the paper. In their dealings over the years, her advice had been uniformly sound. She did not confound law with justice. They understood one another.

Brief greetings over, Wiley said, "Hankie, I'd like to know about forfeiture. What it is and how it is used."

She smiled. Forfeiture had so enriched the funds available to police that they regularly sought her legal guidance. She was as expert in civil forfeiture as any lawyer in the county and cleverer than most when it came to creative application.

"Let me put it succinctly. Civil forfeiture laws apply to property and not to individuals. As crazy as it sounds, inanimate objects are given 'life' and are forfeited to the government for their criminal deeds. Property is subject to forfeiture if there is evidence it is or has been used by anyone, not necessarily the owner, for any criminal activity. The innocence of the owner is not germane. His property is forfeited. Owners are expected to police their property against all criminal activity. If I used this telephone to arrange a drug purchase unknown to you, this building could be seized."

"It sounds incredible. How does it work?" Wiley asked.

"Let me try to list the important points," Panky said. "Federal law allows the government to seize property without notice or a hearing solely on the basis of 'probable cause' which covers such things as hearsay, innuendo, and rumor, none of which would be admissible in a court of law. 'Probable cause' makes it unnecessary for the government to prove anyone's guilt in order to get a forfeiture judgment on his property. Quick action by the government gives it immediate possession. The burden is on the owners to prove they are entitled to have their property returned. Possession being nine-tenths of the law, they don't get it back. It's illogical and victimizes innocent citizens—but that's the way it is, appeals to reason are futile.

"Police have enriched their departments by billions since Congress passed the forfeiture law in the seventies. They probably had mob bosses and drug lords in mind at the time, but it's now used far beyond their original intent. In a word, it's turned some cops into robbers."

This was music to Wiley's ears!

There were three rooms on the ground floor of the house: the parlor, a dining room of equal size, and a kitchen. The windows in the room where Hawkins did his painting and Pag his sculpting faced a southeasterly light. Having been once the parlor of the house, it provided adequate space to work and had a large fireplace which reeked of age. Its contents of easels, the odor of turpentine, clay sculptures, and paintings clearly identified it as an artist's workshop. The walls had been newly painted a uniform light beige color, and two large pine tables, made for outdoor meals, held their tools and materials.

They roughly planned their days: cool summer mornings and long summer evenings for labor, late mornings and early afternoons for art.

"We'll have things in good shape for next winter," Pag said as they sat in the shade of the oak, finished with the morning's labor.

"We need wood for the barn and for framing and siding a woodshed," Hawkins said, "shall we get it new or secondhand?"

"There's a barn on the South Road we can probably get," Pag replied. "It collapsed with the snow. One end of the roof is on the ground, but what's still standing looks pretty good. I'd rather have a shed that looks old."

"So would I. Let's go take a look at it after lunch!"

They drove to a plain-looking but tidy house and were greatly surprised when a dirty-faced Matilda Dawson answered the door in overalls, her gray hair held in a red bandana. "What was she doing in Hemlock Harbor?" they wondered.

"I'm getting organized," she said, wiping her soiled hands on her overalls. "Moved in last week!"

"Moved in! Permanently?" Pag asked.

"Yes," she said, taking a seat on the top porch step. "Sit down!"

"You're probably wondering what I'm doing here. Sometimes I wonder myself." The features of her stalwart face transformed in a broad smile. "Martha suggested it. We've been close ever since college. I liked the idea, so here I am."

"I'm glad we found you," Hawkins said, highly pleased, "and we have a deal to propose. We're interested in your barn."

"Barn! What barn?" she laughed. "You mean that wreck out back?"

"We want to look at it," said Pag. "If there is any salvageable wood, we'll tear down what we can use and burn the rest for you."

Matty was pleased. That tumbledown barn had been on her mind, and she'd be glad to get rid of it.

"That takes care of our barn and woodshed," Pag said as they drove back.

"It was a good idea," said Hawkins, complimenting his comrade, "and we found Matty. Four friends in a year . . . maybe we should give lessons on how to meet people in Maine."

Pag laughed.

The two friends were frequently in town and found pleasure and amusement listening to what went on among the elderly patrons of the Wicked Good Café; the Wicked Good, locals called it. They had no suspicion these same people were not without interest in them and would have been amazed at what was said about themselves.

While most folk were trying to stay warm and dry, they had seen Hawkins and Pag at work outdoors. They were seen on the South Road in slickers and storm hats, pulling down a barn in the pouring rain. This made the "old fahts" chuckle, but they knew what hard work was and admired them for it.

"Old fahts" referred to the retired men in baseball hats, who sat at the counter every morning, rain or shine, a term of unsentimental affection. "They may be from away," said one, "but damned if they don't work like they was bohn heah!"

"Hey, Chahly," said another, "fix one of 'em up with your granddaughtah. Maybe he'll cart off that pile of cow shit settin' by your barn for ya."

"No," replied Charley, "it's been there so long it just wouldn't be home without it!"

Shortly after their arrival in Hemlock Harbor, Hawkins had donated one of his student studies of a professional model to be auctioned at the annual craft show of the Hemlock Harbor Fire Brigade Ladies Auxiliary. Though painted while he was a student, he was rather proud of it. It elicited high praise from Boofy Quimby as he stood admiring it during the presale exhibition.

"Not bad," he said to Mabel Trott, "not bad at all. In fact real good!"

"But, Boofy," answered Mabel, "she's naked!"

"That's what makes it good aht, Mabel. Put clothes on 'er and it's just ordinary. Go look at 'em calendars in Jake's Garage if you want to see real high-class art. I like the one from '78 best." He winked at her and trudged off leaning on his cane.

Boofy and Mabel had been classmates in the Hemlock Harbor Grammar School graduating class of 1935. Boofy had never married and had fished the ocean forty years for a living. Mabel married a farmer who had died several years before. In old age they were usually seen together. Hawkins admired the pair: Boofy in his overalls and baseball cap, Mabel in a plain dress and sneakers. They epitomized a homely, good-natured, even affectionate social bond that struck a responsive chord in Hawkins. Not only were they typical of the Mainers he liked best, they brought to mind something of the bond between his grandfather and grandmother. Would they sit for him? The only way to find out was to ask.

He slid into their booth at the Wicked Good Café one morning to ask them about posing. You could have heard a pin drop after Mabel uttered an audible gasp of surprise. The old fahts turned in a body to hear what that was all about.

"I won't take my clothes off!" Mabel said quite loudly; she was somewhat deaf. "I might take off my dress but not my underwear!"

The old fahts were stunned!

With a red face, Hawkins slid out of the booth, touched the brim of his slouched hat to the men at the counter, beckoned to Pag, and departed.

"Well, I'll be damned," said Charley Bates to his fellows at the counter. "I'd never say anythin' against Mabel, but she ain't what I'd call a real shahp lookah!"

That episode elevated Hawkins in the eyes of the Wicked Good Café regulars to the status of a dashing libertine with a damned peculiar taste in women, and Pag never let him forget it.

Chapter 14

BUTCH FLINT, GUS Gold and Wiley were the only men in the lush bar and bordello which Wiley maintained on the upper floor of the Conservation Group building for entertaining clients. The three men conversed quietly but not quietly enough not to be overheard by the courtesan-barmaid standing by the bar.

It's a quiet night, she thought, *Butch Flint is the only certain client. He never leaves without having sex.* She returned his lecherous smirk with a smile.

"We've made contact with some students who will work for us as our agents," said Flint, "and we're working to get them into leadership positions in the protest groups organizing at the colleges."

"That's good," said Gus Gold of the state police. "Have them keep us up to date on the plans as they develop."

"The sharp agents have already insinuated themselves pretty well," replied Flint. "This is their first operation since leaving the academy, but they've been well trained. I try to keep an eye on them when there's a large enough group so I won't stand out or be recognized. Not all the kids are enthusiastic about them, but most are.

They act every bit the part of concerned conservationists, pushing for the most radical actions every chance they get."

"That's good," Gus said, lighting a cigarette. "Get 'em to warm those kids up to push as hard as they can! It makes our job a lot easier. The harder they push, the harder we can shove."

"Yes," added Wiley, "it makes my job easier too. The more extreme they are, the easier it is to exaggerate what they do and to editorialize about the hardships imposed on the law-abiding public."

"Yeah," said Gus, "we like the public on our side. It makes what we do look good, like we have to do it, like we don't want to, but we're forced. We're moderate, and they're extremists . . . maybe even terrorists.

"By the way, what cover have you given them in case someone checks up on them?"

"Home office has seen to that. Each of them has a fake student identity card from an out-of-state school and a bona fide membership in a respected conservation organization." Flint smiled. "All the state offices have several agents planted in all the major organizations, student and nonstudent. So long as they don't forget their correct alias, their backgrounds are bulletproof."

"Is anything planned?" asked Wiley.

"They are trying to coordinate a demonstration in front of the statehouse and block the traffic on State Street," answered Butch Flint.

"Not in front of the governor's mansion!" exclaimed Wiley.

"Our boys will push for that location," said Flint with a knowing smile. "It shouldn't be too hard to do that."

"Wonderful!" Wiley's eyes glittered sardonically. "Let's think how we'll handle that. We certainly don't want to do anything to stop it or interfere with it. Every stymied commuter will be furious with them and, more importantly, with what they're demonstrating against!"

"We'll have to tell the local police what to do," said Gus.

"When cars are really backed up and horns are blasting," Wiley advised, "but not until then, have them put up roadblocks and detour traffic around the Capitol. Make sure there are plenty of cops! It'll make the demonstrators look more ominous."

"Okay, I'll take care of that," Gus Gold said with assurance.

"I'll get plenty of pictures," Wiley gloated. "I'll make them look so bad even their mothers will turn against them! A couple of similar actions will put Old Woods in the palm of our hands."

Wiley then turned to Butch Flint and asked, "Anything new on other protest groups?"

"Other than encouraging the college kids," replied Flint, "there isn't much we have to do. The conservation lobbyists are regulars at the statehouse, badgering the politicians, but we don't have anything to worry about there. Let them waste their time!"

"Do you have agents in all the organizations involved?"

"Yeah!"

"And the members . . . they're all quiet, law abiding? No dirt to report?"

"Yeah!"

"Can't you do something about that?" Wiley's irritation showed in his voice.

"We've been trying, but they're all law-abiding, clean-living citizens as far as we know at this point. Matilda Dawson has recently moved to Hemlock Harbor. She's been an irritation to the paper companies for years. There isn't much, if any, chance she left any dirt behind her, but we have a man on it. He watches her come and go and follows her if he suspects anything. By the way, Wiley, she's pretty thick with your sister and that fellow Shortreed you're not too fond of. So far that's all he's had to report."

Wiley was surprised but hid his astonishment well. "Lilly has been my inside contact. She doesn't know it, but I've taken in every word she's had to say about Old Woods and any of the people around Shortreed, but I'm not concerned."

"What?" exclaimed Butch Flint. "Why not?"

"That, my friend"—Wiley glanced sidelong at Gus Gold—"is my business."

Matty Dawson met with an ad-hoc group, "Save Our Forest," shortly after the students returned to Chamberlain College for the fall term. She intended to discuss possible sites of protest and how they might be carried out but was surprised to learn a site had been already selected and details of a protest mapped out.

Two men in the group were particularly outspoken. Kurt Kissanger was short and stocky. Thick, closely cropped, black hair left little forehead above thick, protruding eyebrows which shadowed small, closely set black eyes. He spoke in a slow, guttural monotone. Nat Grinch was as colorless as Kissanger was dark. His light brown hair, pale complexion, and washed-out gray eyes would have rendered him indistinguishable except for the notable way he blinked, rapidly squeezing his eyes closed, and for the vehemence of his speech. They reported the planned protest at the statehouse would draw students from five other colleges.

"How do you know that?" Matty asked. There was something about these two men that made her instinctively suspicious. She was familiar with men of that ilk who, without exception, were among the opposition. She must discover what they were up to!

"Nat and I," Kissanger replied in a slow growl, "have been there. We made it our business to inform them what our group had planned. They were glad to know and enthusiastic to join in."

"Damned eager and full of spunk," added Nat who spit out the words in rhythm with rapid, grimacing blinks of his eyes.

Matty found this disturbing. Students mobilizing independently without guidance and consultation from seasoned members of established organizations could do more harm than good.

"What are your plans?" she blandly asked, not wishing to convey her apprehension.

"We'll gather in the parking lot behind the state museum," intoned Kissanger, "and proceed from there to the front of the Capitol."

"Waving our signs and shouting like hell!" interjected Nat.

"Our objective is to block commuter traffic on state street," Kissanger continued, "in order to force the media and the public to take notice of our objections to the sale of Old Woods."

"And the indignation of our members and our collective anger!" added Nat. "A few broken windshields and slashed tires will get their attention!"

Matty was dismayed. "Anger and indignation? What are you talking about? Our objective is to focus attention on what is happening to Old Woods. Violence will turn the public against, not only us, but the efforts of every protest organization. The media will use it to blacken every constructive action on our part."

"What if it does?" cried Nat. "It will wake them up! They'll know what the scumballs will do to Old Woods if they're not stopped!"

"Will you give me the names of the students you've talked to at the other colleges?" Matty hoped her reason for asking would not occur to them.

"What for?" Kissanger replied warily.

"So I can speak with them and get an idea how many students will be taking part and how things are shaping up."

"I'll think it over," Kissanger droned.

Boos and hisses went up from the other students. "Give her the names!" someone demanded. "We're not a secret society, and Matty's on our side."

"Yeah!" the others responded in one voice.

Kissanger took a sheet from a notebook he carried and gave it to Matty. A quick glance before she folded the paper revealed a list of names which she could examine later.

The meeting was brief, and as it broke up, Nat exhorted them, "Get with it, guys! Contact as many friends as you can. We need all the people we can get!"

Two students, Sandra Desmond and Jeffrey Schrader, lingered to speak to Matty.

Sandra was an attractive black young lady of nineteen dressed in jeans and a tan jacket. Her hair was pulled back into flowing tresses which graced her slender neck and accentuated her high cheekbones.

Jeff was an amiable, soft-spoken twenty-year-old with sentimental dark eyes, who was obviously very attached to Sandra. *He must be a poet,* thought Matty, *at least he looks like one.*

Sandra introduced Jeff and herself and then asked Matty's impression of Kissanger and Grinch.

"A student protest in front of the statehouse is a good idea, but I'm afraid if those two men have their way, it will play into the hands of the opposition."

"We think so too," said Sandra. "Ever since those two showed up, they've tried to goad the rest of us. I'm opposed to disorder and senseless provocation. Rowdy behavior will discredit rational objections which might attract some public support."

"How do the rest feel?" Matty was anxious to know how much influence Kissanger and Grinch had.

"It varies," Jeff replied. "Most of the students at the private colleges are from out of state and had never heard of Old Woods before they came to Maine. Their schools have ecology demonstrations and research projects in Old Woods. It's their ecology laboratory, and the students who use the forest are upset about losing it. Until Kissanger and Grinch came along, discussion was reasoned and constructive. We were searching for some way to make a responsible statement, but they're not interested in reason, just in venting anger."

"I'm going to tell you something which I suspect is happening, which incidentally, is why I asked for the list of names." This riveted their attention. They drew three chairs together and conversed in low voices, which did not echo in the deserted classroom.

"The bill to lumber off Old Woods," Matty confided to them, "is the product of a conspiracy involving companies that own big tracts of the North Woods, others with big money to spend on their lackeys in the legislature, and the media. We have proof of that which I can't go into. It's just business as usual in Maine and not of undue importance in this instance. What's crucial is the involvement of the state police and the FBI in the conspiracy.

"I suspect that Kissanger, Grinch, and the others on the list are working for the FBI with the object of provoking violence. That will supply fodder for the media, making it much easier to turn the public against us."

"What should we do? What can we do?" Sandra asked.

"We can't accuse them," said Matty. "We have no proof that we can make public. However, I think you might speak to your friends and tell them of your suspicions so they can be on their guard. That might throw cold water on their influence.

"I plan on visiting the other campuses and seeing how the people on this list are behaving. If they're provoking their organizations, as I suspect they are, something must be done to stop them. If I don't happen to run into students like you, that something must come from this group. Our protests must be symbolic and persuasive, not confrontational if we can avoid it. One rowdy, confrontational demonstration, like the one they've planned at the statehouse, will feed right into the hands of our opponents. It's what they're trying to make happen."

Late on a Friday night in the beginning of October, the bill giving the timber in Old Woods State Forest to the Great Amalgamated Pulp and Hardwood Company was passed and signed into law. Within days, over two hundred students from five colleges arrived at the statehouse in Augusta.

Matty was there along with Bob Ballard of the North Woods League, Lottie Courter of the Appalachian Alliance, and Herb Smith of the Woodlands Council. They came as observers hoping for a peaceful, orderly demonstration which would garner support for saving Old Woods for the people of Maine. Matty was disturbed to see the arriving students rally around the men on Kissanger's list. She had interviewed these men and found them as arrogantly abrasive as Kissanger and Grinch.

"This doesn't look good," Matty said to Ballard, Courter, and Smith. "You can see who the leaders are. I've talked with them, and I'm convinced they are FBI informants hired to provoke as much trouble as they can."

"If you're right," said Lottie, "the police will have been informed. Let's walk around and see if any preparations are evident. If so, then we'll know."

"The students may be walking blindly into a trap!" Herb exclaimed.

"Is there anything we can do to protect these kids from police violence?" asked Bob.

"We can try," answered Matty, "but let's follow Lottie's suggestion and look for evidence of police preparations."

The four adults crossed State Street and entered the public park, where they discovered rows of traffic barricades painted bright yellow, waiting to be deployed. In the street at the far end of the park, a long row of squad cars from the Augusta and the state police were parked. About fifty policemen armed with revolvers and clubs gathered in groups around a coffee wagon or leaned against their autos listening to the messages crackling from the radios.

"This looks threatening!" Lottie remarked, "Why are they carrying gas masks on their belts?"

"They're expecting a riot," Herb replied, "and are ready to use tear gas."

"Good god!" cried Lottie, "We must do something!"

By this time, the students had formed into an uneven line before the statehouse, preparing to march to the governor's mansion in the next block. They hurried to the assembled students to warn them of their danger.

"Let's divide and each take a quarter of the line," Matty shouted in order to be heard in the rambunctious, chanting crowd, "and tell them what we've seen."

Lottie started at the tail end of the line. "The police are waiting for you," she shouted, "don't do anything to provoke them!"

Kissanger ran to her side and followed her down the line. "Don't listen to her," he yelled. "We have our rights! Save Old Woods!"

"They're massed in force on the other side of the park. They have guns and clubs and tear gas. They are in full riot armor. Don't give them an excuse to use them!" she pleaded.

"Screw the pigs!" Kissanger bellowed. "Are we cowards? We're not afraid of the bastards!"

Matty, Bob, and Herb met with similar objections from the provocative agents of the FBI. However, when the bulk of the students marched off, some remained behind and gathered around the four adults, Sandra Desmond and Jeff Schrader among them.

"Tell us, Matty! What is happening?" Sandra asked.

"Listen to me!" Matty said mounting a step so all could hear. "The men who have been goading you are FBI agents. They want mayhem and violence in order to discredit our efforts to save Old Woods. Spread out and try to reach your friends, but come back here before any trouble starts. Keep your eyes open! Watch what happens! We may need witnesses.

"There are barricades in the park. The police are ready for you. There are at least fifty of them behind the park ready to come down on you. They mean trouble, and there isn't a single ambulance in sight. Be quick and be careful!"

At that, the students ran to find their friends. The overcast sky had threatened rain all day, and a light shower began to fall as the students returned with a few others. They formed along the sidewalk where Matty and her friends waited leaving ample room for pedestrians to pass.

The other demonstrators linked arms, formed into two lines, back to back, each facing oncoming traffic and surged across State Street. "Amalgamated Pulp . . . No! Plunderers . . . No! Save the people's forest!" they chanted as traffic backed up on either side.

The clouds opened up, and a cold, drenching rain poured down. Matty sighed with relief. It was sure to bring an early end to this misbegotten effort. Horns blared which obscured the chanted message. Cardboard signs wilted into soggy, unreadable pulp. A cold, bone-chilling wind made continued protest impossible. The lines so boldly strung across the street now backed reluctantly to the curb, and traffic started to flow slowly again. Kissanger, Grinch, and their fellow conspirators were pummeled by some of the soaked students who then departed.

"Rain beat the FBI!" Matty declared thankfully. "But one thing is certain: we've got to lead these kids. They need us. Let's pick a date to meet in Lottie's office and make solid plans. I think most of the students will follow our guidance."

Matty's relief was premature. She and the others watched in horrified disbelief as Kissanger, Grinch, and the FBI conspirators from the colleges, the agent provocateurs, gathered into a coherent group and, by blocking the street again, caused gridlocked traffic. At the same time, the police divided into two sections, one group of about ten men met the conspirators head-on in a mock battle. Like a TV wrestling match, the bogus hand-to-hand encounter was played out before the horrified motorists.

The larger group of police swarmed into the students lining the sidewalk and began beating them with their clubs. The bewildered students, protecting themselves as best they could, covered their bloodied heads with their arms; then they were struck behind the knees which threw them to the pavement where they were quickly handcuffed and dragged off to the waiting police vans, with their sirens blasting and strobe lights flashing. Red, yellow, blue flashed the lights, sirens screeched, the police beat the students and dragged them like sacks of dead-weight flour. Some of the young men fought back, but not many, mostly those trying to protect their girlfriends.

The police donned masks and, over their bullhorns, commanded the motorists to close all their windows. Tear gas blew thick and heavy, blinding and choking the students, who hurled canisters and stones back at the police. Shots rang out as the police fired rubber bullets into the defiant students, destroying one young lady's left eye and inflicting painful bruises on many others.

Then it was over as quickly as it had begun. With blaring sirens and flashing lights, jail-bound police vans and cars containing handcuffed protesters screamed away. A few police dressed in fluorescent vests placed barricades around the sections where blood had been spilled, pushed those students luckily unharmed out of the area, and waved the traffic back into motion.

Matty bandaged the girl so badly injured, and her friends hastened her to the hospital. She and her colleagues went among the students who had not been arrested, shouting, "Eight o'clock . . . the Chamberlain gym . . . we must help our friends who have been arrested."

Overhead, state police helicopters videotaped the conspirator-police staged fracas and provided Wiley and a staff photographer a bird's-eye view.

Wiley rushed his story of the protest on to the newswire. The next day, it made headlines throughout the state: "Student Violence in Augusta," announced the headline.

> Without warning, students massed at the statehouse yesterday and brought rush-hour commuter traffic to a halt. Their blockade of State Street backed up traffic in a radius of half a mile from the Governor's Mansion. Trucks and cars sat motionless on Memorial Bridge, Western Avenue, and State Street for over an hour.
>
> Police efforts to reason with the protestors were met with threats and rude, sarcastic taunts. Undaunted by this outlandish behavior, they set up barriers to detour traffic around the obstruction and skillfully untangled the gridlock. This left hundreds of vehicles still halted on State Street, which could not move so long as protestors continued to block it.
>
> Once again, the police urged the students to disperse but were met with violence. Using their stout signs as clubs, they beat any unlucky policemen who came within their range. Turning the other cheek, the

officers defended the protestors from the wrath of drivers who left their vehicles, intending, as one put it, "To teach these kids a lesson." Police were left with no alternative but to remove the protestors by force. A pitched battle ensued in which several police were injured. One elderly officer received a hard blow in the abdomen from a burly football player, which sent him to the hospital. To disperse the protestors without injury, the use of tear gas was reluctantly brought into play. After motorists were warned to close all the windows in their vehicles, canisters were fired into the massed protesters.

The vengeful protestors smashed headlights and dented the hoods of any vehicles they could reach. This destruction of property demanded intervention. At this point officers, hampered by gas masks and unmindful of personal injury, bodily removed the students. Warning shots were fired to disperse the rioting students, which, in the confusion of the pitched battle, unfortunately resulted in the wounding of one of the student rioters.

One weary officer, his face bloody and his uniform torn, spoke to this reporter. "What a shame!" he said. "The law has been passed. Everyone benefits. Everything was legal and orderly. Now . . . we have a bunch of rowdies disrupting people and damaging their property. It's not fair. It's not the way things are done in this country. It's un- American! People must obey the law, and all but a few do."

This is the first time violence has been used to obstruct the people's will regarding the Old Woods State Forest. We, at this paper, hope that it will be the last.

No mention of the military helmets, face and body armor, clubs, and guns in the hands of the police . . . No mention of the role of the agent provocateurs planted by the FBI and so on . . . The truth, of course, and nothing but the truth!

Chapter 15

MARY AWOKE FULL of zest on a dew-bejeweled, late summer Sunday morning. From her window overlooking the blue flood tide, she saw waves, tipped with shimmering silver, dancing shoreward in an endless minuet. Fulgent late summer greenery shone beneath a brilliant sky. She dressed hastily, eager to go to Hawkins and share this splendid overture of vibrant color, light, and shadow.

Their house is weather tight, she thought. *The barn has been repaired, the woodshed is finished, and the winter supply of wood is nearly all gathered. Surely, he has time now for other things. I wonder if he'll have time for me?*

Though the morning was superb, Hawkins felt somehow incomplete, an aching emptiness he could not explain. He wished for someone with whom to share these lovely moments.

The moment Mary stepped from the car, he felt a surge of warm tenderness. His emotional conflict between practical necessity and the power of love vanished in the realization he would never cease longing for her! They must marry, if she would have him. It might be a long engagement, but that impediment no longer mattered.

Beaming with happiness, he hastened to greet her but was suddenly struck dumb by a sudden sensation that he was unworthy of her.

"Hawkins, what's the matter?" she asked, coming closer to him. "Say something!"

Hawkins laid his hands on her shoulders, slowly drew her to him and enveloped her in his arms.

"Mary," he whispered almost too overcome to speak, "Mary!"

He needed to say no more. She wrapped her arms about him, and they stood in a clinging embrace. There was no need for words; their hearts were, at last, in harmony.

They wandered hand in hand, trancelike across the meadow to the sparkling sea.

Pag, having heard the sound of an auto, peered from his window and smiled. It had to happen; who could have seen them together and not known it was inevitable?

It was only a matter of time, he thought, withdrawing from the window, *and it looks like the time has come.*

Thoughts of Lilly came to mind, and he wished she were there. "Now that won't do!" he told himself. "There's no point in a penniless sculptor thinking of a rich princess! To her, I'm just a Marxist moose, whatever that is. Something silly to joke about."

Had Lilly been there and seen the sad look in Pag's warm brown eyes, she might have felt a twinge of regret; her innocent expression of good-natured affection had been misunderstood.

"It looks like Hawkins' road and mine will soon diverge. I'd better start thinking about where I'll go when I must."

Had Hawkins known what thoughts Pag entertained, he would have been aghast. To part from Pag was not to be thought of; they had become so close, it would be like losing a brother. But Hawkins did not know.

The dreamlike, intense happiness which settled upon Hawkins and Mary eventually mellowed enough for them to speak in immortal strains, the "warring sighs and groans" by which lovers pledge their love. By the time they returned to the house, they were engaged.

"Dear Hawkins," Mary sighed, "I'd like to go to Halifax and tell our grandparents the wonderful news."

"Don't breath a word to Martha, my darling," said Hawkins, "or if you do, ask her not to call or write. They must learn of it from us!"

Joy, the ecstasy of loving and being loved, glowed in every word, every movement, every expression of guileless Mary. She attempted not to mention her engagement and thought she succeeded, but concealment was not within her power. The moment she stepped back into the house, Martha knew immediately what had happened and pressed her warmly to her breast.

"My dear," said Martha tearfully, "I'm so glad . . . but hardly surprised. The first time I saw you two together walking hand in hand, I knew how it would be."

Mary's happiness was foremost; Martha did not write nor call.

Lilly was overjoyed to see Mary glowing with happiness and guessed the cause at once. Mary's admission and Lilly's wholehearted participation in her dreams made them sisters forevermore. Mary was surprised to find Lilly too had long regarded their engagement as inevitable. Did everyone know Hawkins loved her? Was it so obvious to everyone but herself?

Lilly laughed and said, "I saw it in his eyes. I heard it in his voice the day you told us about Old Woods. I didn't think I should say anything, and I'm glad I didn't. Wasn't it best the way it happened?"

Even Wiley was warm in his congratulations. "Take a week off? Only a week? Take all the time you need and don't hurry back!" Mary thanked him but wondered why he was so unusually accommodating.

Within days they were ready to depart for Halifax. A stabbing sadness struck Hawkins on leaving Pag. For the past two years they had lived together and worked together in steadfast friendship. Had they been brothers, they could not have felt for each other a more manly affection.

Mary read their attachment in their parting embrace and sensed Hawkins' unease at leaving his friend. She was certain she had done right in asking Lilly to keep an occasional watch on Pag.

He's like a great big, cuddly dog being separated from his master, she thought. *Lilly will let him know we care about leaving the dear fellow and don't want him to be lonely.*

But it was Wiley, not Lilly, who came calling the day after Hawkins left. His research on coinage used in colonial eighteenth century America revealed it was indeed of Spanish mintage. Therefore, that could not be the reason why the treasure had not been spent lavishly. The amount must be so large it would have excited dangerous suspicion unless it were hoarded and spent in careful allotments. He would find that hoard! He had to, for since his discovery of the Bible, the quest, the treasure hunt, had become an overmastering obsession. Whatever he had coveted had always been acquired by his clever, ingenious plotting. Why should this be any different?

Pag knew who he was. Hawkins had pointed him out after they had discovered the grave.

What the hell does this crooked bastard want, Pag wondered when Wiley knocked on the door with pencil and notebook in hand.

"I'd like to look around," Wiley said affably, "to get details, human interest details, for a follow-up story on that mysterious grave."

"Sure, go ahead," Pag said. The request seemed reasonable, "but at your own risk. We won't be responsible if you hurt yourself."

Wiley noted the barn had been repaired and the grave filled in, then headed for the graveyard.

The boulder monument showed evidence of having been cleaned sometime before, and the dirt at the base appeared to have been recently disturbed. *Probably to clear away vegetation,* he thought.

"Why has he exposed that grave?" he asked himself. "What does he know? Has he found anything or was it just that story about shipwreck and treasure? Unless he has laid hands on something, which I doubt, he's just fishing in the dark."

Wiley chuckled. He had the Bible. He was certain there was a hoard stashed away somewhere; his object was to find it.

He copied the epitaph. *Just a pious homily, he* thought, *but at the moment, there is nothing else, other than the Bible, directly connected with this man Abner Gibbs. It might possibly mean something, but I doubt it. If Gibbs had buried the treasure, what better place could be chosen than a graveyard? It would make sense to bury it shallowly in an existing grave, where it would be easy to retrieve and unlikely to ever be disturbed. But which one?*

He laughed. *He couldn't put it in his own grave which eliminates that one at any rate!*

He could have put it in there, he thought, peering at the grove of cedars, *but that doesn't make sense unless it were somehow marked so he could find it again. After two centuries, it's unlikely any marker he had used would have survived. Why should it be durable if he meant to regularly tap the hoard? If he put it in a marked grave, he'd always be able to dip into it. I can't see any reason to complicate matters. The question is . . . which grave?*

The other graves were either partially or entirely concealed in overgrowth. In the worst case, due to the ravages of time and the inability to discern many of the graves, the entire burying ground might have to be cleared and excavated, in which event Wiley must own the property. His conversation with Gold and Panky provided a means which he would not hesitate to use if he needed to.

Cursing the thorns, beggar's-lice, and burdock which clung to his trousers, Wiley trudged across the meadow toward the ocean, where he came upon the rope coiled against the tree to which it was tied.

What have they been up to here, he wondered. *They were in the water—I saw them. They must have been looking for something to corroborate that legend about a shipwreck! Did they find anything? Had Shortreed found something in that grave which he didn't turn over to the coroner? Something pointing to a hiding place near the ocean?*

He looked over the cliff edge and saw no obvious place where anything valuable might have been secreted. *No, he thought, if it's not in the house, then it has to be in the graveyard. It doesn't seem likely people could live in that house for two hundred years and not stumble on it. It has to be in one of those graves!*

Through gritted teeth, his features contorted with malicious determination, he said, "Shortreed can kiss this place good-bye!"

"I'm glad it's you and not your brother again," said Pag, delighted Lilly had stopped by the following day to see how he was getting along.

"My brother!" Lilly said with surprise, "What was he doing here?" Knowing his perfidious role in the Old Woods conspiracy, Pag had kept Wiley in view until he left and imparted to Lilly what he had said and done.

"He wants something!" Pag declared.

"I know he does," Lilly responded. "That's the only reason Wiley does anything. I wonder what it is."

"Why don't we take a look at what he found so interesting?" Pag suggested. "He spent most of his time in the old graveyard."

When they came to Abner's grave, Lilly knew what Wiley was after, for he had told her of his purchase of the Gibbs' family Bible. She should have asked him more about that at the time, but he was uncommunicative for a reason she could not divine. It was now clear to her it somehow concerned the legendary treasure. Wiley was after it and so was Hawkins.

Hawkins knew and was thus forewarned how black and devious Wiley's character was. Lilly blushed, recalling the villainy and greed of her father and her brother. Wiley, she knew, would stop at nothing. Would Hawkins be able to cope with him? She backed away from the stone, gave a cry of pain, and crumpled to the ground.

A broken, tottering headstone, which had balanced precariously on the remains of yet another, both hidden in the long weeds, had given way under Lilly's foot. In falling, her ankle had twisted under her and bore the wrenching force of her body. Pag was instantly at her side.

She tried to stand, but the pain was too great. Pag gently picked her up and carried her in his arms toward the house. She weighed nothing to Pag whose gentle heart swelled with both pity and delirious exaltation. Lilly was in his arms, not in the most agreeable circumstances, but in his arms nevertheless!

Though her ankle throbbed, Lilly felt something she had not felt since her great-grandfather had died, a sense of being cared for by a man. Her father and her brother treated her with neglectful tolerance and always had. She had no reason to expect anything else. Her independent spirit sought nothing else . . . and yet . . . . Pag was gentle and diffident; there was something almost motherly in the way he held her. Dared she think it? Something loving!

Pag's foot caught in a groundhog hole, and he lurched forward almost stumbling.

"Dammit, Pag," cried Lilly, "be careful!"

Then she buried her face against his chest and began to cry.

Chapter 16

"WHERE SHALL WE go first?" Hawkins asked as they approached Halifax. "I guess the courteous thing is to tell your grandparents and then mine."

"It's been a long drive. If you don't mind, I could freshen up there and drop off my things." Mary snuggled against him. "Oh, Hawkins, just think! We were children the last time we were together here, and we've come back in love and engaged. I feel like Cinderella returning with her handsome prince!"

Hawkins slowed down and put his arm around her. "And I feel like the ex- frog returning with his beautiful princess!"

At the loud honk of a truck horn behind them, Hawkins returned both hands to the steering wheel and proceeded to the Duncan residence.

It had been two years since Mary's brief visit on her way from British Columbia to Hemlock Harbor. Flora and Andrew Duncan were elated to have her back. Flora took both Mary's hands and held her at arm's length; her engaging smile and bright eyes betrayed her curiosity. Mary knew at once what was on her grandmother's mind and could not refrain from imparting her joyous news.

"Oh, Grandma! Hawkins and I are going to be married!"

"I knew it!" Flora cried. "I've always hoped you would find each other!"

She impulsively embraced Hawkins. "How often Andy and I have talked about you and Mary, how close you were as children, and what a pair you would've made if only she hadna' moved so far away. Now our wish has come true!"

Tears of happiness welled into her eyes, and Andrew gave a hoarse cough, choking back a surge of emotion . . . their wee Mary to be a bride.

"Congratulations, lad," he said again, grasping Hawkins' hand. "She's a . . . she's a wonderful lassie."

"Ha' ye told your mother and father?" Flora asked Mary.

"You're the first to know," replied Mary. "Our next stop is the McLeods. Please don't give us away. Hawkins wants to tell them. I'll call Mom tonight. We have settled on the date of June twentieth. I hope they'll fly here and make it a family reunion . . . all together again after so long. Wouldn't that be wonderful!"

Driving down the modest street on which his grandparents lived, Hawkins felt a pang of remorse. The past two years had been filled with events he had not foreseen: buying the Gibbs' property, making it habitable, and the shipwreck saga. How thoughtless and negligent he had been!

Nothing mattered to Will and Bella but their beloved Hawkins was back. Not only was he back but betrothed to Mary. Bella was beside herself with joy; her fond wish he and Mary would wed was going to come true. Will looked at the happy lovers with contented satisfaction; even memories of drum and bagpipe practice now sounded sweet in his ear.

"Grandpa," Hawkins said when they were gathered in the parlor that evening, "will you give us a tune? If Mary's not forgotten how, perhaps she'll dance for us the hie'land fling or sword dance?"

"Oh, yes, do!" said Mary, kicking off her shoes.

Bella glanced apprehensively at Will.

"My fingers are not as nimble as they were, lad, age and a touch of arthritis," Will said, stroking his chin thoughtfully. "I've not had the fiddle out for months."

Bella rose and retrieved his violin case from beside the shoes in their bedroom closet and laid it on his knees.

Will opened the case, removed the cotton pad covering the instrument, and drew forth the fiddle. He fondled it in such a tender, loving, caressing manner that all eyes were fixed upon him, and the room grew silent. Will's thoughts flew back in time. He was young again fiddling at a Saturday dance in the 'auld country,' once more experiencing the pleasure, seeing faces and hearing voices now, like youth, gone forever. Lost in a moment of abstracted reverie, he plucked a string, then slowly adjusted its tuning peg.

Hawkins' heart went out to his grandfather. He saw that Will had aged. He recalled him as he was when Hawkins was a boy; he was much changed but had never lost the kindly sparkle in his eyes. The love Hawkins felt was intensely painful. He saw a day of final parting; it must come when he would see his beloved grandparents no more. How he wished they could know what he felt for them!

Mary saw with dismay the look on Hawkins' face; she had never seen him appear so desolate. She reached for his hand and held it tightly. He looked at her, and liveliness returned, his momentary mood of impending sorrow over.

The suppleness of youth returned to Will's fingers, and he finished tuning the fiddle with vigor, placed his handkerchief on the chin rest, cradled the fiddle against his neck, swept the bow over the strings, and struck out a jig, simultaneously mimicking the bass and melody of a bagpipe as only he could.

Bella watched the faces of Mary and Hawkins light up with the delight they'd displayed as children when Will charmed them with the magic sounds he drew from his fiddle. Will's fiddle was his voice; it talked for him, sang for him, and was as much a living part of him as his grateful, caring heart.

Bella rose to fetch a glass of beer which she set beside him as he let loose his fingers on a lively reel. Will was happier than she had seen him in years. "Never again," she vowed, "would the fiddle be hidden away in the closet!"

It was an evening Hawkins would never forget. Will played with the verve and zest of bygone years. Mary danced until she could dance no longer. They laughed; they sang until the old clock on the mantel struck one.

Will's Methodist piety, his comfort and strength, now surprised Bella and Hawkins. Though he had attended the little church and had sung in the choir, he had always kept his beliefs to himself. He laid the fiddle across his knees and said in his soft, mellow voice, "Lord, bless Mary and Hawkins as you have blessed Bella and me. I can't ask more than that."

He looked at them and smiled. "'The iron tongue of time has tolled One upon the drowsy ear of night,' if I may roughly quote Sir Walter Scott, and it's time we were all in bed."

Hawkins embraced Bella and Will and said, with tears in his eyes, "Dear Grandma and Grandpa! How much you mean to me!"

On the following day, Mary told Hawkins of her conversation with her parents.

"Of course, they will come to Halifax for the wedding. Mother was so excited for a moment she was at a loss for words. 'I knew that shorthand would be good for you,' she said."

Hawkins looked at her. It sounded an odd thing to say.

Mary laughed. "I know that can't mean anything to you, darling, but I know what she meant, and I have to agree with her. If it weren't for shorthand, we might never have met again."

"If I owe you to shorthand," he said with a grin, "then all blessings and praise for it. But did it really bring us together?"

"I'll tell you all about it on some cozy winter night before the fire," she whispered in his ear before she kissed him. "When we're settled and growing old together."

Will sat on the porch steps smoking his pipe, basking in the unusually warm Indian summer afternoon when Hawkins came and sat beside him.

"Grandpa, do you remember sitting here and telling me how you felt about sport?"

"Oh, aye," he replied, "you were just a wee lad. Something about baseball, wasn't it?"

"It was more than just that, Grandpa. It was about honesty, playing honorably, trust, and good comradeship, the way games should be played and life, lived."

Will nodded. "Oh, aye."

"Mary's run up against some people who don't play that way or live that way. There's one sly fellow of whom I'm particularly distrustful."

"Oh?" Will said with a concerned look.

"I've a favor to ask," Hawkins said. "I've been to a bank here and taken a safe-deposit box for the original of my birth certificate, the deed to the property of mine, my insurance annuity, things that I'd like to put in both our names when we're married."

"Oh?" Will said again.

"There's a nasty bit of skullduggery afoot in Maine, the giveaway of public property to the Great Amalgamated Pulp and Paper Company, a private business. I'm upset over it—it's a rotten, dirty game!

"Mary," Hawkins said, extracting a key from his pocket, "is a Canadian citizen, and I would feel better keeping our important papers here. I'd like you to keep the key for me, if you will."

"Oh, aye."

Will took the key. "You're an honest lad, Hawkins, and it does you credit to be thinking of Mary. The key will be here when you want it."

Will was curious about Hawkins' unwillingness to leave his papers in Maine and was on the point of asking about it when Bella announced supper was ready.

Ah, well, it's not that important, Will thought as he entered the house.

Mary and Hawkins were back in Halifax where they had met and grown fond of each other as wee tykes, where those they loved who had come "fra' the auld country" had settled and to whom they had imparted news that gladdened all their hearts. It was the springtime of life and the time of love's ecstasy. Hawkins waited patiently until the joy they imparted to their grandparents mellowed into sublime certainty that the road ahead for Mary and himself was strewn with the fairest petals of the fairest flowers.

Gently taking her hand, he drew Mary aside and whispered, "Come walk with me in the gloaming, sweetheart, for there is something I must tell you."

Mary gladly clung to his arm, and they walked beneath a sky filled with a glowing cloud cathedral, painted sublime hues of pink, blue, and gold by myriad fairy hands. They took their seats on a bench secluded from the house. In later years how often their minds would relive these days, these moments so sweet, stored forever in the albums of their hearts.

"Mary, you must know how difficult it would be to leave you at this special time, but go I must." He was soft and gentle but, she sensed, inflexible.

She laid her arm on his and her head on his shoulder.

"You may ask me where I am going, but I can't tell you. You would want to come with me, and I wish with all my heart you could, but that's not possible."

She waited.

"I can't tell you how long I'll be gone, for I don't know myself, but it will be no longer than absolutely necessary." He paused and waited. "You haven't said anything."

"Hawkins, I hear you. I have questions. But I know you wouldn't leave me unless it were dreadfully important and you'll tell me all I want to know when you return. So I'll miss you and probably will cry for you every day but with complete confidence all will soon be right. For you are going with the purpose of ensuring we're safe from any harm which Wiley may inflict on us . . . aren't you?"

"I am, my love, and have no doubt of my success."

The disappointment of the grandparents at so brief a visit was intense. That the pair would return soon was a great consolation. Hawkins' assurance that the task he willingly would be undertaking carried no personal risk of retaliation satisfied Will and Bella. The only reasons Mary had to return to Maine were her job and to await the implementation of whatever Hawkins had in mind to do. Hawkins and Mary would be in Maine for most of the winter, and it seemed a long time to await their return, but separation was something they had all experienced. This separation was a less unhappy and less uncertain one than the emigration of Will and Andrew had been. All things considered, spring would bring with her more than her usual abundance of delights. They would wait patiently.

Hawkins was taking his dearest Mary back to Maine to the reliable, safe hands of Martha and George and intended to leave at once on his mysterious journey. But a dreadful event awaited him in Hemlock Harbor which would take immediate precedence over everything.

Chapter 17

PAG WAS LONELY. Hawkins and Mary had been away in Nova Scotia for a week; Lilly was indisposed with an ankle fracture, and he missed them all. *Maybe,* he thought, *we should get a dog. That would be some company. If we had a telephone, she might call me, but she probably wouldn't. Why would she?*

Lilly was lonely too; she missed seeing Pag. *What is he doing?* she wondered. *Does he miss me?* She recalled how tenderly he had carried her to her car and stayed by until she hobbled out of the emergency room, her foot wrapped in plaster, and then driven her home. Did he love her? She thought he might.

"What are you doing?" Esther asked as Lilly was about to leave with her car keys in her hand.

"I want to check on the shop, Mother, and make sure everything is all right."

"Do be careful, dear!" Esther knew remonstrance was futile. Once Lilly was determined to do something, she usually did it. "That cast will make driving difficult."

Lilly passed her shop but did not stop. It was Pag she had to see. She wondered where he was when she parked by the oak tree; the house looked deserted. Then she heard untrained baritone strains of Italian opera, hobbled up the granite steps, and pounded on the door. A stunned Pag opened the door, saw Lilly was a dreadful white, about to faint, and took her in his arms.

"I'll be all right," Lilly muttered. "The pain just turned my legs to rubber and things seemed to be drifting far off."

Pag did not release her; in fact, he drew her even closer. Lilly rested her head against his brawny chest. He held her in one arm and gently caressed her hair with the other. Lilly raised her eyes to his, and their lips met. She reached as far as she could around his chest, clung to him, and pressed her mouth against his. Pag almost crushed her in his eager, passionate embrace.

"Oh, moose," Lilly gasped, "don't! I can't breathe!"

She saw the pained look in Pag's eyes. "I meant that kindly you big, cuddly moose." She pulled his head down and kissed him again. "If you help me down these steps, I can sit on the bottom one.

"Now that you've crushed three of my ribs, moose, are you going to marry me?" Lilly demanded, looking Pag squarely in the eye, her heart beating so rapidly she again felt giddy.

Pag was speechless. He would give everything he had to marry Lilly, but . . . he had nothing to give. He was caught between poverty and an overwhelming love for her. Words failed him.

Lilly reddened and looked at her cast. She was mistaken; he did not love her! Neither of them said anything; the silence was ominous.

Pag bent forward and hid his head between his knees. "Christ knows, Lilly," he blurted, "I don't want to live without you!"

Lilly's heart bounded. Pag felt ashamed to look up and stayed as he was, his head still between his knees. "I love you, Lilly," he muttered. "I knew it when I carried you back here the day you fell."

She ran her fingers through his raven locks and stroked his neck. "If you'll stop talking to your feet and speak to me, I might believe you," she said with feigned indignation.

Pag sat up. His face was as red as a tanned and swarthy face could be. He looked so pitiful that Lilly could not restrain herself; she had to laugh.

"Well, are you going to marry me or not?"

"Yes!"

"When?"

Pag hesitated. For a man without any money, especially a fledgling sculptor without any money, that was a daunting question!

"When I'm rich and famous!" Of course, that would be the right time! He had no doubt he would be rich and famous, but it might take a while.

"We can talk about that later," she said with such a sweet, winning smile it made Pag's head swim with ecstasy, "but first things first! If you'll help me to the car, I'll go tell Mother."

Pag watched Lilly's car disappear down the forest lane, his mind in such a swirl of confused thoughts it took him several minutes to collect himself and go back to the house.

"Wahoo! Yeah!" he shouted, kicking the door shut with a loud bang.

Wiley heard what Esther told him with utter disbelief. *That does it!* he thought. *Their goose is cooked. I'll get that property! They'll both be out in the cold, and I'll kill two birds with one stone. I hate those two bastards, and no sister of mine will disgrace this family with a down-and-out communist bum!*

With the aid of one of his shady contacts, Wiley committed an illegal offense. He bought several marijuana cigarettes. With the joints in his car, that vehicle was liable for seizure, but this did not worry him. His car was well known; his powerful connections were well known; he was immune.

The night was pitch-black as he slowly passed down the lane to Hawkins' house and parked just before the roadway exited from the woods. Walking quietly, guided by the lighted window of the house, he pitched the cigarettes into the long grass beneath the oak tree.

The following morning, while Pag was loading wood into the shed, three police cruisers stopped before the house. A group of men, some in police uniforms, others in civilian dress, left the cars and stood looking at the house. He went up to them.

Taking no notice of Pag, they entered the house and began a search. Hawkins' paintings were each examined and carelessly flung into the middle of the floor. The same was done with the model clay horse, which Pag had nearly finished. It took two grunting men to lift it and throw it to the floor, shattering the beautiful piece. Upstairs men tore apart their beds; mattress and blankets were flung down the stairs and added to the pile of paintings and the destroyed statue. Their clothing was also strewn onto the growing pile. Ashes from the parlor fireplace and kitchen range were scooped out and discarded on the pile of debris.

"Hold on!" Pag shouted with rage, "What in hell's name do you think you're doing? Who are you?"

"Buddy, we got a tip that drugs are here," a man in plain clothes said with a snarl. "This is a raid!"

Pag advanced toward him, shouting, "Get the hell out of here! This place belongs to us! You've got no right to be here! Where's your warrant?"

Two burly policemen grabbed his arms. A third struck him across the lower left chest with a large, heavy police club. The pain was intense. He gasped for air, suddenly unable to fill his lungs; he was suffocating. The law enforcer had struck him with such force it doubled him over, and his wrists were immediately handcuffed behind his back. Pag sank to the floor, unable to stand erect and bear the pain. The intruders paid no attention to him and left him lying amid the rubble they had made of the contents of the house.

"Get the dog!" one of the men in plain clothes commanded.

A dog was brought in and led from room to room in a fruitless effort to pick up the scent of marijuana.

Pag lay on the floor, his arms manacled behind his back. The knifelike pain in his chest now spread to his abdomen as well. It was so severe that he laid suffering among the scraps of his creation and was without sufficient breath to ask for help.

"Nothing here! Bring the dog outside!" commanded the plainclothes detective of the state police.

In moments the dog had detected the scent and stood motionless over the spot where Wiley had thrown the cigarettes the night before. The raiding party flocked to the spot and began searching through the long weeds. They documented the details of their search, gathered up the cigarettes, released Pag's handcuffs, left him lying on the floor, got back in their cruisers, and drove away.

Pag was in agony. The pain was almost more than he could bear, but he felt if he could stand and stretch, it would be a relief. He crawled to the door, grasped it in his strong hands, and pulled himself to a standing position.

Hawkins and Mary returned from their idyllic visit to Nova Scotia two days after the attack on Pag had occurred. Hawkins found their work and belongings despoiled and his friend lying on the floor sprawled across a mattress, dirty with ashes, so weak and dehydrated that it took all Hawkins' strength and Pag's heroic fortitude to get him into the truck.

Hawkins raced to the Maine Seal Point General Hospital. Pag was rushed away on a stretcher, and Hawkins waited and worried for hours. In the first light of predawn, a physician finally came to report Pag's condition to him. She was Dr. Collette Devereaux, a young French-Canadian surgeon, very lovely and very kind.

"We had to operate as soon as we could, monsieur," she told him in halting, lilting English. "But he was very acidotic, dehydrated, and had lost much blood. To correct this before Monsieur Doctor

Thomas, a thoracic surgeon, and I operated took much time, but it was essential.

"Three lower ribs are fractured. The lung, it was punctured by the upper fractured rib and has been repaired. The spleen was likewise torn by a very sharp rib. I had to remove it, but spleen cells have seeded the abdomen, so if he lives, he will not be unduly susceptible to infection. He had lost a vast quantity of blood internally. It is a miracle he was still alive when you found him."

"What will happen to him now?" Hawkins asked, fearing the worst.

"He is a young man, very strong and very healthy before the accident. Otherwise, without doubt, he would have been dead when you found him. You arrived at nearly the last moment of time. His condition is critical, monsieur, but not without hope. We will do everything we can. It is best that you prepare yourself for the worst." She grasped Hawkins' arm. "But don't give up hope yet!"

For several days, Pag's fever remained elevated; blood stained the fluid in the airlock sealing his chest tube and stained the bandages over the drains placed in his abdomen. The care he received was expertly appropriate and solicitously administered. His pain medication was carefully dosed so it did no harm yet rendered him comfortable. Most of the time he slept while essential fluids and medications were administered intravenously.

Lilly sat in the waiting room directly adjacent to the intensive care unit so she might not miss a moment of the brief times allotted to visitors. In spite of her fears and internal quaking, she was the staff of strength and comfort to Pag's parents. His mother wept and could not eat; his father, more stoical in his sorrow, bore up before her with manly strength.

Lilly was the strongest incentive in Pag's fight for life, but as he gained strength, another source of strength was born, vengeance! Gradually he began to regain color; his fever abated. Soon he was able to walk haltingly and with support to a chair.

After he was transferred to a room, ambulation was essential. Hawkins took one of Pag's arms while gallant Lilly, her ankle still encased in a walking cast, did her best to lend her support to the other. Once started on the road to recovery, Pag gained momentum daily. Eventually the day came when with copious tears of hope and happiness, Pag's parents flew home, assured of his recovery, and the three friends gave silent thanks to Providence and to skillful, dedicated medical care.

What had happened to Pag could be told in few words: the attack was carried out with trained precision; the men were experienced police bullies. Why it had happened was a mystery to Hawkins. It seemed inexplicable. How did the drug come to be there? How did the authorities know that marijuana was on the property? What was the reason behind it? He suspected only one person evil enough to perpetrate such an outrage: Wiley Williams. However, suspicion was not proof.

There was no question in Lilly's mind that it was her brother and that his motive was to drive Pag away from her. Hawkins was less sure. Pag might have been Wiley's unintended victim, an unfortunate bystander. Hawkins believed that unrestricted access to his property was Wiley's purpose. How this raid and attack would provide him that, Hawkins was unable to guess, but he knew why he wanted it.

After ten days, Pag was discharged, his abdomen swathed in surgical dressings, his wounds still oozing. At the moment of leaving, Pag tenderly embraced Dr. Devereaux before Lilly made him comfortable in the wheelchair. Hawkins pushed him to the hospital entrance and helped him into Lilly's car.

Hawkins drove to Hemlock Harbor where Pag was to reside with Matty during his convalescence. Pag requested they first be allowed to revisit the Gibbs' place. One brief look would make the horror of his attack and the fear it could happen to anyone, at any place, at any time, indelible in the minds of all three.

Chapter 18

DAILY REITERATION OF details of a "drug bust" in the *Dirigo Vigilance* sent repeated tremors of apprehension through the residents of Hemlock Harbor, during the time Pag's life hung in the balance.

Since Hawkins had remained faithfully by Pag in the town of Seal Point during Pag's time of danger, both were absent from Hemlock Harbor when their presence would have mitigated the effects of Wiley's daily repetition of unattributed allegations, the media breath which kept the embers of suspicion glowing.

Wiley's malignant lies, the so-called news, were variations on a consistent theme: two New York City artists, presumed guilty unless proven innocent, dwelling in a lonely and run-down farmhouse, were discovered to possess illegal drugs. Allusions to this litany were restated daily: interviews with the captors, reminders of the penalties for illicit drug use, and that such use nourished criminal danger to the community, the pernicious effects on the youths of the community, and a local preacher's prediction of perdition awaiting those who scorned the laws.

By implication, Hawkins and Pag became desperados, pariahs, tolerated by townsmen at their peril.

Mary was keenly angry. Where was the fact of the brutal attack on Pag reported? Where was Hawkins' denial of drug use or possession? When did any explanation of civil forfeiture, an inconceivable travesty that applies to property only, appear?

She was well aware of Wiley's character, of his despicable policy that people should know only what they were meant to know—meant to know or not know, by whom and for what purpose other than public delusion? She suspected Wiley was as deeply involved in this case of official immorality and injustice as he was in the rape of Old Woods. What could she do? More to the point, what could she not do? She could not remain passive!

Wiley eyed her with scorn. "You're biased!" he exclaimed, making no attempt to hide his anger. "This paper is objective! I won't tolerate any biased, one-sided, unsupported hearsay!"

"But that's exactly what you've already printed!" Mary pleaded.

"What I printed came from reliable authorities! Tell your story to them. If they buy it, then I'll publish it!"

"What they did was horrible—it was wrong! Do you think they'll admit that?"

"I will not debate the matter, and that's final!" Wiley glared at her.

Suddenly she saw his expression undergo a remarkable change: a scowl transmuted into a smile; patronizing affability erased the angry snarl in his voice.

She's my link with Shortreed, he thought. *Where could I find a better unwary spy than her?*

"Mary," he said in his newly altered, conciliatory tone, "interview Shortreed! Take your time. Give me a complete article: background, human interest, where the ten marijuana cigarettes came from, everything you can find out! I'll give it my personal attention."

Back in her office, guileless Mary's pleasant reaction to Wiley's turnabout gave way to suspicion. How did Wiley know there were ten cigarettes? The exact number of cigarettes, even that the so-called drug cache consisted of cigarettes, had never been released by the police. Reference to "a cache" of an undisclosed amount of marijuana sounded more ominous and impressive. She had no doubt Wiley was not only part of the guilty conspiracy directed against Hawkins but was actually trying to use her to spy on Hawkins' plans and intentions!

After she had told George about her confrontation with Wiley and particularly of his reference to ten cigarettes, he slowly shook his head.

"I'm reminded," he said, "of an old Spanish proverb. 'The law's a spiderweb. It catches the fly and lets the rat escape.' It seems Pag and Hawkins may be two flies caught in a web spun by a very nasty spider."

"What shall I do?" she asked.

"Frankly, I can't see anything can be done. The despicable law of civil forfeiture is impervious to constitutional defense. I'm afraid the Gibbs' place is in jeopardy of being seized. But wait until Hawkins gets back from Seal Point with Pag. When his anxiety about Pag has resolved, give him time to sort things out. He has friends to advise him. He's not quite the naive dreamer he used to be. I feel sure of that. We must leave the immediate future to him."

Martha Cottager was a member, though rapidly becoming a disillusioned member, of the political party known by the euphemistic cant of "loyal opposition." Martha was disgusted with the ever more important "loyal," bipartisan aspect. In her estimation, too many of her fellow members were too excessively loyal, a bit too tolerant of social inequity, more interested in winning elections than what they would do should they obtain some power. She found it more than a little difficult to determine just which aspects of government they would change in comparison with the agenda those in power were presently pursuing. Opposition? Opposition to what? Clear- cutting the forests? Widening concrete truck ways for more of the beasts? Ignoring the need for public rail transport? Pocketing graft? Though on the point of doing so, Martha had not yet actually withdrawn from the political farce, for which Matty was thankful.

"Would it be possible," Matty wondered, "for Martha to move enough of her colleagues to demand an investigation of police brutality in the attacks on the students and on Pag?"

Martha had enthusiastically pursued this suggestion and today had given Matty her answer. "Unfortunately, no! I have met nothing but polite refusals from my colleagues. Not frank refusals but the sneaky, oily, specious refusals made by politicians who are too cozy with the source of power—money! The situation is hopeless."

Discouraged, beaten, impotent, and irate, Matty tried valiantly to compose herself. She stopped on the way to her car to exchange a few words with George who was raking up the last of the year's leaves. His calm manner would surely ease her indignation!

The sky was overcast, and a cutting north wind reminded them that snow was possible any day.

"Have you heard anything from Hawkins?" Matty asked.

"He phones often to speak to Mary, but you know how lovers are. Right now, she makes him forget about everyone for a bit, even Pag. Just what he needs, poor fellow. As though Pag's condition were not enough, being continuously raked over the coals by Wiley Williams' scandalous lies and what those lies have done to their reputations has greatly concerned him." He looked significantly at Matty. "And now there is more. I'm afraid the poor fellow's in for a shock when he does get back!"

"Another shock!" Matty could have screamed. Was there to be no end to his troubles? Was he being purposely persecuted? If so, by whom? "What do you mean?"

"If it weren't for the terrible and brutal attack on Pag, Hawkins would have been here to defend himself and initiate legal action. Now it's too late. Their home has been sold out from under them."

"Oh, no!" Matty exclaimed, "That can't be possible!"

"I'm afraid it is," George said sadly. "The seized Gibbs' place was put up for a sealed bid auction by the treasury department, and Wiley Williams was the only bidder. The closing was yesterday. Wiley's now the owner."

"That's outrageous!" Matty angrily exclaimed. "I haven't seen anything in the paper, not a word about any auction. I wonder why?" It was now becoming clear to her who was persecuting Hawkins. Why he was doing it, she did not know yet. "The sinister, sneaking bastard," she said to herself.

"It's all very mysterious," George said annoyed. "Mary happened to learn of it from the reporter who covers the federal court in Augusta and who knows she and Hawkins are engaged and called to tell her about it."

"That must have been a shock," Matty said.

"There's more," George recalled with anger. "Mary stormed into Wiley's office demanding to know what right he had to the property, and Wiley fired her on the spot. She was giving him a piece of her mind when he flung open the door and pushed her out."

"The fiendish devil!" Matty cried.

"That's not all," George said indignantly. "He fired the court reporter as well for not, as he put it, 'keeping his damned mouth shut.'"

George and Matty were not aware that even as they spoke, Hawkins and Pag were returning to Hemlock Harbor.

Driving Lilly and Pag home from the hospital at Seal Point, Hawkins looked eagerly forward to returning to the Gibbs' place, their home, their refuge by the sea. Leaving Lilly and Pag in the car, he raced up the steps. What was this? New padlocks secured the door. Locked out of their own home! Who dared do such a thing? Was it possible? A notice was nailed to the door:

"Property seized. No trespassing under penalty of the law."

What did it mean? What had occurred to bar them from their own home? He stood in silent amazement, dumbfounded, while indignation welled up within him.

At the bottom of the poster in large red script was the ironic message admonishing him to "dare to keep kids off drugs."

Matty and George were both delighted and worried when Lilly's car drove up before the house, and Lilly gently assisted Hawkins in getting Pag out of the car with the least discomfort . . . a wound-stretching maneuver. Hawkins' face was pale with anger, but he was strangely composed.

"Matty! George!" he said in hurried greeting, "You must have heard. Our property has been seized by the police!"

"Hawkins," George said hurriedly, "come inside!"

George held the house door while Lilly and Hawkins assisted Pag to enter the house. Matty flung off her coat; this was no time for her to leave! Mary rushed from the kitchen at the sound of Hawkins' voice and stopped abruptly when she saw the lock on his face. "He's been there and found out from someone else before I could tell him," she said to herself, presuming he had discovered that Wiley owned the Gibbs' place.

Pag was comfortably placed in a chair. "You and Lilly had better sit too, Hawkins," George commanded. "You poor devils have suffered incredibly, but you're among friends!"

It had to be told; there was no way around it. "You probably don't yet know . . . Wiley Williams is the new owner of the Gibbs' place."

Hawkins did not respond. "Why doesn't he say something? Why isn't he angry?" was foremost in everyone's thoughts.

"Well, I'll be goddamned!" Pag sounded like his old self. "The son of a bitch!"

"The son of a bitch!" Hawkins echoed. "Pardon my profanity, but that's what Wiley is, a low, sneaking, conniving, son of a bitch! I'm certain he was primarily responsible for having a lot of young students molested and arrested, that he planted false evidence, indirectly having Pag nearly killed, and now . . . he owns our home. It's outrageous!

"But," Hawkins said, regaining his composure, "the most urgent thing right now is to find a place for us to live after Pag is recovered."

"Fiddlesticks!" said Matty, donning her coat. "You're both going to make your home with me!"

"Come on, George! Quick, Mary!" Martha cried, hurriedly grabbing her coat. "Pag and Hawkins are going to board with Matty. This is no time to sit home. I want to hear everything!"

When Pag was settled on Matty's sofa with his hand in Lilly's, Hawkins dropped his figurative bombshell.

"I'm exceedingly grateful to all of you, but I'm not going to pursue any sort of legal action against Wiley Williams. It would tie us up for months and doubtless prove fruitless in the end anyway. His network of corrupt cronies is too strong. I will not have our lives disrupted, not one bit more of our time taken up by that scoundrel. Let it end right here, right now, a new beginning, and no looking backwards!"

In spite of Pag's severe injuries and their terrible loss, Hawkins' words were like a brisk, clean wind off the ocean blowing away clouds of a life- draining miasma; an oddly happy mood prevailed. The theft of their property did not weigh on Hawkins. It had happened. Since there was now nothing he was willing to do, everything was swept behind them. Of importance now was the future before them, to look ahead to the happiness awaiting them!

"Hooray!" cried Matty. "They can lie, steal, even kill, but they can't take away our will to rise above their crimes. We can escape through 'the eye of the needle,' they can't! Hawkins, there is a bottle of wine in the refrigerator. I'll get some glasses, and we can drink to that!"

They did, and it was like ringing down the curtain on a bad act. "To hell with materialists," cried Pag with his old verve, "let 'em stew in their own dishonest juice. Unless we voluntarily let them intrude into our lives, they can only prey on each other . . . . And I'll be damned if they'll ever get into my life again!"

After Pag had tired and was settled in Matty's soft and comfortable guest bed, Hawkins asked Lilly for a private word.

"Do you think your ankle will permit you to look after Pag for a few days?" he asked. "He doesn't need help. He even changes the dressings himself, but I'd feel better knowing you were here to keep Matty company and to stop him from doing too much while I'm away."

"Of course," Lilly replied, "but where are you going?"

"First, I must take Mary back to Halifax, get her as far away from your brother's influence as I can."

"I understand," said Lilly. "I'd also like to get as far away from him as possible."

"I'll have something to say to you about that sometime soon," Hawkins said with sympathetic kindness.

Lilly looked puzzled. "What do you mean?" She was totally unprepared for yet another mystery.

"There isn't anything more that I can say now, Lilly. There are too many imponderables. But after I get Mary to her grandparents, I must be away for several days. I don't know how long. When I return, you and I will have a serious talk. You can depend on that!"

Their eyes met. She saw Hawkins was deadly serious. "It has something to do with that scandalous 'drug bust' and Wiley! I know it does! Oh, Hawkins, be careful!"

Hawkins eyes narrowed. "I'm not man enough to turn the other cheek, Lilly. He'll pay for what he's done to Pag. He's taken all the rope he needs, and it will hang him!"

"What do you mean?"

"Pag and I will have our revenge," Hawkins declared. "It won't be violent. It won't happen all at once. He won't even know we had anything to do with it. There's only one way to deal with dishonest cheats: Make sure they don't win the game!"

"And you can do that?" she asked, "How?"

"That's what I want to talk to you about when I get back. I'd like to depend on you while I'm away?"

Lilly reached for his hand, gave it an earnest squeeze, and said, "Okay!"

When Hawkins was ready to leave for Halifax, a weeping Martha put her arms around Mary; she had become very close to this sweet young woman during the short time they had lived together. "I have happy news for you," Mary said. "I saved it for a last-minute surprise. You and Mother will both be coming to Halifax when Hawkins and I are married! It's been a long time since you sisters have seen each other."

Mary saw with pleasure the bright change in Martha. She kissed her and George, jumped into the truck, and waved a heartfelt farewell.

After she was again settled with her grandparents, Flora and Andy, and looking forward to seeing her parents again in a few months, Hawkins recalled to her their conversation on the bench. "Do you remember, my darling, that I must leave you here for a while?" She said nothing, hung her head, and nodded.

Hawkins departed without informing anyone of the reason. Even Will had not been made privy to it. His faith in Hawkins was unperturbed; it was only a matter of time.

Hawkins was gone much longer than the anticipated few days. A week passed. In Maine, away from the center of activity, Lilly and Pag became concerned. Could Hawkins cross swords with Wiley and come away unscathed? What was he doing? Surely there was no harm in Lilly telephoning Mary, not to pry, but to reassure herself.

Lilly hung up the telephone and sat thinking about what she had learned. Hawkins had stayed only one day in Halifax. He said he was going to Quebec. What could he possibly have to do in Quebec? Mary had no idea; he had only asked her to trust him and be patient.

"I don't know what he has in mind," Mary had said, "but I know Hawkins. He doesn't want to confide in me now, but when he's ready, he'll tell me everything."

She was sure it had something to do with Wiley, but what?

Another week went by, and Hawkins still had not returned, nor had he called or written. Pag was now up and about and asking for Hawkins. Where the hell had he gone? Where the hell was he? It had now been over three weeks since Hawkins had left Halifax.

Three days later, Lilly looked out the window at the first blizzard of the season. Only shadowy forms of trees along the road and indistinct headlights of passing cars could be seen through the fog of snow. It was growing dark, and she was about to leave for home while the roads were still passable when she saw headlights turn into the drive. It was Hawkins' truck.

Lilly, Matty, and Pag rushed to the door. Hawkins entered with a look of happy satisfaction written on his face.

"Where the hell have you been?" Pag demanded with obvious relief.

Hawkins grasped Pag's hand and searched his eyes intently. "How are you, old fellow?"

"Couldn't be better," Pag replied in his usual hearty manner, which reassured Hawkins more than his words. "Ready to do battle with the scurrilous curs which plague this place."

"What have you been doing?" asked Lilly in high excitement.

"Are you hungry?" was Matty's first question.

Hawkins laughed. "Yes, I'm hungry. I'll tell you about it after I've had something to eat, and then I must be on my way to see Mary as soon as I can."

"Hawkins," Matty said, "you and Lilly can't drive until the plows have been out. You must stay the night! Lilly can sleep with me, and you, with Pag. You can be off at first light, but now let's have some supper and hear what you have to say!"

The wind picked up and howled around the old farm house, rattling the windows in their casements, adding to the snug comfort of Matty's dining room.

"Okay," said an impatient Pag, "where have you been?"

"I don't want to tell you right now. In fact don't ask me about anything yet," replied Hawkins with a broad grin but leaving no doubt that he was in deadly earnest. "You'll find out when the time is right. Now I've a question for both Lilly and Pag." How nonchalantly Hawkins proposed his surprise for them.

"Would you have any objection to being married next spring in Halifax, Nova Scotia?"

Pag's jaw dropped.

"No!" said Lilly.

"Pag," continued Hawkins, "you're now the protégé of a well-to-do Canadian patron. You will be able to marry. What do you say?"

"No!" said Pag.

"No?" gasped Lilly. "Why not?"

"I mean," said Pag, "no, I don't have any objection."

"Will you make it a double wedding, you and Lilly, Mary and me?"

"Yes!" said Lilly.

"Well, if that's settled, I have a request of Lilly." Hawkins looked inquiringly at her.

"Let me hear what it is," Lilly answered.

"It's important Pag and I know everything that Wiley does at the Gibbs' place. I drove in on my way here. 'No Trespass' signs are plastered on the entrance road. Pag or I would be arrested on sight. I need a spy. Will you do it?"

"Spy on my own brother?" Lilly asked. "After what he's done to Pag and you! I know he was behind it   I'd be delighted!"

Lilly was as good as her word. She recorded all Wiley's actions in a journal for Hawkins to read when he was ready.

In spite of the snow, Wiley was having the graveyard carefully cleared by a two-man crew. The weather was dreadful; the peninsula and graveyard were entirely exposed to the frigid northeast winds, which roared in off the ocean with raging force and cut like a knife. Wiley, afraid to leave the men lest they discover the treasure and steal it, rarely left the site.

He had an ice-fishing shack brought in with a kerosene stove; distrust and suspicion kept him glued to the small plastic window. The men in ski masks and snowmobile suits worked in relative comfort. When Wiley returned to his office at the end of each day to oversee the next day's edition of the *Dirigo Vigilance*, his overcoat, his tweed jacket, his button-down collar shirt, and even his tie, reeked of kerosene.

Wiley was miserable. Greed burned like fire within him, but it was fire which threw no heat. He was a man possessed by unbridled, overpowering self-interest, a passion which kept him fixed to the foot square plastic window. He entertained no doubts; the treasure was there, and every moment of every day, he expected its discovery.

As the winter progressed, the temperature plummeted, and the winds continued to blow with gale force. Pag listened to Lilly's reports with eager delight. Nothing pleased him more than hearing them over and over, savoring every discomfort and disappointment which Wiley encountered.

"Is this Hawkins' revenge?" Lilly whispered to him while Pag was in the kitchen, getting himself a beer.

"I'll bet it's part of it," Pag said with a smile, "but I'm sure he's saving the best for last."

"Is our marrying a part of it too?"

The question startled Pag. "Part of his vengeance? Is that what you mean?" He took her hand. "Lilly, if you knew Hawkins as I do, you could never suspect such a thing!" The pained look on his honest face told her it was the truth. "He knows the strength of my love for you and yours for me. I couldn't marry you unless I could support you. Whatever he's done, he has done it to make that possible."

Chapter 19

WILEY'S APPARENT OBJECTIVE was to dig the upper foot or two of dirt beneath the sod of all the visible graves in the burial ground until he found either the gold he sought or a clue to wherever it was hidden. Winter intensified the frustrated greed which gnawed deep into his scheming soul as the barren search continued. Carpenters had stripped every wall of the house down to hand-sawn studs; still, nothing had been found. Every room had been measured, searching for concealed space. He had the fireplace hearths torn up, the bricks of the fireplaces and the mantels torn down, subjecting everything to minute examination. The earth floor of the root cellar, trodden upon for centuries, was completely turned over as was the floor of the barn. If he became hopelessly desperate, demolition of the house was not out of the question. But he remained convinced the graveyard was still the most likely place of concealment, for it was the only place which contained identifiable sites. These, marked by headstones, would allow whoever buried the treasure to readily relocate it. Thus far, he had excavated around the base of the boulder and found nothing and had the decaying vegetation which cloaked the burial ground carefully cleared away.

"Damn that Gibbs," fumed Wiley. "Couldn't he have put something explicit in the Bible? Who would think of looking in the book of Jonah! Could that itself be a clue?"

Every headstone with the name "Jonah" would now likely be investigated first. The tediousness of piecing together the fractured gravestones and placing them in what might have been their nearly correct positions grated upon his raw and tender pride. This was real work, not his work of clever lying and deception. His magic wand of guile was of no use to him. Cold reality which he could not twist and distort stymied him, and he hated it with a red-hot but futile wrath. It gnawed at his brain like a foul rat consuming a ripe and stinking cheese. His pride and vanity turned inward, and he cursed the fate from which he was unable to free himself; such was the power of his greed and imagined omnipotence.

Where else could a treasure of gold coins be hidden? Where else could a hiding place for a map to it be hidden? he thought back, reviewing what Hawkins, Pag, and Mary had done. *They had been in the graveyard, had dug up the grave by the barn. Had they been any place else? . . . done anything extraordinary?*

Yes, they had! He had seen them diving at the foot of the cliff. Suppose Gibbs had put the treasure in a metal box and put the box in a crevice on the cliff face above tide level? Perhaps, there was a recess behind the ledge where the body was likely found. He would make every effort to find out, but this project would have to be delayed until spring, for scrambling about on that cliff face in winter was unthinkable. Ice, wet rocks, cold sea spay, and frozen fingers . . . suppose the rope about his waist or the scrub tree at the top was poorly knotted due to numb fingers? No, it was out of the question during the winter.

There was no alternative but to continue his search without interruption, which he did without discovering anything worthwhile, until a massive ice storm in late January caused a temporary cessation. The two men whom he employed made little progress once the ground froze as hard as granite, unable to do more than hack out chunks of frozen earth and pile them near each grave until they could be sifted in the spring. Wiley hired a security company to supply watchmen for three shifts. He took no chances, yet he suffered from the age-old worry of who would guard the guards. Sleep and rest were impossible; thoughts of the whereabouts of the gold, which he was certain existed, perpetually occupied his mind.

Earl was concerned. Wiley's work on the newspaper and broadcasting stations now fell heavily on his shoulders. Wiley himself had acquired a different aspect. No longer was he the supremely confident, omnipotent potentate of a corporate domain . . . but short-tempered and beginning to acquire a wan and desperate air. How long it would be before Earl's associates began to suspect something was amiss was beyond his power to guess.

Wiley was beside himself. To what extent should he go in pursuit of the still elusive goal? Having gone thus far, defeat was unthinkable. Would a treasure have remained hidden and intact or had it been made a legacy and been passed to subsequent generations? If so, what had they done with it? None of the family had lived in a wealthy manner. In fact, they had worked as hard to survive as their neighbors; it must still be intact, having been well hidden by someone and then somehow forgotten.

Thus far, he had unearthed the surface of the graves of Abner, his wife, and his children with pitiful results. In several instances, the burials were unexpectedly very shallow due to the encounter with ledge rock in burying the dead. Nothing remained of the coffins except stains which could be easily missed in the earth. As particles of bone were discovered in a particular grave, all work there ceased, and the hole was covered with a heavy frame made from railroad ties and a tarpaulin. After the ground dried completely, sometime in late June or early July, each shovelful of earth that had been removed, as well as those still to be excavated, would be thoroughly sifted and carefully examined. Work of this type would usually be the responsibility of trained archeologists from the Maine State Museum, but Wiley had the connections necessary to obtain a permit to proceed independently of any such interference or supervision. He retained enough wisdom in his state of increasing mania to realize it would be in his interest to turn over anything not pertaining to the treasure to the proper hands. Thus far, only the fragmentary remains of two pairs of spectacles, a belt buckle, and several ivory buttons had been recovered in addition to bones, all of which had been given to the grateful museum.

On a particularly frigid, gray day, when the kerosene heater failed to keep Wiley from suffering bone-chilling cold, he saw one of the workman running excitedly toward the ice-fishing shack. In one of the frozen chunks of earth, he had spied a dull bit of nondescript stone which he had struck with his pickax. This slight wound shone brightly silver. He chipped away with his knife until he had freed a circular disk which he brought at once to Wiley. Though he had no idea what it was, Wiley sent it to the state museum. After a considerable period he received a reply stating in part the following:

> The submitted object is an early eighteenth century Spanish coin of the Cob type. Examination of the mint mark and of the assayer's initials indicates that it was issued from the mint at Potosi, circa 1700. These coins were common tender in colonial America; however, it could indicate the existence of archeological remains of interest. If anything further remotely suggestive is discovered, please be assured of the enthusiastic cooperation of the Maine State Museum, etc., etc.

More intense visions of bags and bags of golden Spanish doubloons or French Louis d'Or, not silver coins, now fired his imagination. Ever more powerfully captured by gold fever, his greedy imagination was exacerbated to a fever pitch. Nothing could nor would impede his search after this!

Although winter storms had slowed Wiley's efforts, they were no hindrance to the Great Amalgamated Pulp and Hardwood Company, which had immediately moved their trucks and forest harvesters to Old Woods and attacked it with a vengeance. The only trees remaining unfelled that could be seen from what had once been the parking area lay far distant across a now stark plain of stumps, snow, and mud, crisscrossed by dirty imprints of heavy machinery treads and truck tires. Other than the faint sounds of the motors and saws of the distant harvesters and the crashing of trees as they fell, sounds further dampened by snow, all was as silent as a graveyard at midnight, a graveyard of stumps, a desolate, ravaged wasteland.

Nothing moved among the stumps except the wind; not a bird nor a squirrel was to be seen, for the life of Old Woods was gone, eliminated for profit. Until recently deer and moose had browsed the branches, living as they had when only Indians roamed these glades which the white man had now twice laid waste.

When the breezes which attend the springtime awoke Mother Nature from winter slumber, where would be found her violets, where her arbutus, that beloved mayflower of New England? No poet, in his wildest distorted visions, could picture the Queen of the May dancing in that wasteland of ugliness created by the Great Amalgamated Pulp and Hardwood Company. What had been beautiful was now vile and repugnant. The voices which had promised jobs and prosperity to the working people of the area were heard no longer; the lies had done their job.

In early March, Hawkins and Mary drove down from Halifax to Maine for the pleasure of driving back for the wedding with Lilly and Pag. The night ferry landed them rested and fresh in Bar Harbor from which they continued their journey. But while in Hemlock Harbor, probably for the last time, thereremained one sad duty which they felt obliged to observe: to see for themselves the ravage which had been wreaked upon the forest they once had loved.

Lilly suddenly braked the car. Old Woods Forest was no more!

"Oh my god!" she gasped, choking back tears of sorrow and anger, "Nothing remains of Old Woods except the ghosts of beauty and serenity to which we must bid farewell forever. It will not regrow in our lifetimes."

"'Render unto Caesar that which is Caesar's,'" said Pag with the sarcasm felt by all. "Render your laments and tears while greedy, cruel men in three- piece suits toast their success in carrying out this dastardly deed."

"Oh, Hawkins," Mary spoke through her tears, "if I close my eyes, I can see it as it was just a few months ago. It's heartbreaking!"

"This is wrong!" Hawkins was afraid to close his eyes and bring back the beauty which had once adorned this place. He too could weep over the wretched scene before him. "What monsters drive this country? Is there no limit to their outrageous cupidity? Is there nothing which cannot be sacrificed to make a handful of men rich? I'm glad Matty isn't with us to see this. It would break her heart."

"This wouldn't happen with a socialist government," Pag exclaimed. "The scum who make war on other people, killing them in order to steal what rightfully belongs to them, would be in jail. Our government, that abominable gang of thugs, 'toadies, and humbugs' . . . hell! Call them what they are, psychopaths, murderers, and crooks, who hand power to their obedient clients on a bloody platter. For christ's sake! Won't the people ever wake up and take control of their own lives?"

"I don't think so," said George, his equitable good sense overcome by sorrow and anger. "It's not in the nature of the beast to be either sensible or civilized where the pursuit of money is an epidemic mania."

"I fear you're right," said Martha tearfully. "Capitalism is like fire. Unless it's controlled, the same fire that cooks our food can burn down our house. A little capitalist greed may be a good thing, but when it runs amok, this is what happens."

"Good-bye, dear Old Woods." Lilly kissed the fingers of her right hand and laid them on a woeful stump surrounded by tire-matted underbrush, mud, and snow, churned up by the forest harvesters. They departed for home as though from a bereavement.

March saw Wiley still determined to find a bonanza in the graveyard at the Gibbs' place. While in intimate contact with the dead, it did not occur to him that death awaited every mother's son, be he a greedy capitalist, military sadist, or pauper. His arrogance and his madness rendered him indifferent to that inevitable fate.

"Wiley," asked Lilly indignantly, "why are you desecrating this burial ground?"

"Desecration!" he scornfully exclaimed. "I'm working under a permit. This is historic preservation!"

"But why?" persisted Lilly.

"None of your damned business!" Wiley snapped.

"I have something for you, Wiley." Lilly handed him the shoe box she had found under the truck seat and had thoroughly examined. "It's from the house and is very valuable. Please have the museum people go over it for you."

That will inflame his passion, she thought, *and add nothing material to whatever he hopes to find.* An arch smile flitted across her face.

At that, Lilly walked off, leaving Wiley glued to his vigil, standing in several inches of sloppy mud. She looked back to see him. There he stood in the cold fog, not the old Wiley but a thin, shivering madman, shielded from the icy drizzle by his umbrella, obsessed by his search for something. Hawkins must know what he hoped to find; she'd ask him.

Later that evening, as they sat about the fire at the Cottager's, Hawkins laughed heartily at the picture she painted of Wiley. "Giving him the box was inspired, Lilly. The museum will find good use for the ancient garments, and it will kindle Wiley to white heat!"

"It's not having a hole blown in your spleen, Pag," Hawkins said, "but like the proverbial Chinese water torture, it's effective revenge. It warms my heart to think of him chained there by greed, freezing his butt off, hoping every minute to find a treasure that isn't there."

"Treasure!" exclaimed Lilly. "What treasure?"

Pag briefly explained to her what he had been told by Hawkins before being seriously injured and losing possession of the Gibbs' place.

"I don't know what kind of a treasure he has in mind," Hawkins replied, "but that's what he's searching for."

"How do you know?" demanded Pag.

"Remember the legend about the shipwreck and treasure?" They nodded.

"However, he got hold of the Gibbs' family Bible," Hawkins continued, recalling what Lilly had observed. "He must have found something in it which convinced him there was a treasure, and that ignited his greed. He robbed the title to our property which nearly got Pag killed. We weren't interested in selling the Gibbs' place, so he planted the marijuana cigarettes which enabled his cronies to lay their filthy hands on it for him."

"The unmitigated scoundrel!" exclaimed Lilly.

"I have no doubt of his actions, but alas, no proof," Hawkins said regretfully. "And it probably wouldn't do any good if I had. But I'm absolutely certain that he did it. It fits his crafty, mean, and worthless soul."

"But suppose the bastard finds the treasure?" Pag smote the table.

"He won't!" Hawkins smiled.

"How do you know that?" Pag was dubious.

"I think you should tell us about this rich patron you found," Lilly said. "We really should know!"

Hawkins leaned back. It had to come sooner or later. "You have all been very patient. Some things I can tell you now, but not everything, not yet.

"Pag is a permanent artist in residence of the WIM Art Foundation . . . resident in   " He paused unable to go on.

"Well, where?" demanded Lilly, grinning from ear to ear. She loved surprises.

Hawkins looked at them. "Skunktown, Kansas," he replied.

Pag scratched his head. "I've never heard of that place," he said. "Where is it?"

Lilly looked downcast.

"Corn Country," Hawkins replied, "endless vistas, wide-open spaces, you'll love it!"

"Oh," gasped Lilly, "my god!"

"If you don't like Skunktown, there is one other option."

"Probably Las Vegas, Nevada!" moaned Lilly.

"No," said Hawkins, hoping the real location would come as a welcome, if not a wildly acceptable, relief, "it's Florence, Italy!"

They were stunned!

Lilly was the first to recover her wits. "What of my early American antiques," she wondered aloud. Then her face light up in a bright smile. "European antiquities!" The blood of her maverick great-great-great-uncle Ben coursed through her. What a new, exciting opportunity!

"We'll take the second choice!" she was bursting with enthusiasm.

"My Italian has been getting rusty since I left home." Pag looked pleased. "And what a place to work!"

"Who runs this foundation?" inquired Lilly, "How big is it? How many artists does it support in Italy?"

"It's endowed by a Canadian family, and there is only one other artist."

"Who is it?" asked Pag. "Anybody we know?"

"I think you might," Hawkins answered with a smile.

"I know!" cried Lilly. "It's . . . Hawkins Shortreed!"

"That you'll find out after the wedding!" Hawkins was in high good spirits stimulated by the accounts which he had been told of the scheming and despicable Wiley. Inwardly, he was overjoyed to contemplate the contemptible Wiley led on by his monstrous greed, unable to enjoy the soft luxury of his usual mode of life, forced into the painful cold of a Maine winter at its worst, and lured by limitless covetousness into, what had to be by now, soul-gnawing anxiety and fearful doubt. Oh, the sweetness of vengeance! Perhaps it was morally wrong, but he felt in no mood to entertain that question, which he would present to his grandfather in the near future.

"I think we've enjoyed the spectacle of Wiley's suffering long enough," Hawkins addressed himself to Pag. "What do you think? He'll continue his masochistic search whether we're here or not. The fool is unable to help himself. If you want to stay longer, we can. If not, we can go get married!"

"When?" Lilly asked joyfully.

"June 20," Mary said. "Mother is in Halifax now, and if I call to tell her we're coming, she'll take care of the arrangements. What do you say?"

Mary rushed to the phone. She returned beaming with joy. "June 20 it is, if it's all right with Pag."

For answer, Pag gathered Lilly in his arms.

"Burn your bridges!" Hawkins commanded with a smile. "Get passports! For after the wedding, we leave for Florence!"

Chapter 20

THE WEDDING MONTH of June was all they might have wished for, a world bathed in days of sunshine under clouds of billowing white set in an azure sky. What busy hives of joy and gaiety the modest McLeod and Duncan homes became when the brides and bridegrooms-to-be arrived.

The meeting of Heather and Angus Ayrshire, Mary's parents, with Martha and George Cottager, was an exuberant exchange of hugs, kisses, handshakes, laughter, and tears, celebrating the joyous reunion of sisters separated for a good round dozen of years.

Pag's parents, Dominico and Angelina, jovial, soft spoken, with that Italian flare for turning any gathering into a convivial celebration of wine and food, added their unique effervescence. Dominico destroyed any preconceptions of what a tough and pugnacious union organizer from Newark, New Jersey might be; for he was in everything a most considerate gentleman. On the other hand, Angelina, who prided herself on the reputation of her cooking, invaded the McLeod and Duncan kitchens, where, with singing and gusto, she prepared superb meals. Her robust kindness, her hearty laugh, the blessings of wine and joy made Pag, on more than one occasion, embrace his mother, the red-blanket daughter of his blacklisted grandfather; a grandfather in whose philosophic footsteps he trod, but whose outspoken profanity he transiently forbore.

Nothing could dampen the lovers' happiness, not even the arrival of a dour Earl Williams. He met Hawkins and Pag with restrained formality; had Lilly honored his advice, her marriage would not be taking place. He was greatly relieved to learn she would live abroad; distant disgrace would become distant glory in his country club tales. Thereafter, he was genial though condescending, but that could not last. His naturally jovial nature prevailed, and everyone enjoyed his company except Pag.

Esther, on the other hand, was her usual delightful self; and even Pag was not immune to the charm of her generous, genuine nature. She judged not, that she be not judged; and when she saw, as everyone must, how Pag and Lilly loved each other, it brought tears to her eyes. Many and many had been the years since she, though tolerably happy, had experienced such joy. Lilly and she embraced as they had never embraced before; mother and daughter had found one another at last.

"Lilly is going to take you for better or for worse, God help her," Hawkins said in the hope of diminishing Pag's evident dislike for Earl, "and you must take her on the same terms. There's nothing of her father nor her brother in her. She's her mother's daughter with added spunk and spice . . . don't forget that! You would have fallen head over heels in love with her no matter who her relatives were!"

"I know," a confused Pag replied, "but a snake oil salesman for a father-in- law and a damned cobra for a brother-in-law . . . ?"

"Look on the bright side, Pag! Lilly knows what they are and doesn't like it any better than you do. It might help to think Wiley didn't know you'd be attacked."

"The son of a bitch wouldn't have cared if he did!" Pag retorted.

"Wiley's not here," Hawkins said, "and Earl is just a typical businessman. Okay, you're a Marxist, and he's an enemy, but think of Lilly! Can't you be nice to him for her sake?"

Pag thought it over; a broad grin spread across his face, "For her I can do anything!"

Thenceforth, Pag thought only of Lilly, the dazzling gift of her love, and the joyful, inexpressible wonder that she would soon be his bride. Thenceforth, this oh-so-brief interlude in the oft times turbulent stream of life became that idyllic moment in Longfellow's vision when, " . . . The Night shall be filled with music and the cares that beset the day, will fold their tents like the Arabs and as silently steal away." And so stole away resentment, anger and dislike, banished by more lofty and worthy sentiments.

Hawkins found his grandfather in his usual seat on the porch, preparing to enjoy, as was his custom, the melancholic beauty of the gloaming. How often they had sat there together in bygone years. When, if ever, would they again share such moments? Though a sharp pain of longing and regret caught Hawkins by surprise and brought tears to his eyes, he forced a smile and took his usual seat beside him.

He wanted to recount to Will his personal evidence of the conspiracy to destroy Old Woods, the brutality of the police, and Pag's brush with death; he needed the old man's wisdom and moral judgment. He must somehow reconcile that travesty of justice, that upending of right and wrong, the role of the unscrupulous, with Will's philosophy which had long ago become his own. In addition, there was another's actions on which he badly needed Will's absolution, his own.

"Grandpa," Hawkins asked when he had told all there was to tell, "was that wretched saga only the tip of the iceberg? Is it an example of how the world is really run?"

"To my mind," Will replied with his kindly Scottish burr, "it's one pole of human nature."

Hawkins saw Will was deep in thought and waited patiently for him to proceed. Minutes passed; shadows disappeared with the sun; radiant pink and orange clouds graced the sky; the gloaming had begun.

"As I see it, lad," Will resumed, "there's a top and a bottom to the pillar of human nature; it's predetermined and never changes.

"On the bottom are what drives or misleads men into barbarity: stupidity, dire want, military cruelty, lust, greed, lies, the drive for wealth and power . . . . I can't name them all. On top are civilizing forces: kindness, justice, reason, love of learning, wisdom, and a sense of community . . . . Again I'm no philosopher; I can't fathom them all.

"At the best of times, man strives for civilization; at the worst, his barbaric nature is unleashed. Most of the time there is a mixture of the two forces."

Will paused, unsure if he should finish saying what he felt to be true. He rose, started back into the house and stopped. He owed it to Hawkins to place the Old Woods tragedy in sharper context, to tell him precisely how he felt. He sensed that was what Hawkins was seeking.

"I'm no historian, lad, only a simple working man. I can only tell you about what I have lived through.

"World War II was a period of barbarism," he began slowly, thoughtfully, "forced on the world by wealthy capitalists who built up the German Military and a political party whose members called themselves Fascists. It was a terrible period of suffering for common people, especially the Jews of Europe. Fascism is a useful term for the despotic union of the rich and the military. Although now called 'The Military-Industrial Complex, it's the same thing.

"At the end of World War II, Hawkins, there was a strong sense of solidarity, of community; people felt, having just beaten the fascists by working together, that by continuing to plan and to work together, they could and would make a more perfect world. That was a good and noble task.

"But the rich capitalists would have none of that! They organized the McCarthy purge with the purpose of forcing out all the ablest men in the American Government and blacklisting the idea makers, the 'intelligentsia.' Why? Because the 'intelligentsia' believed in Marxist

Socialism, not Capitalism, and many belonged to the Communist Party which was then legal, so who was to say they couldn't. It was no one's business but their own.

"From there the rich went on to organize 'The Cold War' to create dissension in the world and get a hot war economy going. Throw fear into people, and it's easier to steal their tax money. The public treasury has been looted ever since by 'The Military-Industrial Complex'. The people followed the loudest drums, lost their ideals and put an end to any idea of community in the country or in the world!

"Since then the fascist forces fostering barbarity have held the upper hand, especially in the United States . . . the rich are more secure and content with a strong army and a disorganized and barbarous population. A fearful population is more easily duped and controlled than an informed and knowledgeable one. Fear makes people responsive to propaganda and less of a threat to the wealthy and to what they own. It's been an ongoing oppression from the dawn of history and will never, ever cease.

"In a personal way, it seems to me, you've witnessed an example of the force pushing toward barbarism at first hand, and I'm sorry for that."

"Grandpa, knowing what you know, feeling as you do, would you still play the game squarely and fairly?"

Will looked at him with surprise. "Oh, lad, there will always be ignoble, dishonorable, evil men! Shun them! Always listen to what's noble and honorable in your nature; let it guide you down a path you can be proud of! You'll never regret it!"

With manly honesty Hawkins then told Will of his treatment of Wiley. He was not proud of seeking vengeance nor did he expect Will to be. When he finished Will smiled. "Lad, God must not have cared too much for saints since he made so few of them. I canna' say I would ha' done differently."

Hawkins took the gentle, little man in his arms. "Grandpa . . . ," his voice was choked by unbounded love for this humble man to whom he owed so much.

"I know, lad . . . no need to say anything. Your grandmother and I are thankful for the happy years the three of us have had together. You know how we feel . . . and we know how you feel!"

A strong embrace, into which he poured the strength of his love, ended their conversation. They returned to the house with lighter hearts, each knowing that what had to be said had now been said.

The day before the wedding Hawkins gathered together Mary, Lilly and Pag. They walked to the university and found a shaded, sequestered place on the crowded campus where Hawkins spread a blanket for them to sit on. Around them students sunned themselves while cramming for final exams, sailed Frisbees, and walked or cycled by. None paid the slightest attention to them.

"I wanted to get us together for a very serious purpose," Hawkins began when they were all comfortable, "and I must pledge everyone to the strictest secrecy."

"Mary?"

"Of course, darling!"

"Lilly?"

"Cross my heart!"

"Pag?"

"Hell, yes!"

"Mary, can you remember the epitaph on Abner's grave?" Hawkins smiled recalling how little it meant to them at the time.

"No, but I have a copy of it in my purse," Mary replied withdrawing a small notepad.

LET NONE FORGET

In truth let all ye

Befriend each lost

Outcast wanderer

"Let's try to look at that epitaph in the light of all we now know. In 1761 there was a shipwreck. Abner Gibbs found something. What could it have been? Something consumable would be my first guess except for the legend. So let's say it was our 'treasure' which he secreted someplace. Why? Of course, no one can be certain, but there probably was some unpleasant consequence connected with it he was unwilling to risk. The next thing that struck me was there was no evidence anyone ever benefitted from the 'treasure' or, as a matter of fact, even knew anything about it. Now if it was not some contraband consumable and if no one even suspected its existence, why then I think probable that whatever it was, it was rather small and easily concealed."

"Of course!" ejaculated Mary. "I begin to see what you're driving at, the epitaph!"

"Now I will tell you something else. Given what I have said . . . then how did the idea of a treasure originate? You remember Howard Desmond, the postmaster in Hemlock Harbor, Pag?"

"The man with the beautiful black daughter. Of course, I do."

Hawkins continued, "George got the three of us together, and I told him I was frankly interested in his family history. He is a very intelligent and amiable man and told me all he knew. To be brief there is a hazy family remembrance of a black man who came from the sea wearing a slave anklet and who spoke a language no one understood. He apparently repeated the word 'diamonte' so frequently people thought that it must be his name so he was called Diamonte. He lived with the Indians close by, communicating, I suppose, by signs."

"That's very interesting, Hawkins," said Pag, "but what does it have to do with what you want to tell us?"

"Mary, you tell him! What does 'diamonte' mean in Spanish?"

"Hawkins, you take my breath away," Mary gasped. "It means 'diamond.' Is that it, Hawkins? An intertwining of two stories: that of the shipwreck and that of the black man called Diamonte."

"Mary," Hawkins looked into those gentle blue eyes, "look at your note of the epitaph. Suppose it did refer to a diamond. Does it make any sense?"

They all closely examined Mary's note but said nothing until Mary exclaimed, "Hawkins, sweetheart, I think I have it. 'It lay below' . . . below that scratch?"

"Right you are, my darling! I don't know what got me started," Hawkins began, "I was looking at the epitaph in a daydreaming reverie. 'Let none forget.' The words kept running through my mind when a light dawned. It turned into the command: 'Don't forget!' Don't forget what? Then . . . I have no idea why . . . I put the first letter of all the words together: Lnfitlaybelow."

She looked at the sketch in her hand. "That's what that odd scratch at the bottom pointed to!"

"Exactly!" said Hawkins. "That's where it was!"

"Where what was?" the others asked.

"About six inches below the surface I found a clay vessel filled with dirt."

They gazed at him in wide-eyed attention.

"In god's name, what was in it?" Pag ejaculated.

Hawkins motioned for them to bring their heads closer and said in a whisper, "A large . . . beautiful . . . blue . . . diamond!"

They were stunned into amazed silence.

"That's part of the secret you must not reveal!" cautioned Hawkins. "It's gone. I smuggled it out of the country in my pocket and sold it."

"Without telling me!" said Mary with sorrowful disappointment.

"I didn't know if what I planned to do was legal, my darling, and I couldn't risk involving you as an accessory to a crime . . . if it was a crime. You don't know how hard it was to not confide in you! I just couldn't take that chance!"

The touch of Mary's hand and her loving smile told him that he was forgiven.

"You see why it must always be a secret?"

They nodded.

"There is another reason," Hawkins laid his hand on Pag's arm, "Wiley will drive himself crazy looking for a treasure he'll never find. He'll keep at it until he deciphers the epitaph; he's too deviously smart not to. When he finds nothing and realizes we are prospering without . . . as they say . . . 'any visible means of support,' it will drive him to distraction wondering what we found! All his dishonest scheming for nothing!"

Pag roared with glee, "That's why we'd hung around Hemlock Harbor! You wanted me to know the bastard was freezing his ass off, that we were paying him back for what he did to me! Thanks, Hawkins!"

"My grandfather didn't disapprove of what I've done," Hawkins said with emphatic seriousness, "but it's not how he taught me to play the game. However, we know how Wiley and his ilk play. He stole our house and land, but I was determined he would not steal the diamond nor our happiness. We've seen what power can do; is there any justice left in the US? After what we've been through, I doubt it . . . I couldn't take any chances. It had to be done as it was, but . . . I've got to live with my conscience! I'll never stoop to their level again.

"Maybe things aren't so bad abroad; I hope they're not!"

The others said nothing. He read understanding and sympathy in their eyes; it was all he asked for.

"Now I want to make the rest of the story brief. I flew from Quebec to Antwerp where I sold the diamond. The sale was expertly handled; my name was never disclosed. It caused a minor sensation you may have read about: 'The Aqua Adaman' rediscovered after two hundred years. Reporters hit a stone wall; not a word was released about where it was found or who had discovered it. There was a lot of speculation, but the reporters never came near the truth. As Mary knows, that doesn't make much difference to newspapers.

"The money was wired to a coded Swiss bank account, and I left Antwerp as soon as I could and flew to Zurich. The money was split three ways: one part to the 'William and Isabella McLeod Foundation' and equal parts to accounts for Hawkins and Mary Shortreed and for Anthony and Lilly Pagliano. It took longer than I anticipated to establish the WIM Foundation, which is why I didn't get back as soon as I had planned."

"We're all wealthy!" gasped Pag lifting Lilly off her feet in jubilant embrace.

June 20th, the day of the wedding, was as glorious as its predecessors. Bella and Flora cried; Esther dabbed at her eyes; Will and Andy beamed; Pag's parents both sobbed.

After the reception, which the McLeods and Duncans held at the 'Celtic Brotherhood Lodge,' sad good-byes were said, and the happy couples took flight to a Caribbean honeymoon then on to another land, a land where they hoped to shed dark memories of corrupt power and to find renewed faith in mankind.

Chapter 21

IT MAY BE of interest to know what happened to the Gibbs' place after the newlyweds embarked for Italy.

Wiley continued his search through that summer until one evening when he, thin, wan, rung out by greed and discouragement, stared hatefully at the grave of Abner Gibbs. At that moment a dim idea finally occurred to him . . . the epitaph might be a message. When the truth struck him, he sat down on one of the toppled gravestones, his mind whirling and wandering. Night fell, and still he sat until the cold night air drove him to his car.

All became clear to him. The treasure, whatever it was, had been recovered . . . all his scheming, his illegal planting of marijuana, his unjust use of the unjust law of forfeiture, his frozen vigil, the ridicule of his prolonged search, and his prolonged frustration proved too much for his disturbed mind. He reached into the glove compartment and extracted a revolver. A gunshot through the heart was the reward for his perfidy . . . his suicide, a vindication which removed any lingering stigma attached to Hawkins and Pag.

Earl inherited the Gibbs' place, and in his haste to be rid of what he saw as the cause of Wiley's ruin and death, quickly deeded it to Lilly. She immediately donated it to the WIM Foundation.

The Gibbs' plateau is now somewhat changed. The old house has been restored; a gallery, studio and visitor parking area have arisen at the cliff edge overlooking the sea, and two new cottages have been erected . . . one for the Shortreeds and the other for the Paglianos. The grave yard has been put to rights, as much as it could be, and the picket fence, repaired and restored to its original stateliness.

The Shortreed and Pagliano families return to the Gibbs' Place to spend their summers. Hawkins and Pag exhibit and sell their creations. Hemlock Harbor has become a landmark to which art dealers and visitors now flock in increasing numbers as the fame of Hawkins and Pag grows.

Lilly imports European antiques to her select little shop which now flourishes under her direction and the on-going management of Sandra Desmond.

Mary finds the Gibbs' Place a relaxed and peacefully inspiring locale where her vivid and abundant imagination finds outlet in novels dealing with dramatic episodes in Florentine history.

The Gibbs' Place . . . they formally named it such . . . has become a summertime Mecca!

Were it not for the efforts of George Cottager and Hawkins, who repeatedly urged responsible zoning, Hemlock Harbor would have become a miscellaneous honkey tonk of gift shops, coast grabbing hotels, ocean recreations, restaurants and bars. The people of Hemlock Harbor demanded that it remain as little changed as possible and let politicians know that if they yielded to the bribes of business entrepreneurs, they would be retired at the next election. To everyone's surprise, Earl Williams spearheaded that movement which mellowed his aggressive capitalist philosophy somewhat . . . enough in fact, for he and Esther to be welcome guests at The Gibbs' Place.

POSTSCRIPT

I OWE THE reader, whom I suspect may associate the word "conspiracy" with a derogatory noun such as "nut," (guess whose interest that association serves?) an explanation of my thoughts on the matter.

They are based on the idea of Abstraction, Occam's Razor and task force organization.

Since the adjective "abstract" is used so freely, I pondered for many years what, precisely, is a scientific abstraction. This became clear to me when I read the following by Herman Hertz written in 1894:

> "Within our own minds we create images or symbols of the external objects, and we construct them in such a way that the logically necessary consequences of the images are again the images of the physically necessary consequences of the objects."[4]

That perspicuous statement may take you a bit of time to puzzle out, and be comfortable with . . . hopefully a bit less time than it took me. When you have it clearly in mind, it may occur to you that it is the arch stone of deductive knowledge, ranging from Sherlock Holmes to Science itself. Observation, reliable facts, and the process of abstract thought lead to what we call the Truth (subject to revision as new data are acquired). In the absence of reliable facts, effective reasoning is fruitless.

Woefully, if one relies on the corporate print and electronic media, reliable social, political and environmental facts, what with commercial censorship and spin, are very hard to come by. One must search and search for hidden reliable facts.

One reliable fact is that our governments, from the municipal to the federal, ignore the voices of the people and using every means in their power, from restrictive ballot access, rejection of instant run-off voting, to physical attacks by paramilitary forces (erstwhile police forces) seek to silence it. Why? Try using the following!

> Occam's Razor: " . . . a philosophical or scientific principle according
> to which the best explanation of an event is the one that is simplest,
> using the fewest assumptions or hypotheses."[5]

When Occam's Razor is applied, along with what I call the Hertz abstraction, to historical or current political events, conspiracy, it seems to me, becomes an essential consideration.

When legislative bills are written by corporate lobbyists and enacted into law, what is the simplest explanation for that dastardly practice? When a league of corporate-hack ventriloquists concocts lies for their collective dummies in order to wage an aggressive war to steal another nation's resources for its corporate backers, what is the simplest explanation for that?

An additional consideration is this: many people are required to achieve any significant goal. The more difficult the goal, say putting the first man on the moon, the larger the number of people involved. To be effective, these people must be organized; hence planning, and a hierarchy of leadership are requisite. What is true of a moon landing applies with equal force to, say, keeping our country on a bogus war economy for over half a century, an economy financed by people's taxes which returns little material benefit to the people. When the purpose and the goal are unworthy, the necessary organization, planning and leadership, clandestine . . . what have we but a conspiracy? " . . . a combination of persons for an evil or unlawful purpose; a plot . . ."[6]

I don't wish to belabor the point, only to offer a plausible defense of one episode in this novel. Perhaps you don't agree with my reasoning. Nevertheless, I hope you have enjoyed the story. It may be a tiny influence, for some readers, shedding a bit of light into the murky darkness of propaganda.

NOTE REFERENCES

1. (Pg. 4 to Pg. 33) H. Carter, A. Mace: The Discovery of the Tomb of Tutankhamen, Dover Publications, 1977

2. (Pg. 5 to Pg. 72) "Taken For a Ride":
http://www.culturechange.org/issue10/taken-for-a-ride.htm

3. (Pg. 1 to Pg. 130) Forfeiture in England and Colonial America Drug Control and Asset Seizures: A Review of the History of. Forfeiture in England and Colonial America, By Cecil Greek, Ph.D. University of South Florida. *http://www.fsu.edu/~crimo/forfeiture.html*

   Other sources:
   http://internet.ggu.edu/university_library/if/outrage.html
   http://www.zmag.org/ZMag/articles/jan96meeker.htm

4. (Postscript Pg. 197) H. Behnke, F. Bachmann, K, Fladt, W. Suss (Ed): Fundamentals of Mathematics, Volume 1. MIT Press, 1983.

5. (Postscript Pg. 198) V. Neufeldt, D. Guralnik (Ed): Webster's New World Dictionary, 3rd Edition. Prentice Hall, 1988.

6. (Postscript Pg. 198) C. Barnhart, J. Stein (ed): The American College Dictionary, Random House, 1960.